Sunday Lunch

He watched her speaking, her great solemn grey eyes glowing as if lit by an inner fire, her whole face transformed by her memory of Larry, which brought her joy, not sorrow. He thought her marvellously beautiful. When she turned and smiled at him he felt a sharp pang which he recognised as jealousy. This love of theirs must have been unique; it was something special, not at all like the affection he and Mary had once felt. He supposed that Larry and Lizzie's was romantic love, something sought after but very rarely attained, like the Holy Grail. Once you've had it, he thought, any other love would inevitably be second best. He was not surprised to hear Mary's acerbic voice warning him: 'Now just you watch your step.'

Nora Naish was born in India, one of seven children of an Irish father in the Indian Civil Service, and did not come to England until she was eight years old. She qualified as a doctor at King's College Hospital during the war. She married and brought up four children in Gloucestershire. In middle life she went back to medicine as a GP in Avon. Her elder brother was the late P. R. Reid, the author of *The Colditz Story*.

Sunday Lunch

Nora Naish

Mandarin

A Mandarin Paperback
SUNDAY LUNCH

First published in Great Britain 1993
by Sinclair-Stevenson
This edition published 1994
by Mandarin Paperbacks
an imprint of Reed Consumer Books Ltd
Michelin House, 81 Fulham Road, London SW3 6RB
and Auckland, Melbourne, Singapore and Toronto

Reprinted 1994

A CIP catalogue record for this title
is available from the British Library
ISBN 0 7493 1558 X

Printed and bound in Great Britain by
BPC Paperbacks Ltd
A member of
The British Printing Company Ltd

One

Dr James woke late that Sunday morning. He had been called out at 2 a.m. to see a child with febrile convulsions and in great pain from an acutely inflamed ear-drum. He had spent rather a long time with the mother talking to her and showing her how to cool the little boy's body by sponging him down with tepid water. 'Like this,' he said. The mother was half crazy with anxiety, her hand trembling, so he grasped it firmly and swept it over the child's hot skin. He'd been surprised and suddenly pleased when he felt her tremor disappear. 'You'll have to do it again next time he runs a temperature, so you must know how to do it,' he said. He gave her enough antibiotic doses to cover the weekend, when the local pharmacy was closed. She had already administered some painkilling syrup she kept in the house. He was dog-tired by the time he got home, but the mother's face full of gratitude and the boy's quiet breathing as he fell asleep were recompense enough for his efforts. He reminded himself as he lay in bed that he must ring Julia and pass the case over to her as she was on call now.

He thought without pleasure of the day ahead. He would have to get spruced up in time for that lunch party next door. He didn't really like Sunday drinking; all that uninteresting small talk with people you didn't particularly want to meet! But he liked his neighbours, Larry and Lizzie, he liked the house Larry had built for his little nesting-bird of a wife, and he more than liked the excellent food she always provided for her guests. Good food in James's widower's existence was a rarity to be relished. Although they were neighbours he didn't know Larry very well. They usually met on the grass verge that united the ends of their gardens when Larry came down from London for the weekend. Leaning on the open wooden fence between them and the stream which flowed round the edge of their properties they would pass the time of day commenting on the farmer's livestock in the field beyond, or exchange idle village gossip and occasionally news from the wider world. Most of the land surrounding the two houses was owned by the farmer who had sold them their pieces of land; but James had a garden of about an acre, which he and his wife had redesigned, replanted and carefully tended all the time Mary was alive, but which James had allowed to slip back into the wild since her death because he lost interest in it.

He groaned inwardly as he thought about it: that overgrown lawn which he must mow today before it got too hot. It was already hot, but in two or three hours it would be much hotter. The July heatwave had already lasted six days and showed no sign of breaking. He got up and went into the bathroom which dear Mary had proudly installed in what had once been a dressing-room adjacent to the main bedroom of their dilapidated ancient house. He looked at himself in the mirror over the basin, at the shadows under his eyes, at a few grey hairs appearing at his temples and thought: I'm still in my forties and I look over fifty. He decided to cut that blasted grass, get the job over and done with as soon as he'd had a cup of tea. That would still leave him enough time to shave, shower, cool down and dress himself in clothes suitable for a party.

'And see you comb your hair properly!' He could hear his dead wife's voice in his head, her teasingly sharp Scottish intonation, and the little placatory laugh she used to give after her orders when she was being bossy.

When he was finally ready for social life he emerged into the street and shut his gate behind him. Cars were being parked, and a few guests were strolling up the drive next door. He turned for a moment to survey the scene, glancing up at the façades of the two houses.

They stood at the western edge of Fossbury. Owl House, the doctor's home, originally a farmhouse built of the fabled honey-coloured Cotswold stone which he and Mary had bought not long after they married and long before the property boom had blown prices to absurd heights, had been lovingly restored by them. The adjoining barn was the house that Larry built, or rather rebuilt, only a few years ago; and since he was an architect of talent and vision he'd made a good job of it, using local stone for the exterior and installing many modern conveniences not too obtrusively fitted inside. He named it Owl House Barn, which very soon became simply the Barn. Windows were let into the solid walls, each window with its traditional overhanging drip-course carved out of stone: 'An eyebrow for each eye,' as Larry put it. The central entrance, originally high enough to allow passage to a wagon loaded up with as many bales of hay as it could balance, was closed with two storeys of double glazing reminiscent of tall windows seen in some Cotswold houses built by wealthy wool merchants long ago; but the narrow stone ribs of those medieval windows he replaced with ribs of steel. This great glass wall threw light on the hall inside, its wide staircase, and the landing above. On the ground floor two large rooms were separated by wide archways on either side of the hall, on the right the kitchen-diner floored with red tiles, on the left the drawing-room, from the west end of which big sliding glass doors led out to a terrace with a view of the garden and the river beyond.

Guests were crowding into the drawing-room where Larry was dispensing drinks when James edged his way through knots of smiling people, all talking at once, towards the sliding doors. After being waylaid a few times to exchange the necessary pleasantries, he reached the people he wanted to talk to: Liam Tiernan, an amusing if slightly unreliable fellow who made agreeable half-promises you knew he'd no intention of keeping, but was never boring and always excellent company at a party, and that attractive woman Amanda, whom he'd spied from across the room. She looked even more attractive than usual this morning in a cool, cream-coloured shirt of some semi-transparent material, with a string of bright multicoloured beads round her neck, which rose firm and softly rounded from the open collar.

'The extraordinary thing was,' Liam was expounding to a small circle of listeners, 'that the painting was so clean! There it had lain forgotten in a corner of the cellar for over a hundred years; the scrap of curtain material over it was grey with dust and in shreds, but the colours on the canvas were as fresh as when they'd been put on!' He spoke with a slight Irish accent, the terminal T's softened more than usual by the alcohol he'd drunk.

'How can you explain that?' asked Amanda's clear-cut voice.

'Well you see, Amanda,' he replied, smiling at her before lifting his shoulders and looking round the room to see who else was arriving, 'that painting had been isolated from human kind for a long time. It's people who pollute the atmosphere of museums and galleries. All that secret farting by the culture vultures adds sulphides to the atmosphere as they stroll and gaze. . . . It's all that gas in the guts of art lovers that blackens the faces of the Old Masters.' A ripple of laughter applauded him. 'In churches it's even worse. A packed congregation and centuries of praying wreak havoc with the priceless painted triptych above the altar.'

'The pious are great farters,' said the man at his elbow.

'The kneeling position is conducive to farting,' said another.

It was during the burst of laughter following this

that Dr James joined the group. He smiled at Amanda, admiring her blonde, well cut hair, nodded greetings at the men, and tried to turn his back on the rest of the party. He had already caught sight of two women on the other side of the room who, he knew, would try to corner him in conversation if they could. He had seen them both at the surgery and suspected they would be even more boring socially than they were over their minor ailments. They might even (God help us!) bring these up as matters of interest, and without his notes he would be unable to recall the details. He determined to stay clear of them if at all possible. Socially he liked to remove the physician's mask and assume another persona, but this was not easy to do in a small country town. He knew all the old inhabitants, and a few in the outlying great houses still referred to as gentry, as patients, as well as an increasing number of commuters to London and neighbouring Swinester, and all the farmers. The weekend crowd he was not so familiar with. They usually had their own GPs in London and were seldom ill when they came down to their cottages to become weekend country lovers. They put on their tweeds and wellies and stuck straw behind their ears, and sometimes, in his opinion, stuffed it into their skulls as well. But this sort of hole in the head did not require his assistance. Amanda, he thought severely, was one of them, though he had to admit there was no straw left on her this morning. He cast a professional eye over her health and fitness, summing them up. Although she must be in her late thirties, since she was an old schoolfriend of Lizzie's who already had a son of ten or eleven, and her fertility by now must be beginning to decline she seemed, judging by the glow and quality of her skin and the brightness of her eyes, to be at the peak of her sexual powers. She was at ease with herself, confident and unquestioning. Her legs beneath an olive green skirt he couldn't see very well because they were hidden by the trousers of the men standing close to her; but he knew they were shapely because he had once examined them, that time about a year ago when one Saturday evening he was called out to see her as a temporary resident in her cottage in Frenny Hinton, three miles away. She had twisted her ankle over a dip in the corridor on the first floor of that ancient building. Why she hadn't had the floor levelled when she had the place modernised he couldn't imagine, and said so at the time; but she told him she liked the irregularities for their quaintness. He remembered, too, that she possessed several very good watercolours, and supposed Liam must have seen them. He would be interested, since that was his line.

'What's going on in the Great Wen?' he asked Liam. James sometimes went up to London by train on his day off, to visit exhibitions, occasionally to see a new play. He liked to keep in touch with the metropolis and the wider stream of life, as he thought of it.

'I believe you missed the Egon Schiele exhibition?' asked Liam.

'Never heard of him,' admitted James.

'Pupil of Gustav Klimt. Viennese. Got in trouble with the obscenity laws, and was actually imprisoned before the First World War. No longer considered obscene enough for that in our day and age,' Liam laughed. 'But very explicit sexually. And a marvellous draughtsman. Nobody can draw pubic hair like him.'

'I don't know that I want to travel to London to inspect drawings of pubic hair,' said James. 'After all I can see quite a lot of that in the surgery down here in Fossbury.'

The men laughed; but Amanda didn't. She detached herself from the group and wandered off into the crowd, exchanging little flattering comments with the women and drinking salutations with the men.

Amanda knew a thing or two, thought James, watching her as she moved through the room. She was a successful accountant earning a high salary, with a flat in town as well as her little country retreat in

Frenny Hinton. He could almost hear Mary's voice warning him: 'She's not your type, Jamie. She's really too sexy. And it shows! And she probably screams when she can't get her own way!' Mary had always had a way of cutting people down to size. He himself had often been included in that cutting, he remembered ruefully. In his opinion women could never be too sexy; but this he kept to himself during the conversations he held with Mary in his head.

'Hullo there, James!' his host greeted him, claret in hand. 'So glad you were able to leave the care of the less fortunate for a bit. What'll you drink?'

'Just a glass of wine, Larry,' said the doctor. 'Dry. White. Thanks.' He looked about for Lizzie but couldn't see her in the crowd.

'She's in the kitchen,' said Larry, answering his unspoken question. 'Fussing over some last-minute touch. You know what these perfectionists are!' He laughed, and immediately James was glad he'd come. It lifted his spirits just to see how much Larry was enjoying his party. He sometimes wondered why he liked this man so much. Mary would have said: 'He's not your type, Jamie. He's a hedonist. He's not a man of fine feelings.' But James admired his big frame, his great animal strength, his ready laugh and exuberant good nature, and most of all the wonderful health and vigour which seemed to emanate from him. He was a hedonist. So what? He loved life and all the good things about living, and wanted everybody else to enjoy them too, for he was nothing if not generous. To James, Larry was something of a prodigy, a completely natural, warm-hearted human being with no hang-ups, no fun-spoiling inhibitions. He was the sort of man who increased the tempo, the exhilaration and noise of any party simply by his presence. He was undeniably good-looking too, even if his flesh was a bit too solid for his forty-odd – no must be knocking fifty – years, and his thickly curled dark hair and frank blue eyes gave a look of appealing boyishness to his face, so how could anyone help loving him?

'As a matter of fact it's my Sunday off,' said James.

'That must be a relief.' They sipped silently.

The Reverend Foster, a tall man, was beaming in his direction over the heads of other guests. Gerry Foster was not one who thought the Sabbath could be rendered unholy by the consumption of good food and drink. The subtleties of Christian theology did not concern him overmuch anyway. What he chiefly believed in was brotherly love, and practical demonstrations of it at that. During his years as an army chaplain he'd found he could talk to the chaps more easily over drinks than anywhere else, so, unlike what he thought of as these damned puritanical Muslims we were all having to think about a bit these days, he found alcohol an aid and a helpmeet. He rather wished his other half or helpmeet had come to the party too; but Maisie – bless her! – didn't like parties and refused to attend them excusing herself on the grounds that she had two girls to look after and remembering her habit of looking like a tramp even in her best clothes he considered that perhaps her decision was not a bad one. She was of course invaluable in more important areas of living, and at this very moment was doing a Sunday shift nursing at the Swinester General Hospital, bringing in much-needed income to their joint account.

The doctor raised his glass in greeting, but turned away from Gerry to the child standing on the terrace outside the window.

'Hullo Timothy!' It was Larry's son.

Timothy offered a formal handshake. He was dressed casually in jeans and a T-shirt but still mentally enclosed within his prep school uniform, and was struggling to behave in a manner which his eleven-year-old experience led him to believe was proper for the occasion.

'Would you like me to show you the cows?' he asked politely.

They sauntered down to the bottom of the lawn and stood at the fence to watch some heifers grazing.

'That one's only got three tits,' said Timothy, pointing to the defective animal. 'Do you think it'll matter? I mean when she grows up to be a cow?'

'Not much,' said James. 'She may not give so much milk as the others, I suppose.' He thought, but did not say, that she would probably be carted off while still young and sold for beef.

The boy turned to look at him. 'I like your suit,' he said. 'Who's your tailor?' He was trying to keep the ball rolling in an adult conversational style.

'I'll give you his address some time,' said James seriously, though his clothes were never tailor-made but bought off the peg from time to time on those visits he made to London. 'School finished, then?'

'I like school, you know,' said Timothy quietly. 'There's not much to do here when Daddy's away working.'

'You could come and play croquet with me next door,' suggested James, wondering how lonely was this only child. Probably he had few friends in the town since most of his year was spent away at boarding school. James felt a painful stab as he recalled his own misery and homesickness at that age, when he was sent away from home to live with alien small boys. Really it was monstrous cruelty committed against children to pack them off at the tender age of ten to be educated by strangers! Why do we go on doing it, tormenting ourselves as parents, and making our children suffer? He remembered his own cry for help, his first letter home to his mother: 'I AM HOMSICK. PLEASE SEND SOME CHOLATE.' His mother kept the letter. She treasured its spelling mistakes, which became a family joke preserved among the family archives; but it was no joke when he wrote it.

'Can I really?' asked Timothy. 'Oh yes! I'd like that.' And then asked: 'I say, do you have one of those bleep things? Can I see it?' And as James took it out of his breast pocket: 'Can I use it?'

'You can hold it and look at it; but for God's sake don't fiddle with it,' implored James. 'It's all set to call me up when they need me.' Timothy looked happily solemn and impressed.

'Is James your first or second name?' he asked.

'Both, as a matter of fact. I always thought my parents rather lazy not being able to think up another name for me. But it's quite convenient really, because people call me that without worrying about whether it's formal or familiar. At school I was always called Jim-Jams.'

'Jim-Jams!' Timothy laughed. He was beginning to relax.

'Let's go and get some grub,' said James, twirling the stem of his empty glass. 'It must be about time for food.'

They made their way to the kitchen by the back door.

'Mummy's a super cook, you know,' said Timothy.

'Oh yes,' agreed James. 'Everybody knows. Your mother's culinary fame has spread throughout the land.'

'Has it really?' Timothy glanced sideways at him, not quite sure if this was true or joking.

'Well, anyway, throughout Fossbury,' said James. 'She is the queen of trifles and soufflés!'

Timothy ran into the kitchen laughing. The last shreds of his school uniform were slipping off him. The kid's all right with his mother, thought James.

Lizzie was sprinkling chopped parsley over potato salad, and Myra Roxby, who cleaned for her once a week and who would always come to help, even on a Sunday if it was for a party, was shredding an apple into a bowl of lettuce.

'Jim-Jams says your culinary is famous throughout the land,' shouted Timothy as he hopped round his mother. 'He says you're the Queen of Tarts!' He'd heard some older boys at school laughing at that and wanted to repeat the joke.

Mrs Roxby burst out laughing. 'I know one or two in Fossbury who could claim that title better than your mum,' she said. 'There's that new young barmaid down at the Fleece for a start!'

James, catching Lizzie's eye over Timothy's head and trying not to laugh, protested, 'I said no such thing! Queen of trifles was what I said.'

'Ah yes,' smiled Lizzie. 'You men! Allowing me to queen it over small matters! But I'll let you two into a secret.' And as they bent towards her she whispered, 'The mackerel mousse is the best thing today. But don't tell the others. There's not enough for everybody. It's made with green gooseberries and whipped cream as well as mackerel. It's a very old English recipe,' she confided to James, as Timothy skipped round the table. 'Parson Woodforde describes it.'

'Who's Parson Woodforde?' asked James.

'A greedy old eighteenth-century diarist who rode about the countryside eating his parishioners' dinners. Perhaps lemons were hard to come by in those days, so they used gooseberries instead. Timothy, run and tell Daddy we're ready.'

When the boy had disappeared and he was left alone

with Lizzie, James was overcome with shyness. He never knew what to say to her. Although he met her frequently with Larry at weekends and greeted her cheerfully across their gardens from time to time during the week he had never talked to her about anything. She was such a quiet, reserved woman. She took no part in local affairs; she seemed to like shutting herself away from the world – almost like a contemplative nun. That made him smile. Hardly a nun! No woman married to that great hunk of jolly machismo could possibly remain a nun.

Hungry drinkers pushed their way into the kitchen, the women uttering little cries of pleasure and admiration on seeing the beautiful display of food. Amanda placed herself in front of a big dish laden with a whole salmon lying on a bed of cress and began to slice it into portions.

'Mind the bones!' she warned, handing a plate to Timothy, who was just behind her. 'And get yourself some of the salads, love.'

Lizzie was being besieged by greetings when the phone rang on the kitchen extension. Mrs Roxby, who was enjoying her glass of white wine, answered it and found the call was for her.

'Oh, Sandra. It's you, is it? You never ought to ring me here. Not now. I can't pay attention to your woes just now. I'm in the middle of the party. You should know better.'

'Sorry, Mum,' came her daughter's reply from the public phone box on the corner of Wistaria Way and Clematis Close at the other end of town. 'Ever so sorry, but it's desperate really. Yes. Could you . . . ? Yes, do – come down here before you go home today.'

'Trouble again is it? Wilf is it? Well don't tell me I didn't warn you!' Mrs Roxby agreed, however, to visit Sandra after the party, and promised to bring with her some left-over delicacies, perhaps a couple of strawberry tarts for the boys.

Conversation was more subdued while people ate. It was then that Amanda said her car had broken down that morning.

'But how did you get here?' asked Lizzie.

'Walked, of course. I just started an hour earlier. I took the country lane way.'

'But it's more than three miles to Frenny Hinton!'

'It was cooler earlier on,' Amanda explained. 'And a lovely walk, looking down from the hill as you go. Banks of ragged robin and meadowsweet all along the hedges. I like walking. I walk everywhere in London, you know.'

'I suppose it keeps you fit. How will you get back?'

'Same way,' Amanda shrugged.

'Oh no!' said Lizzie. 'It'll be too hot – and uphill too. I'll ask Larry to drive you back when the time comes.'

Amanda and Lizzie, although such old friends, were very different. Lizzie was quiet, studious, perhaps over-conscientious. At school she had worked hard and done well. Amanda was more extrovert, more independent, and cared less about the opinion of others; she was not so interested in acquiring knowledge but excelled in sports. She played hockey with enthusiasm, and in the summer term her backhand drive had drawn shouts of admiration from spectators round the tennis court. The girls became buddies at an early age when they discovered similarities in their childhood backgrounds. They were both brought up by tweedy, slightly eccentric aunts about whom they compared notes and giggled secretly. The bond was strengthened when at fifteen they both discovered Keats's poetry and fell in love with the poet, Lizzie with pity for his tender feelings and his tragically short life, Amanda yearning for his caresses and longing to return them. 'Not like that Fanny Brawne.' She was contemptuous. 'Prissy little thing!' She, Amanda Burton, would certainly never have allowed her lover to leave her when he was sick, even if it was to travel south to a warmer climate for the sake of his lungs, and to die lonely in Rome, too far away to be able to lay his head for comfort on her prim virginal bosom. If Keats had called upon Amanda for her 'warm, white, lucent, million-pleasured breast' nothing on earth would have stopped her letting him have it.

After they left school they became separated for more than a decade, although they still exchanged annual Christmas greetings, till they met again quite accidentally one night during the interval of a performance of Donizetti's *Lucia di Lammermoor* at Covent Garden. Lizzie was going up the stairs and Amanda was coming down. In the excitement of mutual recognition they stretched out arms, grasped hands, uttered squeals of surprise and pleasure. Larry looked on, laughing at the girls, and his mother beside him smiling, pointed out that they were causing a traffic jam on the staircase. Lizzie had been subdued and saddened by the music till they met; Amanda was exhilarated by the tension of the drama. Afterwards they picked up their friendship as easily as if they had been sisters; and when Larry and Lizzie left London to live in Fossbury Amanda followed, buying her little weekend cottage nearby.

Although the girls were such old friends there were still aspects of themselves and their lives they didn't discuss; but Lizzie was beginning to think it was time

Amanda settled down, and was on the lookout for a husband for her. She even suggested nice, kind, lonely Dr James as a possible applicant, but Amanda didn't seem interested in marriage. Lizzie observed that men often swarmed after her friend like bees after a queen; but this queen liked flying solo. As for Amanda, she often thought Lizzie was too much the perfect wife who sacrificed ambition and even identity for Larry. She is Fausta, she told herself. She has sold her soul, not for extra years of life but for love. Sometimes she feared that one day Lizzie might be damned for it.

Lizzie glanced anxiously across the table at Larry. 'We'll have to stop him drinking if he's going to drive,' she said.

'No really, Lizzie. Don't spoil his fun.'

But Lizzie insisted. At about 3 p.m. that afternoon after coffee had been drunk out on the terrace, when most of the guests were drifting away from the Barn and those living in the town were walking home, and Dr James had already reached the shade and silence of his overgrown garden and his untidy, womanless house, Larry left with Amanda.

'Be careful now,' said Lizzie, standing by the Volvo. He wound down the window to listen. 'How much have you drunk?'

'Two or three glasses,' he admitted. 'But you know

how much I weigh. The alcohol has to spread thinly over a big area!' He and Amanda both laughed.

'Well, take care,' she repeated.

'Silly Lizzie,' he said, stroking her cheek. 'You know how good I am at looking after Number One.'

'I believe you,' she said. 'Just don't let yourself down, that's all.'

'Bye, Blossom!' he said and started the engine.

'Blossom?' repeated Amanda as the car began to move.

'It's a private name I sometimes use,' he said.

Liam was beside Lizzie as she walked back to the house. He had drunk not wisely, nor too well either, and looked the worse for it.

'You'd better come in and sit down, Liam,' she said. 'You can have a sleep, and then I'll make you a cup of tea.'

'That would be great,' he beamed. 'Just great! Sit me down opposite that lovely watercolour you have.' To his annoyance he was unable in his fuddled state to remember the name of the painter. 'That one of the twenties girl sitting in the garden.'

'I have no intention of selling it to you, as you well know,' she said severely. 'But you can certainly look at it.'

'It'll soothe my troubled soul.'

'I don't think that particular commodity needs much more soothing,' was Lizzie's comment; but she placed a cushion behind his head.

Liam settled himself in the comfortable armchair in the small sitting-room at the back of the house over-looking the doctor's garden. As he put his feet up on the low stool she placed there for him, he thought: She is a nice woman, really. All the hard shell is only camouflage. She's not like Amanda, of course, who is a star in the firmament, unattainable. And by God! He'd have a go there, even if he died in the attempt. Why not be an astronaut? He would make a start that very evening. A pity he hadn't been sober enough to offer her a lift home instead of Larry; but as soon as he was fit for the road he'd call on her and offer to drive her back up the M4 to London. She had probably been unable to get a mechanic as it was a Sunday. He only hoped Larry would keep his hand off her engine, and not fix it for her.

Larry was silent for a time as they drove out of Fossbury and took the main road to Frenny Hinton.

'We shouldn't be doing this,' he said suddenly. 'You know we made a pact to keep Lizzie out of it.'

'I couldn't help it,' said Amanda. 'She insisted when she heard about my car.'

'What's wrong with it?'

'I don't know. Just wouldn't start. And being Sunday I couldn't get hold of any garage to put it right.'

'What about the AA?'

'I said I was going out to a party and it would be all right if they came this evening.'

'Something simple, no doubt,' he said impatiently. 'Why you brainy women can't learn a bit about how to look after your cars I can't think.'

'Sorry! Sorry!' said Amanda. Living in a man's world, as she did during her working life, she had learned that to take the blame was usually the quickest way out of a difficulty. But he wasn't pacified.

'We made a pact to keep everything between us in London – remember? Not let a breath reach Lizzie down here.'

'Yes,' agreed Amanda. 'And that's still a promise.' But she felt annoyed, felt she'd suffered an injustice. So she changed the subject quickly.

'That shirt you're wearing, Larry, it's a bit unusual.' She touched the blue and green pattern on his shoulder. 'You look wonderful in it, though. Makes me think of Othello.'

'Well, it is African. And the fellow who gave it to me in Lagos, funnily enough, I used to call Othello.' He paused for a couple of seconds wondering if he might have told her this before; maybe that had made her think of him as Othello. 'I couldn't pronounce his name. It began with O and was all NBGUs. I couldn't get round it. He protested, of course. Said he'd divorced three wives but never murdered one, though he'd often felt like it. And he laughed. Out there they seem to laugh most of the time. I designed a house for him – a very palatial one it was – and when it was built he threw an enormous party to celebrate.' He remembered that Lizzie had flown out for the event. Amanda must have known that too; but neither of them mentioned it. 'I remember the wonderful spicy food – all sorts of flavours I'd never come across before. And Othello dressed in an emerald green robe, with a small square white hat on his thick hair . . . what a figure of a man. Truly a Black Prince!'

He remembered, too, Lizzie in her midnight blue dress with shimmering silver threads. He could see Othello now, taking her hand and bending over it, but not kissing it, and his great shining eyes eating her up. 'You are Queen of the Night,' he said. Larry had felt his stomach turn over with jealousy. Yes, he had been afraid of that handsome Othello. In a way it was how he thought of her himself. To him she was Joyce's 'heaventree of stars hung with humid nightblue fruit'. It was that remote, enigmatic quality of hers that made him shiver with desire when he was away from her and thought of her suddenly. Though he could, with his eyes closed, have mapped the surface of her body, there was always a small uncertainty, a fear even, that in spite of their having loved each other so well and so long she was, in some sense he never quite understood, still free and unpossessed by him. He could not explain these feelings, these intuitions about her; he thought of them as her paradoxes, for to outward appearances she was dependent on him, a home-loving little bird. She never demanded any special preroga-tives or freedom, had often, in fact, been accused by friends, and especially by Amanda, of living entirely for him, of not being her own true and independent self.

'Well anyway, Othello gave me this shirt as a parting gift when I left Lagos. He called me Scrooge when I reminded him that he owed me money. "We'll keep it literary," was what he said. He still owes me money.'

When they reached the hamlet of Frenny Hinton and the row of stone cottages of which hers was the end but one in the terrace, Amanda said, 'Let me give you a cup of coffee. I expect you're thirsty.'

'Yes, OK,' he agreed, 'but I'd better park the car round the corner, not outside your door.'

They walked back to the house. There was nobody in the street. She unlocked her yellow-painted door and entered the narrow hall, and Larry followed her. He was not his usual relaxed and happy self. He had never been there before; and he was nervous.

'Sit down, love,' she said. 'I'll fix some coffee.'

He drank it with relish, scenting the aroma first. 'Colombian?' he asked. 'You certainly do make good coffee. And it's just what I needed after all that crowd.'

'But I thought you liked giving parties?'

'I do, I do. Just sometimes I wonder why the hell I bother.'

'It's because you do it so well.' She was about to add: 'And Lizzie provides such marvellous food,' but decided not to. Instead she stood behind his chair and put her cool hands over his forehead. She noticed some grey hairs among the black, and smiled, thinking: grey hairs add distinction to a man, only age to a woman.

'Amazing,' he said. 'Amazing how cool your hands are even on a hot summer's day. It makes me wonder if your heart's rather cool too.'

'Try me,' she murmured, kissing the back of his neck.

As he followed her up the narrow staircase he grumbled, 'We shouldn't be doing this, you know. It's against our pact.' But already he was slipping off the Nigerian shirt before he reached the landing. He went straight through the open bedroom door, stooping under the low lintel as he undid his belt and placed his corduroys neatly over her dressing-stool, then stood naked except for his wristwatch. The watch annoyed Amanda. It made her feel the love he gave her was strictly rationed; but when he stood behind her, cupping her breasts in his hands and kissing her shoulders, and she felt his prick hard against her back she forgot her annoyance, forgot time, forgot everything in her overwhelming need for his body. She turned and putting her arms round his neck cried, 'Oh Larry my love! My love!'

He pulled her towards the bed. He was greedy in love, nuzzling her like an infant; when at last they rushed together towards climax and were pushed off the edge of the world in a great explosion of sensation and then went into free-fall, drifting down together in a close embrace, with eyes closed, towards the wine-dark sea of sleep, she was filled with such tenderness for him that she wept, calling out his name several times. He uttered a whimper, and after a while a sudden snore. That sound shook her awake. Surely he couldn't be asleep already? But he mustn't fall asleep! He had to go back to the Barn almost immediately. That was why he'd worn his watch, wasn't it? To remind him of the time. . . . He gave a soft groan and another, louder snore.

'What's the matter, Larry?' she cried. 'Are you all right?' He didn't answer. She pushed him away from her and he rolled over on his back. His right arm fell off the edge of the bed, and his hand dropped on the carpet. 'Larry!' she repeated loudly. 'You mustn't go to sleep, you've got to go home!' She sat up in bed and looked at him. His mouth was open and his eyes stared at the ceiling.

She jumped out of bed, ran round the foot of it and stood beside him.

'Larry!' she screamed. 'Larry!' But he made no reply.

She leaned over him and peered into his unseeing eyes; she touched his lips across which no breath was passing; she moaned, wringing her hands: 'The kiss of life – oh my God! How do you do it?' Then she knelt down and pummelled his chest with her fists. She leaned forward and breathed out a long breath into his wide-open mouth, but he made no movement, gave no

29

sign of recognition. He was forever beyond the reach of her beauty and the grasp of her small, efficient hands.

She began to run wildly about the room whimpering, 'Oh my God! Oh my God!' Backwards and forwards across the foot of the bed she ran. At last she sat down trembling on her dressing-stool, on his folded corduroy trousers, and seeing herself naked in her mirror called out loudly in her clear-cut voice, 'Oh my God!'

After an hour's sleep Liam woke up. He could hear the sound of the dishwasher whirring softly in the kitchen and voices, two female voices. He guessed Mrs Roxby, Fossbury's help-to-all in times of trouble, family crisis or after parties, must be giving Lizzie a hand with the clearing up. He felt better, certainly wide awake enough to look at that nice watercolour. He examined it carefully. Without peering at the signature he knew who had painted it: he'd known all along it was a double-barrelled name. The picture was of a girl with brown bobbed hair in a loose pink twenties dress, sitting on a wide garden seat under a tree. Sunshine filtering through leaves splashed over her. He nodded with satisfaction as his eyes flicked over it. Very few could paint dappled sunlight as well as Margaret Tiller-Mount. By the time he had drunk a cup of Lizzie's tea he was almost himself again.

'I'll give you two thousand for it, Lizzie,' he offered.

'I don't want to sell it,' she said. 'It belonged to my mother. She went to the Slade, you know. She knew a thing or two about painting – could always tell a painter from a dabbler. She was quite a good painter herself too, but she drank . . .'

He nodded. 'Quite a lot of painters do. Ah well,' he sighed. 'I'd best be on my way, my dear.' He kissed her cheek. 'It was a lovely party. You and Larry do give wonderful parties. And thanks for all the tender-loving-ministering-angelica.'

He drove to Frenny Hinton not by the main road but along the winding lane, humming gaily as he watched the flower-decked hedgerows flash past. Amanda had often told him it was a marvellous place for wild flowers. Parking his car outside Amanda's yellow door, he noticed with pleasure that Larry must have gone, since his car was nowhere to be seen. He walked jauntily up the garden path and rang the doorbell. After a few minutes Amanda opened it. She was wearing a towelling bathrobe.

'Oh I say, I'm sorry, Amanda! Were you going to have a bath? I've come at a bad time, for sure.'

Without a word she pulled him inside and shut the door. She sat down on the stairs and burst into tears; then pushing her forehead between bannisters she sobbed.

'For Christ's sake, Amanda, what's up?' Liam asked. 'Can I not do something to help?'

She stopped crying, and wiping her nose on the end of her belt she stood up. 'Come upstairs,' she said. 'I suppose you might as well.'

Larry lay on one side of the big double bed, stark naked, his mouth still open, the knuckles of his right hand on the crushed-strawberry carpet of her ultra-feminine bedroom. Liam couldn't help noticing with half his mind, even at such a time as this, that the room was decorated in what he called a pink-and-pow-der-blue Pompadour style. Around Larry's mouth and nose was a certain purplish colour.

'Jesus!' he hissed. 'When did it happen?'

'About twenty minutes ago,' she replied. The minutes had been recorded for ever in her memory by that same watch Larry had refused to strip off.

'We'll have to call a doctor. And he'll have to inform the coroner. That always has to be done when there's a sudden unexplained death. There might even have to be an inquest.'

She began to tremble violently. Liam, leaving the

bed, put his arm round her shoulders and led her to a chair by the window.

'You'd better sit down,' he said. 'How long has this . . . this affair been going on?'

'One year, seven months and twelve days.' The exactness of her answer revealed how much she had loved him; and although Liam was angry and jealous enough to think of Larry Bassett as that lucky bastard he felt ashamed of his disrespect for the dead, and mighty glad it wasn't himself lying there. He felt pity, too, that such a love as this must have been was wiped out by this terrible event.

'We'll have to think,' he said.

'We've never done – we've never made love here before,' said Amanda. 'We used to meet in town, usually at my place. Lizzie knows nothing about it. I believe it would kill her if she knew.'

'Well . . . about his death she'll have to know. That's bad enough. But the rest – You haven't phoned Dr James yet?'

'No. Why did this have to happen to me?' Amanda broke out. 'And why here?'

'It could have happened anywhere,' said Liam. 'In the car while driving – that's where heart attacks often happen. Or on the garden path. Or at the front door while he was leaving.' He was silent for a moment.

'Come on, Amanda. He didn't die in your bed. He dropped just as he was about to go out through your front door, didn't he? We'll dress him. Yes, you will!' He shook her shoulder roughly when he saw her flinch. 'I can hold him up while you slip on his shirt.'

He picked up the gaudy shirt, its green and indigo streaks and splashes crumpled on the floor, and handed it to her. It was fairly easy getting it on: it was loose-fitting and the body was not yet stiff; but it was difficult putting on his trousers. Liam was thankful Larry had not been wearing tight jeans. He raised one foot at a time in the air for Amanda to slide the trouser leg over the ankle; then he had to roll the body from side to side while Amanda tugged the cloth over the thighs, and finally he had to heave up the trunk, which was unexpectedly heavy, so that she could pull up the seat of the pants and zip up the flies. The sandals were easy to fix.

'I'm glad he wasn't wearing socks,' said Amanda. They were both sweating from their exertions in the late afternoon heat.

'We'll have to drag him downstairs. It won't be all that difficult, Amanda, though he's a big man, I know. We can take our time. What's the time now? Jesus! It's after five. D'you think Lizzie will be worrying why he isn't home yet? We'd better take the phone off the hook in case she rings.'

Amanda ran downstairs to pick up the receiver and let it dangle while Liam edged the body gently off the bed on to the floor. He dragged it over the pink carpet to the bedroom door, which was so narrow they had to squeeze the body through it in the diagonal plane.

'Be careful in the corridor,' Amanda warned. 'There are one or two dips and bumps.'

At the top of the stairs Liam pulled the head and shoulders down a few steps.

'Now hold the feet, Amanda, and don't let go. I'll go down first to stop him falling too fast.' Gravity and Larry's bulk made it easier than they'd anticipated. Liam dumped the body on its back in the hallway, head towards the front door and feet facing the kitchen. 'He had the attack just as he was on his way out. You'll have to describe the attack exactly the way you remember it.'

She kept repeating, 'Oh my God, oh my God,' which in spite of the compassion he felt irritated Liam.

'Now you go and get dressed while I ring up Dr James. And don't take too long. You can look a bit dishevelled. And wear what you had on this morning, or he'll smell a rat. He'll be here in ten minutes.'

'Give me fifteen.'

He put his arms round her and held her firmly. He could feel her trembling. 'Nobody will know exactly what happened except you and me, Amanda,' he said. 'Try to be calm when the doctor comes – though of course it would be natural for you to be upset. Such a terrible thing to happen to your best friend's husband in your house!' No trace of irony crept into his voice.

At 5.30 p.m. Dr James was enjoying a mug of tea at the bottom of his garden, sitting in a dilapidated deckchair under the lofty dome of a lime tree heavy with flowers. Their powerful soporific scent was also heavy and soporific with a thousand bees and the soft continuous boom of their working. It was not yet cool in the garden. He had stripped off his shirt and was wiping the sweat off his chest with it and arguing with Mary in his head. 'Why the hell should I wear a suit at a party like that? I'm a silly bugger to bother over such formalities on a hot day like this,' when he became aware of the phone ringing above Mary's tart reply. Carrying his mug, he went inside to answer it.

An urgent voice jumped into his ear, Liam's slightly Irish voice with its soft Ts. 'I know 'tis your day off, James, but this is desperate. No it's not me. It's Larry. There's been an accident.'

'Road accident?' James sprang into professional alertness.

'No, James. Not a car crash at all. But for God's sake come at once. I think he's had a heart attack. Yes Amanda's house in Frenny Hinton.'

'What's the number?'

'It's the one from the end in the row. Yellow door.'

'I'll be with you in ten minutes.' He picked up his medical bag from the table in the hall, ran out into the garden to get his damp shirt, and sprinted to the garage, where he pulled the shirt over his head as he sat down in the car. When he reached Frenny Hinton he parked opposite Amanda's yellow door, on the other side of the road. He noticed Liam's car, but couldn't see Larry's Volvo.

Liam opened the door and James stepped inside, almost tripping over Larry's head only a few feet away. Larry was lying on his back: his mouth had fallen open and his lips and nose were bluish. The doctor dropped to his knees without a word, put his hand over the mouth to check for breathing, and felt the skin already cold. He clicked open his medical bag, which he placed on the floor, and took out his stethoscope. Although he knew Larry was dead he performed the rituals of looking for signs of life, listening to the heartbeat and for any breath sounds in the chest. Then he stood up and glanced at Amanda, who was sitting on the stairs, her face swollen and red with weeping.

'It's awful. Awful,' he muttered at last. 'He's so young. And there's the boy, too.'

'You don't need to tell me,' she said.

James stood irresolutely swinging his stethoscope.

'Perhaps we'd better sit down somewhere and talk all this over,' he suggested.

Liam, seeing the doctor's gaze settle on the kitchen table, hastened to explain. 'It seems Amanda offered Larry a cup of tea after he'd brought her home from the party.'

'Coffee, actually,' said Amanda.

'You were not here then?' James asked Liam, though he had already noted that there were two used cups, not three.

'No. I followed on later – after I'd sobered up a bit in Lizzie's armchair.'

'He was quite all right while he was sitting here,' said Amanda. 'It was afterwards – when he was leaving – when he was just going to open the front door that he – Oh my God!' She began to cry again.

'Why was he here at all?' asked James. 'Didn't you have your own car?'

'It's broken down,' explained Liam. 'Won't start. She walked to the party this morning.'

'I only wish I'd walked back too,' sobbed Amanda. 'It was all Lizzie's idea, really. She asked Larry to drive me home. She thought another three miles on a hot day would be too much for me. Silly, really.'

'Let's have some tea,' said James. 'I could do with a cup now.' He placed his bag on the table and put both hands on her shoulders. 'You've got some difficult days ahead of you, Amanda. We all have.'

Liam filled the electric kettle at the sink, and Amanda fetched some clean cups from a cupboard.

'I shall have to inform the coroner, you know,' said James. 'Robbie McLean. I know him, fortunately. I'll tell him the circumstances and get him to move the body as soon as possible. I can't give a death certificate, of course, though I guess he died of a coronary. Robbie will send the coroner's officer, a police constable from Swinester. That'll take a little time, since he's not a local man. Will you wait here with Amanda, Liam, till he comes?' He was wondering what had made Liam turn up here anyway, and suspected that perhaps they were having an affair.

'I'll stick around,' Liam promised. 'And when it's all tidied up I can take Amanda back to town. That was what I came for actually – to offer her a lift. Lizzie told me her car was off the road.' He poured tea into the clean mugs and handed them round.

'Natural causes,' said the doctor. 'And there won't be an inquest if that's what's found at post-mortem.' He glanced at Amanda as she gasped, 'Oh no! Oh my God, no!' The image of a post-mortem was not, he knew, a pleasant one for the uninitiated to contemplate.

After he had swallowed some of the scalding tea he used Amanda's phone to call the coroner.

'Robbie? James here. Yes, Jim-Jams. Sorry to break into your Sabbath peace. A really dreadful thing, Robbie . . . man in the prime of life – my next-door neighbour, in fact – a man who was never ill. We'd all been to a party at his house. He drove one of the guests home after it, and fell dead, collapsed, as he was leaving. Oh yes, I know all concerned. Dead man a patient of mine, but never ill. I don't think I've ever had cause to examine him. Seen him for such things as cholera and typhoid jabs and prescriptions for anti-malarials when he goes – went – on foreign tours of duty. Yes. Travelled a lot. Yes. The young woman here has to get back to work on Monday. Or should. . . . Yes, there's someone with her. Yes. Thank you. PC Robinson. He'll get the body moved to the mortuary then? Yes, we're in Frenny Hinton, second from the end of the row. Yellow door. Amanda Burton is the lady's name.'

He hugged Amanda when she stood up as he came back to the kitchen. 'Is there anything I can do for you?' he asked. As she shook her head he grumbled, 'Well, spare a little tear for me. I've got to tell Lizzie tonight.'

Amanda uttered a moan. 'Lizzie,' and tears poured down her cheeks.

James was rather surprised at all the weeping. He had never suspected Amanda of being so tender-hearted.

'Let me know if I can be of any help,' he said. He was slightly envious of Liam's intimacy with her, and sighed as he got into his car. He decided to drive home the longer way by the curved crooked lane and enjoy the cool air now that the day was beginning to fade into its long summer evening. Watching the green fields glide past the windscreen always had a calming effect on him. He would need to be calm when he met Lizzie and the boy. If Amanda, who was after all only a friend, wept so much, what must he expect from Larry's wife? As he turned the corner at the top of the main street he saw Larry's Volvo parked up a side alley. He wondered idly why Larry had left it there, and not outside Amanda's house, and presumed that at the time there had been no nearer parking space. They must have walked back to her house for that last cup of tea that he drank.

Two

Shreds of yesterday still clung to James when his alarm woke him on Monday making him roll unwittingly out of bed and downstairs like a sleepwalker to boil a kettle for his early morning tea. As he sat at the kitchen table he contemplated the day ahead of him with gloom. Monday morning surgery was always the busiest, most crowded session of the week. Despair often settled on people after a weekend spent with their nearest and dearest; the unpleasant sensations produced by misery were interpreted as sickness, so they came on Monday morning to complain, hoping for relief. His patients were mostly women. Dr James knew that statistically as well as in his own experience women came more often with psychosomatic symptoms than men, and had often wondered why, since he was well aware that they were not the weaker sex: not in the matter of endurance, and certainly not in terms of survival. He knew he'd have to do a lot of careful listening, careful because among all the irrelevances there might appear that sign his clinical sense must seize on of physical disease emerging, or that hint that he must not miss that misery had pushed a human being beyond the point of no return. Notoriously difficult to do so, but it was his job to forestall suicide, which was rising among women, as well as all the unsuccessful attempts (if you could describe the ultimate despair of the human spirit as a success) among the adolescent lovelorn.

There would also be a core of elderly men and women with long-standing disabilities which their nearest and dearest were tired of hearing about, and so at Sunday dinner they had suggested, 'Why don't you go and see the doctor, Mum (Dad)? Get some tablets. There must be something can be done.' Not many children with coughs and colds in the summer, but insect bites, occasionally dog bites, cuts and bruises, and after yesterday's hot sun one or two tiny tots with sunburn due to foolish exposure of tender skins. . . . Among this forest of minor ailments, most of which would improve in time without his interference, there was always the possibility of an unexpected and perhaps rare disease presenting and needing urgent attention, or the real diagnostic problem which he must try to solve with observation, analysis and detective acumen, or know when to summon specialist help from the hospital hierarchy. So he had to be constantly on the alert, watchful and kind. Kindness eased the flow of communication from the patient so necessary to the doctor's sifting ear. He sighed again. He didn't feel very kind this morning.

He hadn't slept well. He had stayed up late with Lizzie after poor little Timothy stopped crying, which he did as soon as he climbed into his mother's bed and fell asleep. He had telephoned a number of Lizzie's friends and relatives, including her mother-in-law and the vicar. He was aware that he'd done more for her than was usually expected of a physician, but he was, after all, her next-door neighbour as well as her dead husband's friend. He was worried about Lizzie, who had surprised him by not shedding a tear, too stunned by the news, perhaps, to be able to react normally.

'You may need something to help you sleep for a few nights – just at first,' he said. He gave her half a dozen capsules, which she took without a word and dropped into a small ornamental vase on her sitting-room mantelpiece. 'I shall pop in tomorrow to see how you're both getting on.' She nodded absent-mindedly.

As he shaved, remembering all this, and stared at his own face in the mirror, he thought of Larry. What had gone wrong? How was it he had no inkling of the disaster hanging over this healthy man in the midst of life? He would have to get out the medical record and study it; but as far as he could recall Larry had never been ill.

Mrs Roxby, who came each morning to tidy up and cook for him, arrived just as he was leaving; when she heard what had happened she groaned repeatedly, echoing Amanda's prayers of the previous day: 'Oh my Gawd! Oh my Gawd! Whatever will the poor mite do?' James was unsure if the mite was Lizzie, or Timothy.

'Will you pop in there every day for a week or two, just to see they're going on all right? I'll call every evening after surgery till I know how things stand.' He didn't quite know what he meant by that. He would certainly see that she didn't get hold of enough sleeping drugs to do herself in, which he thought unlikely anyway. But you never could be quite sure. And he intended to offer her emotional support (whatever that was) through the traumatic days of the funeral ahead.

'Of course I will, Doctor,' said Mrs Roxby. 'What a terrible thing. You never know what's round the corner, do you, Doctor?'

James did know what was round his corner that Monday morning. It was a bloody long and harassing day. So he thanked Mrs Roxby and ran out to the garage. He was already a little late.

★

When the Reverend Foster called to see Lizzie at the Barn she was crouched in an armchair in the sitting-room at the back of her house and staring out of the long window at her garden. Perhaps she was watching the field beyond, where the continuing heatwave had driven the cattle away from the dried-up brownish grass of the central expanse to seek shade under the hedge at its furthest boundary. Certainly her eyes were focused on some far-off point. He was rather nervous. Although he admired and even worshipped Lizzie in secret fantasies (feelings he did not share with his wife) he never knew what to say to her.

'Where is Timothy?' he asked.

She glanced at him and made an effort to withdraw her attention from her thoughts to the present time and place. She gave a small smile, grateful that he had not asked the more obvious 'How?', so her reply could be impersonal, matter of fact.

'He's playing croquet with Dr James,' she said, and relapsed into silence.

He brought up a low stool and sat down beside her, hunching his back and drawing his knees up to his chin. He took her hand and held it firmly. She let it rest in his for what seemed to him a long time in silence; but when at last he said, 'He is with God,' she withdrew it quickly.

47

'Do you think so?' she asked.

'I know it,' he replied loudly.

'He is with me!' she declared indignantly. 'Here!' touching her forehead, 'And here!' striking her breast.

He looked at her sadly. She's not going to let God have her husband, he thought; she's going to keep him for herself.

'Shall we pray together?' he asked her hopefully.

'No!' replied Lizzie sharply. That was the last thing she wanted to do: kneel down with poor dear stolid Gerry and mumble clichés, grovelling among dusty bits of worn-out thinking. Seeing his startled expression she added more gently, 'You see, he brought me to his banquet hall, And his banner over me was love.' Gerry was even more startled then. He thought the quotation inappropriate for the occasion, though he recognised it as from the Bible. It was Robert Graves's version of the Song of Songs, which she had recently read.

'Would you like a drink?'

'No, no. Not now.' And they fell silent once more, till he forced himself to speak. 'Have you any particular wishes – I mean, about the funeral?'

'I don't want any funeral,' she cried; then, hearing the anger in her own voice she added, 'I'm sorry, Gerry. I can't think just now. But Larry's mother will be here tomorrow. She'll see to everything. You can work it out with her. I'll ask her to ring you.'

On Tuesday morning Larry's mother telephoned him and arrived at the vicarage soon after, in time for coffee with him and Maisie in the garden, which the morning sun had not yet turned into a green oven. She was a large woman, surprisingly mobile for her size and years, dressed in loose swaying garments of startling reds and purples, and her hair, which was quite elaborately styled, was dyed an unlikely metallic hue somewhere between copper and brass. 'Like pinchbeck,' Maisie confided to him later. 'You know – the poor man's gold of Victorian jewellery. . . .'

Maisie, in a T-shirt and shorts with frayed edges, was watering some wilting petunias from a lidless teapot as Larry's mother swooped through the garden like an exotic bird.

'I'm Elena Watson,' she introduced herself, sinking with a sigh into one of the rickety deckchairs spread beneath the shade of a great chestnut tree. 'I married again after Larry's father died, you see. He was Mr Bassett. As a matter of fact he died young too, and of his heart.' She spoke English perfectly, but with a slight accent he couldn't place. She fanned herself with a notebook she carried. In spite of the heat she was wide awake enough to notice Maisie's attire and consider it rather unsuitable for a vicar's wife, even on a hot midweek morning in July. She supposed they were her garden clothes. People did dress down so for gardening nowadays. She surveyed the place.

'It's lovely and cool in this shade,' she gasped.

'Only in the morning,' said Maisie. 'The afternoon sun burns it up like a furnace.'

'Yes, I can see the grass is pretty scorched. Black please, and no sugar.' She gave Maisie full marks for her coffee, and after sipping it declared, 'What a blessing it is to be with the living. My daughter-in-law is so silent I sometimes wonder if it isn't she who's dead.'

'I think the suddenness of this blow has stunned her,' suggested Gerry gently.

'I suppose so. Well of course, I know she did love Larry very much. She could hardly do otherwise, could she? Everybody loved Larry.'

'Yes indeed.'

Tears gathered in Mrs Weston's large, pale blue eyes and spilled over her rouged cheeks. She didn't dry them with a handkerchief, or blow her nose. She simply went on talking, sniffing now and again.

'Well, somebody's got to do the practical things; and it looks as if that's going to be my lot. The funeral service, for instance – We've got to fix the date for the memorial service as well as for the cremation.'

'Have you found out what Lizzie wants?' asked Gerry.

'Cremation, she said. "I don't want to him buried. That way he'd be in one place where people could tread on him." That's what she said. She wants him cremated so that part of him will be in the air all round her. And when the wind blows she'll feel his arms wrap round her. Quite poetical she is sometimes.'

Maisie shivered, imagining even on that hot day the cold north-easterly that blew down Fossbury Main Street in winter.

'I thought about a month from now for the memorial service. What do you think? That would give time for his London friends and colleagues to gather. And down here. Why not? It's as good as anywhere, and no traffic and parking problems.'

'Would you like to see the church?' Gerry Foster suggested when her cup was empty. Although it was not yet noon he was already longing for the wonderful coolness of his parish church, its plain stone walls and the repetition of stone pillars up the nave so soothing to frayed nerves; but as they reached the porch and pushed open the heavy nail-studded oak door the peace and quiet they were both looking forward to was shattered by children's voices and a loud rattling of metal on stone echoing in the high empty, timber-vaulting. As they stepped inside a small boy on a skateboard rushed down the nave, and a smaller one followed shouting, 'My turn now! My turn now!'

Their mother raised her head from polishing brass near the altar, and came quickly towards them, duster in hand.

'Sorry, sir! Sorry, Mr Foster – but you said I could bring them with me.'

'Well, yes, Mrs Billings,' he admitted. 'But the skateboard! And the noise – !'

Undismayed, Elena sailed in like a windjammer and sank into a pew, unfurling her sails with a great sigh and dropping anchor. 'David, I believe, danced before God in the Temple,' she commented.

'Well, yes. But he had a harp, not a skateboard.' Reverend Foster stood beside her, the little boys and their mother clustered uncertainly about him.

'Joy,' said Elena. 'Joy in a church. . . . That's a good thing.'

'It's the dead I'm thinking of,' he argued. 'Disrespect for the dead. They're skating and rattling all over these ancient graves in the floor, you know.'

'I don't think the dead will object,' she said. 'I think they'll be delighted. All that noise and happy voices

52

shouting will make them think it's resurrection morning and time to get up.'

The vision of the dead rising from the floor decided Mrs Billings. 'Out you go!' she commanded her boys. 'Outside, and play there.'

'It's too bumpy for the skateboard,' the elder grumbled. 'I haven't had my turn,' whimpered the younger.

'You'll 'ave to wait for it,' said his mother shortly. 'Now go on. And don't go outside the gate.'

Grateful for the sudden silence, Gerry sat down in a pew, level with Elena but separated by the nave.

'I should think the acoustics are good,' she said, looking upwards. 'What sort of choir have you got?'

'Medium good,' he said. 'I'm not all that musical myself, but we have a keen organist. He's the choirmaster really. You'd better meet him.'

'I know you can't exactly expect Rachmaninov's "Vespers" in a village church but I do think music is important, don't you? And the Bible – for heaven's sake not the New English. It must be the old King James's, which of course is so poetical. I never realised till it went out of fashion how good it was. People must have something to light up the soul, some little bit of magic to take away after a death – something to keep them going, don't you agree?'

He looked across at her. 'How right you are. Have you anything particular in mind?'

'Perhaps a friend could read that nice piece from St Paul about love not being like sounding brass. That always makes me cry. And music . . . I was a singer myself, you see, so Larry was surrounded by music when he was growing up, and if he's hanging about anywhere he'll expect some good music. Can your organist manage "Jesu Joy of Man's Desiring"? But I'll talk it over with him, as you suggest. And there must be at least one hymn that everybody knows, with words that aren't too silly. A full church congregation singing out loud for him . . . Larry would like that.' She sighed noisily. 'He was a star that fell out of the sky too soon; but I'm not going to let him go without a fanfare.'

'We'll see what we can do,' he said.

When Mrs Weston rose and tottered towards the altar steps he hurried after her to hold her arm; he was afraid she might trip up in those surprisingly high-heeled scarlet shoes.

'Flowers?' she queried, looking over the area.

'We have a very good florist in the town,' he said. 'She knows what's suitable here.' He gave her the name and address to jot down in her notebook when they paused in the porch before plunging into the heat beyond.

'She's taking it badly, Lizzie,' said Elena suddenly. 'She thinks I'm very unfeeling, you know.' She hesitated. She was certainly a talker; and he had the feeling there was something else she wanted to say. Perhaps she wanted to confess. People often did at times of crisis. Well, confessions could be heard, he knew, any time, in any place, even in the porch.

'The fact is I never expected Larry to live. He was born in the concentration camp, you see. I married my first husband' – the H was unexpectedly harsh and breathy – 'Laurence Bassett, not long before Pearl Harbor. We lived a charmed life in Shanghai, outside the real world, though we didn't know that then. I suppose we were rather like those French aristocrats before the Terror: revolution rumbling all around them and they were unaware. Bliss it was in Shanghai then. Days of wine and roses . . . I thought we were immune, protected by the British flag. A British passport was better than diamonds before Pearl Harbor. But that changed everything. After that we were the enemy. The Japs collected us and herded all us British civilians into camps around the city. My parents were sent to a different camp out by Lunghua airfield, where they both died. Malaria I was told. . . .'

'I didn't know,' said Gerry. 'I had no idea.'

'We made a pact, Laurence and I, that we'd work together to survive. We both got very thin, of course; and my – you know, periods – more or less stopped, so I thought I was barren. Stopped and started. Started and stopped. It was a big surprise when I found Larry was on the way. My God! Was I hungry then? Laurence dug out a piece of what used to be lawn, and we grew vegetables. We used our own shit as fertiliser, and our washing water for watering the plot. The Japs liked us growing food. That was something they understood. As a matter of fact they didn't really have much more food than we did at the end. Anyway the soil was full of worms and slugs, which we collected in an old pillowcase. We used it as a filter to wash out the earth. And then we cooked them and chopped them up for mince. It was quite good actually, especially when we added a bit of onion. Sometimes I managed to steal an extra potato from the cookhouse. Luckily for Larry I had breast milk for him – at any rate for a few months.'

'I had no idea that Larry – that you went through such an ordeal,' said Gerry.

'I never expected him to live, you see,' she explained. 'The odds were stacked against him. Some other children in the camp died of diphtheria, of pneumonia after measles, of diarrhoea and malnutrition; but Larry lived.' She paused. 'I suppose the anxiety I felt about him at the time hung over my shoulder even after we were safe back in England. I always used to think it a miracle that he was alive. And so I suppose his death didn't take me by surprise in the way it has poor Lizzie.' She was weeping again, big unchecked tears welling out.

'You did your best,' said Gerry. 'Nobody can do more. God will look after him now.'

She glanced at him sharply sideways, and then stared out into the blazing heat beyond the porch. She braced her shoulders as if about to tackle a palpable obstruction.

'It's really too hot,' he muttered. 'Too hot for you to walk to the florist's. Will you be all right?'

'Oh yes, I shall make it,' she assured him jauntily, sniffing. 'It's nothing like as hot as it used to be in Shanghai. But Lizzie, I believe, will never be reconciled.'

'Give her time,' he suggested. He watched her fill her sails and skim off down the path between the old graves. A card, Lizzie had called her – 'a bit of a card, my mother-in-law. . . .' He supposed that what she really was was a *grande dame* from the imperial past; and as her loose, bright-hued skirt swirled about her, so quickly did she move even in that heat, he saw her as flying the colours.

Dr James decided to pop into the Barn that evening after surgery. He had remembered Larry's car parked in a side street in Frenny Hinton and wondered if anyone had rescued it yet. Larry's keys were probably still in the mortuary with his clothes; but Lizzie must have another set.

The house seemed to be gasping for air it was so still and hot as James walked through the wide open doors of the big sitting-room. He could hear the television from the open door of Lizzie's room, and walked towards the sound.

'Anyone for Moselle?' he asked, swinging a bottle.

They smiled assent. Lizzie told Timothy to switch off the telly.

'I don't think you've met Elena? Dr James from next door,' she introduced them.

'She's my granny,' explained Timothy.

'Your *babushka*,' said Elena.

'What's a *babushka*?' asked Timothy.

'A species of trans-Siberian monkey,' said Lizzie, and Elena added, 'A Russian monkey,' whereupon Timothy jumped up and capered round the room scratching his armpits and uttering small shrill cries. Only Elena laughed.

'Are you half Russian, then?' asked James.

'Wholly Russian,' she replied.

'And I'm a quarter Russian. And Daddy . . .' Timothy suddenly faltered and burst into tears, 'was only half – ' Both women spoke to him at once in soothing voices.

So Larry had been half Russian. There were so many things Dr James didn't know about this lost neighbour of his. Lizzie rose to fetch glasses from a cupboard in one corner, and as James poured out three full glasses and one half-full for Timothy he said, 'But you've lived here all your life?'

'Oh no,' said Elena. 'I spent my gilded youth in Shanghai – though we arrived first in Harbin when my mother fled from Moscow and the Bolsheviks via the trans-Siberian Railway. We were only minimally gilded then. All her fortune was the jewellery and a few coins stitched into the hem of her skirt. I don't remember Harbin at all. I was too little. I don't remember my father either. He was killed before we became refugees.'

'Did he die in a shoot out?' asked Timothy hopefully.

'I don't know how he died. He just disappeared; and

then my mother was a widow and very frightened. She wasn't a widow for very long in Harbin, because the next thing I remember is Shanghai, where my step-father was a rich merchant and British; and I was sent to an English school run by nuns.'

'Was it a very strict school?' asked Timothy.

'Not at all. I only went in the morning. In the after-noon my *Amah* took me for walks in various parks and gardens – not the Riverside Park you always hear about where there was that notice at the gate: No Admittance to Dogs and Chinese. Well, that *was* awful! But the Chinese were always more racist than we were you know. They regarded all foreigners with disgust. They thought we smelt bad and said we had red faces and big long noses.'

Timothy laughed.

'Even now they call us Running Dogs. And the Americans are paper tigers. Very nice,' she added, sipping her wine. 'So good, Moselle, on a warm summer evening.'

'You know, Lizzie,' said James, 'I believe Larry's car is still parked in the street in Frenny Hinton. We ought to drive it back.'

Lizzie, who had been sitting quite still and silent throughout Elena's discourse, stirred herself with an effort. She rose, and after rummaging in her desk produced a bunch of keys. 'Shall we go?' she asked; and to Timothy: 'Turn on the telly again, love. Elena likes it.'

'So do I,' he said.

They were silent as they drove to Frenny Hinton. When James located the Volvo Lizzie came suddenly to life.

'Has it been moved?' she asked. 'It's nowhere near Amanda's door.'

'No. I noticed that before,' said James. 'I suppose there was no parking space nearer. It was a Sunday. People would be at home with their cars then, wouldn't they?' As Lizzie sat down in the driving seat he tapped on her window. She wound it down.

'I hope you're eating all right. Are you?' he leaned over her. 'You must keep yourself well.'

'There's not much point really, is there?' she said, grasping the wheel fiercely.

'There's Timothy.'

She nodded, and as she started the ignition he kissed two fingers and stroked her cheek with them. She drove off, followed by James's car, and parked the Volvo in the garage at the Barn. She sat still then for a few seconds trying to summon enough energy for her next move. She supposed she ought to clear things out of shelves and pockets, and began to search. There were a couple of maps and a large battered engagement diary, which she took indoors. There might be business engagements that ought to be cancelled, something she must make herself do in the next few days. She would go through it systematically soon, but first she must contact his secretary in London, who would have to inform the many associates and clients of his death.

James could not attend the cremation service; but he heard all about it from Mrs Roxby.

'Very private. Only family,' she said. 'Mrs Bassett, Timothy and old Mrs Bassett and me in the limousine be'ind the 'earse. Mrs Garner, that's Larry sister, and her daughter bringing up the rear of the funeral cortège.'

He didn't correct her pronunciation, but asked, 'How was Lizzie?'

'Bearing up wonderful. I thought she might drop, sudden like, when the coffin was slid away into the furnace; but Timothy and old Elena put their arms around her and held her up.'

He nodded.

'Old Mrs Bassett – Elena – she's Mrs Weston really, you know. Twice married and twice widowed, poor soul. Her first husband, Bassett that was, died of a heart attack same as her son, when he were not much more than forty. She's taking Timothy off to the seaside tomorrow. Seems as 'ow her daughter has a boy his age, and they're all going off to Slapton Sands down south.'

'That'll be nice for Timothy,' said the doctor, 'but not so good for Lizzie to be alone all the time, will it?'

'She says she'd rather be alone,' said Mrs Roxby, muffling herself up. She rode a moped from job to job, and liked dressing up in the correct gear: quilted coat, rainproof trousers, and a vast red helmet complete with visor, even on the hottest day. 'What I do worry is she'll starve herself. She's not eating no more 'n a bird.'

'That won't do,' said James. 'That won't do at all.'

So that evening he walked towards the Barn carrying the cold supper Mrs Roxby had provided: a pork pie, a few lettuce leaves and a tomato, and a bottle of Wine Society claret tucked into one of the pockets of his jacket. He decided to take that off as soon as he got there, though it was a lot cooler than it had been since the heatwave broke into scattered thunderstorms soon after the cremation. The sliding doors above the terrace were open, so he walked in shouting, 'Are you there, Lizzie?' A muffled voice answered from the sitting-room.

'I've brought you some supper,' he said. She didn't move from her chair by the window, but he knew where to find glasses, and proceeded to uncork the wine. She drank a glass quite greedily, but only managed to swallow a mouthful of pie.

'I'm going to plant a stand of English woodland cherry,' she said, gazing out of the window. 'Twelve trees, one for each year of our married life. Larry always loved the wild cherry.

> Loveliest of trees, the cherry now
> Is hung with bloom along the bough,
> And stands about the woodland ride
> Wearing white for Eastertide.

He used to quote Housman. He liked that simple, disciplined verse.' She held out her glass for more wine. 'It helps me to sleep,' she explained.

The following evening he brought her a warmed-up toad-in-the-hole with some limp cabbage.

'Mrs Roxby, bless her, is no cook,' was Lizzie's comment, as she drank some of James's Spanish plonk. James ate in silence; and then they watched the nine o'clock news on TV together. 'I'll cook something for tomorrow,' she suddenly offered as he was about to leave. 'I can't bear to think of you having to eat that awful food.'

James was pleased, not only at the prospect of eating some of her excellent grub, but also because he knew that the need to cook would force her into activity. All this sitting and staring out of a window at the past might be a necessary part of her mourning, but he was afraid it was taking hold of her completely.

And so a new pattern of living emerged for them both. He called at the Barn on most evenings with a bottle of wine, and she provided a delicious meal in the kitchen. He noticed with satisfaction that after a fortnight she was beginning to eat a little of it herself. After supper they moved into her sitting-room and after the news he returned home. She didn't talk much; but she didn't seem to mind sitting with him in silence. Once she commented, 'I appreciate your kindness, James. I'm sorry I'm such poor company.' He reached out and squeezed her hand briefly.

When she did talk it was always about Larry. Larry had been away in Nigeria when Timothy was born. He had intended flying home in time for the birth, but Timothy was in too much of a hurry and arrived two weeks early. 'I sent him a telegram to tell him the news; and do you know what he wired back? "Happy,

happy, happiness and love." That was all.' She smiled suddenly, a radiant smile, but James's eyes filled with tears. Theirs was an envied joy. He remembered his disappointment and Mary's sadness as each year of their marriage passed and she did not conceive; but Mary would encourage him now, praising him for his compassion and neighbourliness. 'Poor soul. Poor wee soul!' was how she would have put it, referring of course to Lizzie.

'I hope Timothy is enjoying his holiday in spite of being sad, which I know he is,' Lizzie said one evening. 'I hope he gets some sailing. Larry should have left London on the second. We were to have gone to Salcombe on the Sunday after. Larry promised to take him sailing. Yes, I did remember to cancel that booking.' She relapsed into silence, reminded of the fact that she had not yet written to people mentioned in his diary. 'Anyway, Miss Brockway is coming down here to see me tomorrow. She's Larry's secretary. And the executor is coming too. You can guess how I dread all that.'

'Look,' he said. 'Don't bother to cook anything for the evening. I dare say you'll have to give them lunch, won't you?'

'I'll keep some titbits for you. And then you'll have to make do with cheese.'

'That'll be wonderful. But you'll be tired. Would you rather I didn't come in tomorrow?'

'Oh no. Do come as usual, and then I'll tell you all they said.'

But just before he left his house for the evening surgery she phoned him. 'I'm afraid it's all been rather too much for me, James,' she said; and James knew by the sound of her voice that she'd been crying at last. 'And what they said has been a bit of a bombshell. So if you don't mind . . . .'

'You go straight to bed, Lizzie. Doctor's orders. And it wouldn't hurt to take one of those sleeping tablets I gave you. I'll come round tomorrow.'

'Yes. We'll finish up the leftovers then.'

When next they met her face was ravaged by tears and sleeplessness and she was more than usually silent until it was nearly time for him to go, when she announced, 'Something awful seems to have happened. Not as bad as Larry's death, of course.' She paused. 'He's left a lot of debts, you see. Overstretched, they say. Borrowing money for some time, it seems. I don't know quite how we're going to manage. I'm not very good about money. I'll have to sell something I suppose.' She looked round the room as if seeking help from the walls.

'He must have left some insurance,' said James. He

was shocked to learn that someone as intelligent, as wealthy and successful, as confident and worthy of trust as Larry had seemed to him could leave his affairs in such a mess, with his wife and son unprovided for.

She shook her head. 'It will all be swallowed up by debts, I'm told. They think I'll have to sell the house.'

He waited, he hesitated, then said, 'You'll have to take Timothy away from his prep school. That's the first thing. The cost of private education is a bottomless pit. And – don't look aghast – there's a very good comprehensive in Fossbury.'

'Yes,' said Lizzie. 'Mrs Roxby's grandsons go there.' She looked out of the window. 'I shall have to talk it over with Elena. She's so good at this sort of thing.'

'You can't do anything till after probate, anyway.'

'No.'

They fell silent again.

'Elena and Timothy will be back here for the memorial service at the end of the month,' she said at last. 'Elena's arranging it all – all the music too. She used to have a lovely voice, you know. Larry always said she sang not like an angel but like a whole choir of them.' She laughed unexpectedly. 'Well, if they're all like her in heaven Larry will be all right!'

James wondered if she resented Elena's domineering personality and Larry's strong attachment to his mother; but she showed no bitterness, no jealousy. 'Elena understands about music,' she continued. 'So I'm leaving it all to her. She says Larry must go out with a triumphal fanfare. And I completely agree.'

'So do I. Absolutely.' He was pleased that she seemed to be taking an interest in the coming memorial service.

But that night when she was alone in bed her loss and desolation swept over her like a tidal wave. In the darkness under the sheets she held out her arms, pleading with Larry to come into her. Her yearning for him, both spiritual and physical, was so overwhelming that she uttered shuddering groans, and called out in a loud voice, accusing God: 'Why didn't you take me instead of him?' She would gladly have given her own life for Larry's, so great was her love.

She was emerging from her state of shock into active grieving. Once or twice she slipped a note through James's letterbox while he was out: 'Don't come tonight, James. Couldn't make it today. So no food. Sorry. Come tomorrow.' On other evenings she forced herself to cook a meal for them both; and after a couple of glasses of wine she talked a little, but still it was always about Larry.

'He once told me he was like one of those little Russian dolls, six little painted dolls all carved out of one piece of lime wood, still smelling of summer and lime flowers he said – although of course that was only his fanciful way of talking. When you open the biggest there's another one inside, and another smaller one inside that, and so on. And each doll, he said, was a different person, one for each of his different lives; but in the centre was his secret self. That was only for me. There he was mine.'

He watched her speaking, her great solemn grey eyes glowing as if lit by an inner fire, her whole face transformed by her memory of Larry, which brought her joy, not sorrow. He thought her marvellously beautiful. When she turned and smiled at him he felt a sharp pang which he recognised as jealousy. This love of theirs must have been unique; it was something special, not at all like the affection he and Mary had once felt. He supposed that Larry and Lizzie's was romantic love, something sought after but very rarely attained, like the Holy Grail. Once you've had it, he thought, any other love would inevitably be second best. He was not surprised to hear Mary's acerbic voice warning him: 'Now just you watch your step.'

Maisie visited Lizzie nearly every day, after she'd finished her night shift and had a sleep. She did night work because it was the best paid. They needed the money; and Gerry was so good with the kids, getting their breakfast and packing them off to school. He usually made her tea, too, when she woke up.

'I'm worried about Lizzie,' he told her. 'She's angry with God. And she won't pray.'

Maisie was less concerned about Lizzie's repudiation of spiritual help than about her physical reaction to bereavement. Maisie, a trained nurse, had watched wounds healing. It wasn't only time that was needed, but layer after layer of fine tissue accumulating with the days. So, in Maisie's view, events and even gossip could be laid over and so help to blunt the raw sensitive surface of Lizzie's soul.

'I've got a follower,' she said.

'What do you mean, Maisie? A lover?'

'Well, in a way, I suppose that's it.' She busied herself in Lizzie's kitchen making coffee and finding the tin of biscuits.

'This woman's started following me about. She's an assistant nurse at the hospital. She finds out when I'm going off duty and waits in the car park. At first, when I found out that she lived in Frenny Hinton I offered her a lift. She usually gets the bus to Fossbury and picks up her cycle here somewhere for the rest of her journey home. She's had a lot of bad luck. She's lonely, and I was sorry for her.'

They sat down at the kitchen table and sipped coffee.

'Eat a biscuit too, Lizzie. You must feed yourself, you know.' Obediently Lizzie nibbled. 'I suggested she joined the Mothers' Union. I thought that would be company for her, but she said her own mother was dead and she didn't want union with anyone else's, thank you! So I said, "What about the Young Wives' Fellowship?" "I'm not a young wife," she said, "and I want more than fellowship." '

'What does she want, then?'

'That's what I asked her. And do you know what she said?' Poor Maisie blushed scarlet as she brought it out in a rush: 'She said to me – would you believe it? "It's you I want".' Maisie knew that Lizzie's old self would have burst out laughing at her predicament; her grieving self only managed a smile.

'Poor Maisie. It must have been a shock,' was her comment.

'She presented me with a cake she'd made. And another time it was a bottle of cheap perfume.'

'Good heavens, Maisie. She *is* in love with you!'

'Well, I wish she wasn't. It's sad, I know. But why

can't she find someone more like herself? I can't bear the woman. I mean,' she interrupted herself with an attempt at a parenthesis of Christian charity, 'I feel sorry for her and all that. I don't mean her any harm. But I do wish she'd leave me alone.'

'What's she like?' Lizzie's curiosity was aroused.

'Surprising really – not masculine at all. Quite beautiful in a way. Large dark eyes, and a big mouth. A bit too fat.'

'Perhaps she thinks of you as the masculine one?'

'Oh Lord!' Maisie was startled. 'Do you think so? I don't think I look masculine, do I?'

'Well, you do rather stride about, but you haven't developed a bass voice yet.'

Maisie glared steadily at Lizzie. 'I forgive you,' she said. After all, it was the first joke Lizzie had made in weeks.

'What's her name, Maisie?'

'Melanie.'

'It's sad,' said Lizzie. 'Unrequited love is always sad, and if you belong to a minority group it must be so much more difficult to find another lover.'

'Yes, but why pick on me? There must be some place where they hang out – people with her inclinations.'

'What are you going to do about it?'

'I wish I knew. Gerry says I must carry on regardless. It will all die away if I don't encourage her, he says.'

'What problems vicars' wives do have!' said Lizzie. 'I had no idea.'

'Nor had I till this happened. Fairly plain sailing up till now. Disapproval, of course – lots of that from the old church cats. I don't do all the things vicars' wives are supposed to do. But as I'm no good at flower arranging, I leave that to those who are. I do do my shift at church cleaning, and sometimes I polish the brass. Anyway I don't care much what people say so long as Gerry thinks I'm doing all right.'

'Which he should,' said Lizzie. 'I think he's a very lucky man.'

'So does he, which is nice,' said Maisie, smiling. 'Being a nurse helps. He thinks nursing's rather holy and all that. . . . And some of the parishioners do too. If it was dress designing I did, or running a shop, it would be another story. But we need the money. That's why I have to work – hospital shifts, private cases, anything I can get. Luckily Gerry's so good and understanding. And adaptable.'

'If this Melanie business gets around people will talk,' said Lizzie.

'They're talking already. Talking their bloody heads

off.' Only yesterday Mrs Roxby had told her that old Mrs Sims waylaid her outside the post office to pronounce judgement: 'If she goes round the town wearing shorts that's just what she must expect. Makes you think she's one of them.'

'Lots of women wear shorts!' cried Lizzie indignantly. 'Especially in hot weather. We all wear shorts some time or other. That doesn't make us all lesbians.'

'That's probably what Mrs Roxby said – something like that.'

'How absurd,' said Lizzie; and indignation made her eat another biscuit.

She was grateful for Maisie's visits. It was easier to talk to Maisie than to Dr James, kind though he was, and in need of looking after as well. Easier to talk to a woman than a man, she decided, though it had always been easy to talk to Larry. But then Larry was different, absolutely different from all other men. Then she remembered Larry was no longer there, absolutely *not there*. Suddenly she felt sick, and laid her head on the table and groaned. Maisie didn't ask her any questions; she didn't pester her; she simply took the cup out of her hands and stroked the back of her neck. Maisie was all right, but it was Amanda she really wanted to see. It would be so easy to talk to her because they shared so many memories: the excitement when they found the Barn, the designing, planning and rebuilding of it. . . . Timothy's babyhood, and how good Amanda was that time when she took some of her annual holiday to look after him so that Lizzie could travel to Nigeria with Larry.

She missed Amanda; but for whatever reason Amanda had been aloof and silent since the party. She sent Lizzie a formal card: WITH DEEPEST SYMPATHY in silver lettering, and underneath it a scrawl: *love always. Amanda.* But nothing else. No letter, no phone call. When Lizzie in desperation phoned her London flat an Ansafone spoke in such a cold voice asking her to record a message that Lizzie said nothing at all, and hung up. She supposed Amanda must feel shattered, and perhaps even guilty that Larry had died at her front door after giving her a lift home. But that was not her fault; it might have happened at the Barn had Lizzie not suggested that lift. Nor would she have suggested it if Amanda's car hadn't broken down on such a hot day for walking. It was not Amanda but a chain of accidental causes that decided the place of Larry's death. She would write to Amanda, later, when she felt stronger; and they would renew their friendship. They would talk about Larry and the past. Amanda was the only person in the world who could tell her about Larry's last minutes of living. Had he suffered? Had he murmured no last message for her, no farewell, no words of comfort for the distress he was leaving behind? Did he know he was dying, or did he not have time to think about it? These and many other things she wanted to know only Amanda could tell her. She thought of other deaths she'd read about: of Nelson walking on the deck of HMS *Victory* with his flag captain Hardy during the Battle of Trafalgar and being suddenly fatally wounded by enemy shot, of how he lay dying in his friend's arms and whispered the famous message, 'Kiss me, Hardy', which some interpreted as 'Kismet Hardy'. She remembered Turner, the great painter of sunsets, who murmured as he died, 'The sun is God.' Last words of the famous are recorded. Larry's last words only Amanda knew. Surely, surely, Lizzie hoped and believed, he must have left some significant words for her. And if he had, Amanda heard them.

But when later that day she sat down in her sitting-room and stared out of the window she forgot Amanda, the affair of Maisie and her unusual lover slipped from her mind, and Larry's presence surrounded her. She could think of nothing else; but however much she longed for him, called out his name and cried for him, she could not touch him. He was in her heart and in her head, but not in her arms.

Three

Sunday morning was the time Myra Roxby liked best in the whole week. It was then that she could enjoy, could revel in the little home she'd made for herself, had saved for as well as slaved for, had fought for against all the odds. Now she could survey with pride and pleasure what she'd snatched for herself from hostile fortune. She hummed as she sprayed her house plants.

'There now,' she spoke aloud caressingly. 'That should cool you down.' Then she stood still, suddenly alert and accusing. ''Allo, 'allo! What do I spy with my little eye?'

She put on her glasses for closer inspection. 'Something beginning with P that's what. A whole lot of Ps. A whole lot of nasty bleeding little parasites sucking the strength – sucking the will to live out of you.' She squeezed a layer of aphids off a succulent shoot, and sprayed again. 'Can't have you eating up my lovely greenery!' Ferns were her favourites. So cool and feathery. Carefree, somehow. Not like humans. She noticed they were a bit dry, and took the pots of fern, one by one, over to the sink to soak them in water. Supremo, her big black neutered tom-cat followed her and rubbed himself against her ankles. 'Mind my nylons,' she warned him sharply, but she bent and stroked his back. The phone rang as she straightened up.

'Mum . . .' a familiar voice insinuated itself into her ear.

'Oh, it's you Sandra. . . . Well, I can tell you're going to ask me again. And the answer is No.'

'But Mum. . . .'

'You're brought it on yourself, Sandra.' Mrs Roxby's voice was severe. 'I warned you in the beginning if you took him into your house you'd never get rid of him.'

'But Mum, he is my dad,' objected Sandra.

Mrs Roxby was silent. He was once, she thought, before he washed his marbles down his gullet with all that scrumpy he swallowed over the years, before he came home – fell home – paralytic and filthy and reeking of booze.

'I'm not having any more,' she said. 'Thank you. I struggled with him and all the debts he dragged behind him for fifteen years. It took me all that time to make up my mind to kick him out.'

'I've heard it all before,' said Sandra wearily.

'Well, it seems you need to be reminded.'

'Haven't you any feeling?'

'Not for him.'

'Well, for me then, and for Chris and Darren. If you could just take Dad for the day – for an afternoon – then Darren could bring his friends home. It's his birthday, next month, you know, and I want to make a cake for him.'

'I'm not stopping his friends coming in.'

'Darren's ashamed of his grandad. The other kids laugh at him and call him funny.'

'He's more than funny. He's horrible.' She knew just how his friends felt. Dad would be sitting in his smelly chair by the telly dropping daft remarks and snorting. 'I can't have him here,' she added in sudden panic. 'He'd pee on the carpet, or spit on the cushions. Or worse. Once I let him in I'd never get rid of him.'

Sandra began to cry.

'It was your fault, Sandra, for taking him in the first place.'

'I had to, Mum,' Sandra defended herself between sniffs. 'He was out on the street. He might have died of hypothermia.'

Mrs Roxby secretly thought it a pity she hadn't left him there. She never could understand why everybody was so scared of hypothermia. It seemed to her a nice way to go: just falling asleep quietly instead of hanging on only half alive and being a bloody nuisance. If Sandra had left him in the street the Social Services would have *had* to find him a bed. Now he'd got one they needn't bother.

'What can I do, Mum?' asked Sandra, and immediately began to pour out a catalogue of troubles: how she had to change Dad's clothes twice a day, how the boys kept Vince and her awake half the night quarrelling since she'd put them together in one room in order to give Dad a room to himself. And the washing – ' You wouldn't believe how much washing there was! The district nurse had been ever so kind and given her a pair of her own old nylon sheets to help out – quick drying they were – but he needed a clean pair every day. On a wet day she had sheets draped all over the house and drying on the bannisters. The kids couldn't stand the smell, had given up watching TV and were out in the streets all the time so she didn't know what they were up to; and Vince had taken to going out every night to the pub, which he never used to do. She was at her wits' end. And the mattress was filthy.

'So now we're hearing the truth,' said her mum. 'Have you tried the Social Services again?'

'They haven't got the beds, they say.' Sandra explained. 'I keep ringing them. They've put him on a waiting list for an old people's nursing home. Six months. Maybe a year. Part Three Accommodation is what they call it. Whatever number it is it isn't plentiful.'

If it was Part Three, thought Mrs Roxby, there must be other parts. There were warden-assisted bungalows, weren't there? But he was long past that, and anyway that group of them in Fossbury had filled up very quickly. Then there's the old folks' home, but they wouldn't take him there because he was incontinent.

'Why don't you try Dr James again?' she suggested. 'Get him to move Dad. Make out he's just had a stroke. Make up some queer symptoms so he'll be more interesting. Say he's had a fit and swallowed his tongue and nearly choked himself. Doctors will always do something about an interesting case.'

'Do you reckon so?'

'I know so. And tell you what . . . I'll let you have another pair of sheets. You must be getting short.'

'Short? Desperate, you mean!' And Sandra was off again on another long moan. 'Vince has rigged up a line across the landing for when it rains. Surprising how well it dries over the stairs really. . . . And it does stop him coming down. Dad, I mean – when the washing's drying there, I mean – he can't find 'is way through the sheets. I've got this dread 'e'll fall down-stairs and break 'is neck.'

'Might be the best thing,' said Mum. 'Only the Social Services'd be bound to think you pushed him.'

Sandra was shocked. 'That's *evil*, Mum! How can you say such things? I am fond of him, you know.'

It was something Mrs Roxby could never under-stand: her daughter's attachment to her dad. It was all part and parcel of the same thing: that love makes a fool of you. 'I'll bring the sheets round one of these days,' she said, and rang off.

The heatwave had ended and been forgotten and Cots-wold rain was falling steadily when Dr James visited Sandra Parsons' council house and climbed the stairs behind her. He knew pretty well what to expect; he also knew there was very little he could do. The demented old man was already swallowing hypnotic pills at night to keep him quiet so that the rest of the family could sleep; he was already being taken by ambulance once a week to a day centre in Swinester to give Sandra a few hours free of him when she could get on with other necessary work in the house; and an attendance allowance had been applied for to help her financially – little enough, James knew, but no doubt she was adding her father's old age pension to the family budget too. But he was taken aback by the sight of all the washing hanging over the landing. He had to grope his way through the wet sheets, flipping their cold edges away from his ears, and the toe of a dripping sock out of his eyes.

'Sorry about the sheets, Doctor!' Sandra, ahead of him, called out as she opened a bedroom door. 'I haven't got a tumble-drier you see.'

'Have you thought of the launderette at the other end of the town?'

'I couldn't leave him alone for the time it takes,' she explained. 'He'd fall downstairs, or turn on the gas and forget to light it.'

Dr James put his medical bag on the end of the bed and greeted the old man who was sitting up and grinning at them.

'Good morning, Mr Roxby.'

'George,' said the patient.

'Is his name George?'

'No, it's Wilf. None of us knows who this George is

he keeps on about. Mum used to call Dad Wilf the Wolf. He was a good-looker in them days.'

Dr James strapped the sleeve of his sphygmomanometer round Wilf's arm, put the earpieces of his stethoscope in place and began to pump.

'Poppycock!' said Wilf.

'Poppycock, is it? Now just look at this light. Follow it with your eyes. No trouble there.' He stroked Wilf's cheek.

'Nice. Nice,' said Wilf.

'No paralysis there. He seems to like that.'

'It's just one of his words, doctor. Don't mean a thing.'

'How many words does he have?'

'About ten. The kids counted them once. They say he has ten marbles left. Kids can be cruel.'

'Has Nurse supplied you with incontinence pads?' asked James.

'He just pulls them off and throws them out the window.'

'You'll have to keep the window shut then.'

'He keeps falling down, Doctor,' Sandra began in a breathless rush. 'I think he must have had a stroke. Or perhaps he's having fits. He rolls his eyes sometimes. And sometimes he groans something terrible . . . thrashing about on the floor. . . .' She was inventing wildly, aware that her mum would have done it all much better. He watched her calmly. She was too truthful a girl to be able to make out a good case.

'I know it's difficult for you, Sandra,' he said. He removed the bedclothes from Wilf's knees, and with the sharp end of his rubber-ringed patella-hammer he scratched the soles of Wilf's feet till Wilf pulled them away, objecting 'Bloody racket!'

'Bloody racket, is it? Swing you legs over the side of the bed, George, and let's try your knee jerks.' They were very sluggish, and the ankle jerks were unobtainable. Dr James stood up and, beating the palm of one hand with the heavy end of his hammer, he spoke to Sandra across the bed. 'Blood pressure not up, Sandra. Not too bad at all. No hypertension. No stroke. But he's got some peripheral neuritis. That's why his legs are weak. How much do you think he was in the habit of drinking before you took him in? Beer? Spirits?'

'Scrumpy mostly. The rough sort that's stronger and cheaper. He couldn't afford spirits. Doesn't drink now. We dried him out.'

'He's just an old cider alky, my dear. There's nothing we can do about it now. The alcohol's destroyed his brain – washed away his neurones, really – and must have damaged his liver too. But you're coping very well, Sandra. Marvellously, in fact.

You're giving him all he needs. You've given him a good home, and dried him out. You could say he's home and dry. Wonderful job, you've done.'

'Well I can't do it no more!' she cried angrily. 'It's my home 'e's breaking up. And as for being dry – well, you saw the sheets; and you must have noticed the smell as you came in. It drives most people out.'

'I know. I know, Sandra.'

She began to cry: 'I can't do no more. I wanted to look after 'im. 'E is my Dad, but it all seems to have gone wrong some'ow. The boys are getting so wild, and out in the streets till after dark . . . and Vince never used to drink, but 'e's at the pub every night now till closing time. I can't go on much longer. That's the truth.'

'Shit,' came a squeaky voice from the bed.

'Sorry, Doctor. It's another of his words.'

'It won't be easy to get him away,' said Dr James. 'Beds are scarce, especially long-term beds. And he may last quite a while. Let's see – ' he picked up his notes. 'He's only sixty-four, I see. But I'll do my best. I may be able to get Dr MacTrap to see him as an end-phase alcoholic.'

'Is he a specialist?'

'Yes. Psychiatrist. Knows all about marbles. And if he won't play ball I'll get on to the geriatrician.'

'Nice, nice,' Wilf murmured, grinning.

'That's right, me old dear,' said Sandra, folding back the blankets and tucking him in. 'Just you have a nice nap while I take Doctor downstairs. I'll bring you a cup of tea when he's gone. I talk to him like this,' she said as they left the room, 'but he don't understand a word.'

As soon as the boys came in for their dinner she fed them, and while they were busy eating in the kitchen she ran up to the phone box on the corner of Clematis Close to ring her mum, who at this time of day on a Tuesday was at Mrs Bassett's Barn, to tell her the good news; but Mrs Roxby had left a bit early that day, so she spoke to Lizzie, and in her excitement and relief Sandra poured out her tale of woe as well as her hopes for the ending of it.

The sudden unexpected revelation of Sandra's predicament shook Lizzie out of her own egocentric suffering. She determined to talk to Mrs Roxby about what could be done to help, and as soon as James arrived that evening she discussed it all with him.

'I'm trying to get him away for a bit to give his daughter a rest,' he said. 'But it's not going to be easy. No consultant wants an incurable demented old man blocking one of his hospital beds. And with the present increased pressure for efficient use of what they call resources it's going to be doubly difficult.'

'It's awful for her. Awful!' cried Lizzie indignantly; but James, who was more used to dealing with such crises, took the matter more calmly.

'Tell you what,' he suggested. 'What about letting Timothy play croquet with Sandra's boys on my lawn? Only when you or Mrs Roxby can be there to see that they don't get up to mischief. That goes without saying.'

'What a good idea,' said Lizzie. 'And if it's fine I'll give them a picnic tea in the garden.'

'It's wonderful how your thoughts inevitably revert to food,' he said.

'Feeding is an act of love,' she said primly.

That gave him something to think about when he went back to his own house. Did it mean that Lizzie was growing almost as fond of him as he was of her? He sighed resignedly. No, that was a foolish thought. Love was a word with so many different meanings. Lizzie felt affection for the people she fed; she would feel the same for a dog or cat. She loved Larry, would continue loving him for months, years, possibly till the end of her life. It would be silly to allow himself hopes in that direction. But sometimes when he was alone at night, and sometimes when driving home from his last visit in the afternoon, his imagination escaped from his control, and he enjoyed fantasies about her of a sort that Lizzie would probably strongly disapprove of if she even guessed their nature.

A week later Doreen, Dr James's receptionist at the health centre, stopped a patient as he was about to enter the surgery, because, as she explained with that satisfaction she felt when she was able to boss, or better still thwart a patient, she had to put through an urgent call on the line to Dr James.

'Dr James? It's Dr MacTrap on the line.' Doreen's voice – always loud and clear from frequent rehearsing of the amateur dramatic society's musicals she starred in on Fossbury's Town Hall stage – trilled in his ear.

'Oh yes. Put him through, will you, Doreen?'

After a few clicks and a brief high-pitched buzz Dr MacTrap's gravelly Scottish bass percolated through.

'Is that you, James? You wanted my opinion and advice on your patient – er – Wilfred Roxby? I saw him on Saturday.'

'That was good of you Dr MacTrap. Seeing him on a Saturday, I mean.'

'I have to fit these domiciliary visits into my free time, James. That goes without saying.' James couldn't help noticing that he had nevertheless said it. 'Yes. Well . . . It was the syndrome I expected from your notes. Complete cognitive loss with emotional passivity. You suggested Korsakoff's psychosis as the likely syndrome?'

'He has drop-foot and memory loss,' said James, defending his diagnosis.

'An interesting idea. We don't see much of it now-adays. I also considered the possibility of lead poisoning to explain the peripheral neuropathy. Sometimes old-fashioned farmhouse cider-making adds lead to the alcohol, you know. Contamination from the apparatus somewhere. But it's all rather academic. What I was more interested in was the survival of his vocabulary.'

'Only ten words,' James reminded him, but Mac-Trap was not rebuffed.

'Quite. Quite The question is: why those particular words instead of any combination of others? My point being: why this choice of words, and what is their meaning?'

'They seemed disconnected and meaningless to me.'

'Well, don't you see, man? The sequence of single words put together by the informed observer does make sense.'

'Really? For example?'

'What does poppycock make you think of?' There was an unmistakable note of triumph in that gravelly voice.

'Rubbish. Nonsense. Which is what his speech is.'

'That is the socially permissible interpretation. The real underlying significance is phallic, therefore hidden. Cock (the male genital organ) being the colour of a poppy, i.e. red, and/or erect.'

In a field where there were few scientific surveys or experiments to prove or disprove theory he could speculate, and was, James had to admit, as inventive as a writer of crime fiction.

'There is a blue Himalayan poppy I believe. *Meconopsis Baileyi* . . .' James suggested.

'Well, I don't suppose he'd have heard of that.' Dr MacTrap brusquely dismissed it.

'No, I suppose not.'

'So at once you see that he's remembering something: George – poppycock – Monday – Nice.'

'I see. . . . You mean he had sexual relations with somebody called George on a Monday and enjoyed it?'

'Exactly. And has forgotten the details. The only thing he strongly recalls now is the burden of guilt associated with this experience.'

James was silent. He was reserving his medical right to suspension of belief. 'George might be a pub of course,' he said. 'The George VI for instance? It stands on the corner of Clematis Close and Wistaria Way.'

'That is possible.' Dr MacTrap was always willing

to see the other point of view. 'George might indicate the site where it took place.'

'On a Monday?'

'Quite. Quite.'

There was a long pause, during which James's commitment to truth and his wish to score over Dr MacTrap struggled with his desire for a patient's bed. 'I think I ought to tell you,' he said at last, 'that in youth he was nicknamed Wilf the Wolf. I understand he was attractive to women, and preferred them to men. I believe his philandering was partly to blame for the marital break-up. His wife left him, you know.'

'Sexual ambivalence would of course complicate matters.' Dr MacTrap was unabashed. 'It would certainly lead to greatly increased confusion, with anxiety and guilt.'

'Can you get him into hospital?' asked James abruptly.

'Quite out of the question, James. I simply haven't got the beds. Besides he's better at home in familiar surroundings where he can work out his feelings of guilt and aggression.'

'With the help of his vocabulary of ten words?'

'Do you know what the others are, by the way?'

'Bloody racket I believe sometimes comes out.'

'Ah, I detect a touch of aggression there!'

'What happens if his daughter breaks down under the strain of looking after him?'

'That would be a different ball-game entirely, James. I have some acute beds vacant. I could always admit her.'

'That would not, of course, help him.'

'We try to keep these cases in the community as long as possible.'

'The community in this case means his daughter.'

'And her home and family.'

'Which is beginning to break up. The girl's not a trained nurse. Anyway you'd need several – a team of them, as well as a hospital laundry. I have only one nurse attached to the practice, and she's already doing her best.'

'Quite. Quite.'

Dr James waited again before he asked, 'What do you suggest?'

'There's little I can do, James, at this stage.' Was there a hint of defensiveness? James wondered. 'As far as I can see he's being very well looked after by his daughter. He's in a place sufficiently familiar to be thought of by him as home, and he's not getting any more alcohol, so he's dry. At any rate in the alcoholic sense. You might almost say he's home and dry.' He laughed – rather a prolonged laugh – in which Dr

James didn't join so he continued, 'I can see her difficulties, James; but to admit him to my wards is impossible. Your patient – a chronic case – would block one of my beds for a considerable time, as you know, so preventing its use by an acute case for which I might be able to do something. After all – let's face it – Mr Roxby is largely responsible for his own destruction through years of excessive imbibing. Not to put too fine a point on it, he's nothing but an old soak. And at this stage I can do nothing whatever for him,'

'What happens if his daughter does crack up?'

'Well, as I have already indicated I could offer her an acute bed. But we are moving now to the realms of supposition and hypothesis. It might never happen. She seemed to me a strong, sensible girl.' His kilted Rs reeled confidently over the line, and Dr James suffered a sudden disturbing vision of him doing the Highland fling, jigging up and down between the points of two crossed swords.

'Yes, I think she is,' he agreed.

'Well then, we must await events. My secretary will send you my claim form for the domiciliary visit. I would be grateful if you'd sign it. And thank you, James, for asking me to see such an interesting case. Strictly speaking I think it's one for the geriatricians. Their wards are better equipped for dealing with aged dements than mine are. I strongly recommend that you refer him to Dr Kumar.'

James had already contacted Dr Kumar, who was probably at this moment examining the patient. 'Mr Roxby is only sixty-four,' he said. 'Just too young for the geriatric department.'

'Physically he's well beyond his calendar age,' Dr MacTrap argued. 'In any case he'll soon be sixty-five, I hope. I think that's all there is to say, so I'll bid you good-day, James.'

'Shit,' murmured Dr James as he put down the receiver. It was one of Wilf's words that had not been mentioned. He pressed the buzzer wearily for the next patient. Poppycock indeed! He was still ruffled when an elderly, red-faced farm labourer came in.

'What can I do for you, Mr Blunt?' asked James.

'It's me 'earin', Doctor,' replied Blunt, sitting down. His voice had a marked West Country burr, and he pronounced the word eeurrin. Dr James, who was still battling with the confused emotions the psychiatrist had roused in him, still trying to adjust himself into impartial composure, failed to pick up his meaning. He asked, 'What's wrong? is it painful?'

'Not really.'

'Do you have to get up in the night?'

'Well, I do as a matter of fact, now that you mention

it, Doctor.' He spoke slowly with many pauses. Speech was more difficult for him than shifting bales of hay. 'But then I'm not as young as I was, Doctor, am I?' He grinned, pleased at having found the explanation.

'Quite. Quite. I mean to say . . .' James felt flustered. 'Is there any difficulty?'

'Difficulty with what, Doctor?'

'When you pass water, Mr Blunt. When you pee.'

'Oh none at all there, Doctor! Rather free if anything. 'Tis all the beer I do drink.'

'You'd better pee into this jar,' said James with quiet persistence. 'When you've finished I can test your urine.'

''Tis not me urine!' declared Blunt indignantly. He pronounced it to rhyme with wine. ''Tis me eeurrs.'

'Which ear, Mr Blunt?' The doctor spoke sharply.

'Both bloody eeurrs!'

James had to admit defeat. 'OK, Mr Blunt. Sit down and I'll have a look.' When he did look he saw exactly what he'd suspected. Both ears were blocked with wax. While he was preparing to syringe them out with warm water the phone rang again, and Doreen's happy soprano told him that Dr Kumar was on the line.

'Dr James?' enquired a soft tenor voice which had

uttered its first cry somewhere on the vast Indian sub-continent. R.K. here.'

'Oh yes. Dr Ramesh Kumar. Kind of you to call. Can you hold on a moment? I have a patient in the surgery.' He turned to Blunt, holding the receiver in one hand and scribbling on a prescription pad with the other. 'Put a few drops of this in your ears for three nights running.' He remembered that at their last practice meeting he and his two partners had agreed to delegate as many of the simpler tasks as possible. 'Make an appointment to see Nurse on Friday.' He raised his voice as no gleam of comprehension lit Blunt's face: 'See Nurse Friday for syringing! Try again end of week.'

Mr Blunt, realising that he could get no further that morning, took the prescription and left the surgery muttering, 'Bloody eeurrs! Bloody doctors!' And James turned to the phone and other matters.

'Sorry about that, Dr Kumar. You've seen Wilfred Roxby?'

Dr Kumar had, and thought he was a very nice old chap. Most appreciative and grateful.

'Yes, he doesn't seem unahppy,' agreed James. 'It's his daughter – '

'Telling me all the time everything was nice . . .'

98

'Vocabulary is reduced to ten words. Nice is one of them.'

'He's severely constipated,' said Dr Kumar. 'I think we can do something about that. An enema can sometimes work wonders.'

'Do you think it will restore his mental faculties?'

'Well – ah – um. . . . Sometimes they can surprise you, these old people.'

'He's demented, isn't he? Senile dementia. And alcohol has wiped the slate clean.' Dr James had had a trying morning.

'Alzheimer's is rather advanced in this case,' said the gentle voice soothingly. 'But he's being very well cared for by his daughter. Matters would be worse to move him into strange surroundings.'

'I don't think he notices his surroundings any more. His daughter isn't even sure that he recognises her now.'

'Sad. . . . Well, that is sad, I know. We must offer her all the support we can.'

James waited for any suggestions, but when none came he said, 'What our Wilfred needs right now is a bed in one of your wards.'

Immediately the geriatrician became agitated and began to speak very fast. 'That is not possible, Dr James. All the time more and more people come to me, hammering on my door, isn't it? And I must keep most of them out or we shall all be crushed in the rush. I must use my beds to maximum advantage and market economy, isn't it? This Wilfred would block one of my beds for months, greatly reducing the efficiency of our bed occupancy and slowing down the rate of turnover. In any case he's only sixty-four.' A note of relief crept into his voice.

'He should not come under my department at all. He really is a case for the psychiatrists, you know.'

James pointed out that Wilfred Roxby would be sixty-five in a few months' time.

'Then it will be an altogether different game of cricket,' said Dr Kumar. 'I suggest you refer him to me again when he is sixty-five – unless he expires. Meanwhile try Dr MacTrap. This is really a case for him.' As no reply was forthcoming, he pursued: 'After all, this is a case of terminal alcohol addiction. There are many signs of psychiatric disturbance as well as neuropathy. He is not a straightforward case of Alzheimer's disease, I think you will agree?'

'I agree,' said James.

Trying to be helpful, Dr Kumar then suggested a private nursing home.

'The fees, Dr Kumar. Have you any idea what the fees are? These people are not well off. Part Three

Accommodation is simply unavailable, and the private nursing home, too, has a waiting list of six months – probably longer if they succeed in keeping all their patients alive.'

'Dear me! I am sorry to hear it.' There was a long pause before he added hopefully, 'Perhaps you will arrange with your nurse to give the patient a rectal washout? I'll send you the usual form to sign.'

Dr James hung up and then sat still for a moment breathing deeply and looking straight ahead of him at nothing. Was the whole world mad, he wondered, or was it just he who was out of step? He pressed the buzzer, and as he did so a sudden vision of Doreen prancing about on the Town Hall stage in a black bikini passed before him, bouncing, and – oh horrors! – topless. Such a thing had never happened to him before. He found he was pressing the buzzer non-stop when the phone rang and Doreen's voice shouted at him in a far from sexily seductive register, 'OK, Doctor, OK! OK! The next one's on her way. Can't work any faster than we're doing already!'

'Sorry, Doreen,' Dr James was penitent. 'I'm just rattled, for some reason, that's all.'

'That's OK then,' she allowed cheerfully.

He tried the slow breathing technique again, and by lunchtime was almost back to normal. He poured himself a gin and tonic when he got home. He didn't feel like eating; but Mary's voice nagged him, suggesting a cheese sandwich and a cup of tea. She was always so prudent! He sighed. What would she say about his present state of mind? He needed a woman, that was obvious, perhaps a wife, certainly a woman. He'd been too long alone. He was letting himself go: drinking at lunchtime and not taking any exercise; he was putting on weight, and although still several years away from fifty he looked more. He didn't worry about the grey hairs sprinkled through his dense black thatch. Grey hairs add distinction to a man, especially a doctor, he told himself; but he was worried about the irrepressibility of his lusts. And perhaps he was already in love with Lizzie – a hopeless infatuation that would be, with Lizzie locked forever into that inmost Russian box of loving Larry. He sighed again. One of these days he'd find himself groping a female patient's knickers, and then it would be all up with him: accused by the *Sun*, derided by the *News of the World*, hauled up before the General Medical Council, struck off the Register, ruined. Cast into outer darkness. Abandon hope all ye who enter here! This sort of thing would never do. He wondered what Mary would say, but this time Mary was unaccountably silent.

As he went to the fridge for some ice cubes he heard

the click of a wooden mallet on a hard croquet ball. Holding his drink in his hand he walked out on to his lawn and found Timothy there with two young strangers: Darren and Chris, Mrs Roxby's, Wilf's grandsons, Sandra's boys. They greeted him cheerfully, and Chris, who was only seven, commented, 'Grass a bit long, en it?'

Dr James felt foolishly ashamed, like a schoolboy reprimanded. All through the heatwave that had shrivelled the grass he had no need to cut it; but he'd made no effort to do so since the recent rain, which had undoubtedly made it grow.

'Can I do it for you, Doctor?' asked Darren, who was nearly twelve, and rather tall for his age.

'No,' said James firmly. 'I'll do it myself. This evening. His cylinder motormower was an old one and a pig to start. He was convinced no one but himself could coax it into life – certainly not this lanky boy. 'And I think you'd better all go back to the Barn for some lunch,' he added.

'Leave the balls where they are,' shouted Timothy, delighted to be a leader. 'We'll finish the game after lunch.' They threw down their mallets and trooped off towards the tunnel they'd made in the shrubbery, then climbed over the fence into Lizzie's garden.

When later that evening Lizzie heard the lawnmower

next door make a few false starts and spurt into life she knew it would be nearly an hour before James turned up for his supper, so reluctantly she opened Larry's engagement diary and began to search out names and addresses of people she ought to write to. There were a few scattered through October and September. She worked backwards. *Return Home* was entered in the space for Sunday 18 August, and *Drive to Salcombe* for Sunday, 4 August, and *HOME* in large capitals was scrawled across Friday and Saturday the 2nd and 3rd, which made her cry; but then her eye was caught by a single word on Thursday, 1 August: *Pettigrew*. It was a familiar word because that was where Amanda lived: 7a Pettigrew Place. Amanda hadn't mentioned that she was seeing Larry on that date; but she would have, Lizzie supposed, all in good time, when it came up in conversation, had Larry not died. There was nothing unusual in Larry meeting Amanda in town. She sometimes did audits for the consortium Larry worked for. Lizzie didn't think much about it; and by the time she reached mid-July James had arrived and needed feeding, so she closed the book.

When Myra Roxby called on her daughter to deliver the extra pair of sheets she found her ex-husband sitting on a deckchair in the front garden, smoking. She didn't greet him, and he didn't know who she was.

'He's less likely to set fire to things out here,' Sandra said. 'And he don't make such a mess with his ash all over the place.'

They went into the kitchen, from the window of which Sandra could keep an eye on him. Her mother filled the kettle and lit the gas under it.

'I can't get Dad moved at all,' said Sandra when the tea was brewed.

'That's not surprising.'

'The psychiatrist says he's too old for a bed in his hospital, and the geriatric doctor says he's a case for the loony bin.'

'No loonies in the bin nowadays, dear. They're all being looked after in the community. That means you and me. In this case you.'

'Whatever can I do, Mum? I think I'm going barmy myself with all the work and worry of it.'

Her mother held her peace, which was more effective than speech, for it made Sandra confess. 'I know. I should have thought of my own family before yours.'

'What d'you mean, *mine*?'

'Well, he's your husband, isn't he?'

'Was. Once. When he was a proper man. It's not my fault all those years of boozing have softened his brain.

It's his own fault, isn't it? No one but him has let a tide of cider wash away his marbles. I know I never divorced him, if that's what you mean. What was the point? He'd never sign any papers, and I'd never get any money out of him. But he's not been my husband, except on paper, for twenty years.'

'No, I suppose not. Look Mum, I know you've had a hard time in the past. I'm not blaming you. I'm just desperate, that's all. I don't know where to turn.'

The two women finished their tea in silence. Mrs Roxby turned the dregs this way and that in her mug before she spoke again.

'If he had an accident and you called the ambulance they'd have to take him into hospital,' she said.

'What are you saying, Mum?' Sandra's voice was shrill with alarm.

'I'm just thinking. It's a pity. . . . Well! It's only a matter of time before he falls down those stairs when you're not looking, and then you can send him off to the casualty department straight away.'

'They wouldn't keep him in, Mum. They'd patch him up and send him back to me.'

'Not if you didn't have a bed.'

'But I have, Mum! I gave him Darren's and Darren and Chris have to share now.'

'You wouldn't have a bed for him if you burnt it,' said Mrs Roxby. 'In the interests of hygiene . . . .'

'Well he hasn't had any sort of accident,' said Sandra shortly. 'So we won't be able to have Darren's birthday party.'

'Tell you what, Sandra,' suggested her mother, touched a little by remorse, 'I'll take Darren and Chris to the movies instead.'

'You're like that poor gentle little Mrs Bassett,' said Sandra, 'giving a little useless help. It's Dad I want taken off my hands – not the boys. But ta, Mum, all the same.'

She watched Myra don her red helmet whose vizor she pulled down over her face as they walked down the garden path towards her much prized Honda 50 c.c. scooter leaning against the gate. Sandra couldn't catch her words of farewell, so effectively was the sound insulated by the vizor; but she could see her mum's eyes twinkling with her own peculiar brand of good-will acidified with malice.

Four

Thomas Verdi Parry had played in grander churches
and on better organs than that of St Aldhelm's parish
church in Fossbury. He had played in two London
parishes he knew in his youthful past, and for a mem-
orable six months when he had acted as locum during
the illness of the regular organist to St Mary Redcliffe
in Bristol, described (quite rightly in his opinion) by
Elizabeth, Gloriana, the Virgin Queen as 'the fairest,
goodliest, most famous parish church in England'; but
in spite of its second-rate organ he loved his rural
parish church. He knew its history and he was at home
with its acoustics; what's more he liked his vicar and
inside his heart he hid a romantic attachment to
Maisie, the vicar's wife.

Thomas didn't remember much about his father,
who until he was killed in a mine accident sang lustily
(Mam said) in a Welsh male-voice choir. His mother,
who came originally from Pembrokeshire (little

England beyond Wales) left her home when widowed and migrated eastwards towards a sister living in Bristol, where he grew up. He was a small boy with a shock of wiry blond hair, now white but still abundant; and he was bullied at school; but he had a good ear, considerable manual dexterity and a delight in melody, so he found pleasure and protection in music lessons, which his aunt paid for, first the piano, later the organ. After his wanderings in London and some southern counties he discovered Fossbury, and here he was settled in a small eighteenth-century house in Main Street, alone now, his mam having passed on into fields of paradise, and he was happy. His miserable schooldays and his unsuccessful pursuit of girls during an incoherent sex-tormented adolescence and young manhood had taught him to expect little in life. In Fossbury he found his niche at last. In this peaceful place he was able to get on with what he liked doing, which was making music, combined (to keep the wolf from the door) with teaching music to some of the pupils from Fossbury's school, once a grammar school endowed in 1460 by Dorothy Lady Chippersley, a wealthy wood merchant's daughter who had married into the local landed gentry, but nowadays a comprehensive. He had long ago admitted to his more ambitious self that he was a second-rate musician playing virtually unnoticed in his organ loft to an unmusical congregation in a church which he regarded as far from top-notch. In fact (he sniggered mentally at his own little bit of rhyming slang) it was, architecturally at least, a hotch-potch as well. Nothing of the original Saxon church remained except perhaps the site and the name of its Saxon saint. Its base was Norman, and the best part of that surviving was the Norman west doorway, whose semicircular arch, decorated with the usual zigzag stone cutting, framed a tympanum, much peered at by visiting academics, said to depict the Coronation of the Virgin. To Thomas's eye she was being crowned with what looked like a big flat hat. Undoubtedly a halo represented in the very ancient manner horizontally instead of behind the head, time had stained the stone making it look like a brown beret, or even a cowpat. This thought made him smile secretly. He would never, of course, voice this little blasphemy, even to raise a laugh at his local. The carving was so smudged and rubbed away by wind and rain it was nearly indecipherable anyway. The old Norman building had been replaced by a rich wool merchant (father of Dorothy) in the fifteenth century, who added a tower topped by a stone balustrade, its corners embellished with carvings representative of his trade: sheep shears and a ram's head with great circular horns. He had also built a high chancel arch, and large windows, which used to be filled with brilliantly coloured leaded glass depicting events in the life of Fossbury's patron saint. St Aldhelm was blind, but good at playing the harp, which he did in order to tempt the heathen to listen; when he'd suitably softened them up with music he preached his Christian message, converting many on the spot. Thomas naturally liked the story of this Christian Orpheus subduing the savage Brits. Sadly he had never seen those windows – they were all smashed by Parliamentary soldiers during the Civil War – but because he knew their scrap of history, and had added a few fancies of his own, the stained glass flashed brightly in his imagination. The only window worth looking at today revealed a Pre-Raphaelite annunciatory angel. It had been endowed by a Victorian banker who bought a mansion in the country nearby, and this angel was visible and pleasing to Thomas as he played in his organ loft.

But for all his underlying contentment Thomas sometimes found Fossbury humdrum, even dull, so that when Elena Weston streaked like a comet through his quiet life, talking unexpectedly about real music for Larry Bassett's memorial service his day was shot through with excitement and delight. Of course he was aware that all humanity is but a handful of dust, yet he believed, like Elena, that the dead should not be shovelled out of sight with the scrape of spade on gravel, but should be allowed to leave this world with some dignity, and even pomp. It was important, too, that the image of the beloved dead should shine in the memory of those left behind, should vibrate in the ears of mourners, if only for a short while after his passing, with a big beautiful chord. (His own mam he always remembered now in that glorious soprano aria from Handel's "Messiah": 'I know that my Redeemer liveth'.)

Shy and nervous when Elena called on him, he ushered her into his small parlour with its bay window overlooking the pavement of the busy Main Street, and offered her a cigarette.

'Oh no!' She recoiled from the packet. 'I've never smoked. Smoking ruins your voice – thickens the vocal chords. A smoking soprano couldn't possibly hit top C.' After that he knew where he was, and they settled down to serious musical business.

She arrived with the quartet of singers from her London choral society the day before the memorial service, so they were able to rehearse the music together in the church all through that afternoon. The two ladies and the bass, who was married to the soprano, stayed with Lizzie and Elena at the Barn, but the tenor lodged overnight with Thomas. He was not much of a cook himself so he took his guest for supper to the Portcullis, where they ate a good homely meal of meat-and-two-veg washed down with Guinness, which was Thomas's tipple. The tenor drank lager. A darts match in progress gave them the opportunity for a little desultory conversation; but they didn't have much to say to each other. They felt little need to talk: already they were benevolently united in an unspoken determination to produce the best possible music on the morrow. They turned in fairly early, Thomas expressing the hope that his guest would sleep as well as he always did himself. After a silent breakfast they walked to church. Elena and the rest of her singers awaited them, and they had another good hour for more rehearsing before the service at eleven o'clock. At 10.30 they left the organ loft to meet Elena in the porch for a breath of fresh air and coffee, which she provided from a large thermos flask. They were joined by St Aldelm's church choir, who were to sing the introductory motet.

Before he sat down again at the organ, Thomas watched from his loft as the church began to fill up. There at the front on the right sat little Lizzie Bassett, a black lace veil falling over her head and arms, on one side of her Elena Weston wearing an enormous black velvet hat, on the other the boy in his school uniform plus black armband. In the pew opposite was Dr James in his working clothes, and beside him the vicar's wife Maisie, looking surprisingly attractive in a little black dress with a long necklace of pearls she'd picked up for £1.50 at a church jumble sale. This was certainly a change from her usual grubby jeans or frayed shorts; and it gave Thomas quite a thrill simply to see her from afar. A great crowd of London folk, none of whom Thomas knew, was filling the pews, the men looking formal, the women fashionably well heeled, colleagues no doubt, and business associates of the deceased. There was a scattering of locals too, and at the back underneath the organ, invisible to Thomas, were Mrs Roxby and Sandra, who had managed to persuade her next-door neighbour to keep an eye on Wilf and the boys for an hour or so. Near the door there knelt with bowed head a stranger known only to Maisie and the vicar. Melanie had rightly assumed that Maisie would be at this service, and had come to devour her with hungry loving eyes, which nobody could stop her doing, and hopefully to snatch a few words from her when it was all over and the throng moved outside.

At 11 a.m. sharp, Thomas, feeling rather important, was playing some structureless meandering music of his own invention until Gerry, dressed in simple white surplice over his cassuck with a purple stole around his neck, stood at the altar and reminded the congregation of why they'd come together on this day: to remember Larry, and to give thanks for his short but happy and splendid life. Then they all knelt to pray silently, until after a single chord from Thomas his Fossbury choir sang softly the beautiful words of that old prayer, 'God be in my head/ And in my understanding.' Immediately afterwards Thomas moved into the introit of the Mass. It was not a rich and solemn requiem but Beethoven's simpler Mass in C, which was to be sung (or some of it) by Elena's four voices, which now embarked on the Kyrie. The sweet soprano sang her solo section, her voice soaring ecstatically into the high timbered vault, and then the tenor, easy and confident, took up the melody; the mourners, surprised into silence, sat listening. Elena and Thomas had decided to omit the Gloria, which they considered too jolly for the occasion, and also the triumphant Credo. Elena said she wasn't at all sure that Larry believed in all that Credo stuff, and Thomas more circumspectly added that Credos were usually omitted from requiem mass anyway. So they left a space here for Gerry to lead a prayer.

Then there was the Agnus Dei. When the tender

soprano voice pleaded: '*Agnus Dei qui venit in nomine Domini . . .*' and the cry was echoed by the other voices one after another: '*Qui tollis peccata mundi . . .* who comest in the name of the Lord, who takest away the sins of the world . . . have mercy on us all' every word was audible in the hushed church. Not a cough was heard, not a chair leg scraped across the stone floor as the mourners listened and Thomas's compassionate heart was wrung with musical anguish.

He had been firm about the Sanctus.

'We'll leave it out,' he said to Elena. 'Any more Latin will be too much for Fossbury. We must have a hymn here with a good swing to it.'

'What about "Jerusalem"?' she suggested. 'Everybody knows that.'

'By Charles Hubert Parry? No relation. Beautiful words by Blake, and a good resolution to build a better world for people to take away with them. Yes. That's a good idea.'

But first Larry's brother-in-law from Guildford, Surrey, who stood with his wife and a son and daughter behind Elena, left his seat and went to the lectern to read the lesson which had been Lizzie's choice. She had insisted that he read from the old Bible; she couldn't bear the dull prose of the new: 'Though I speak with the tongues of men and angels, and have not charity, I am become as sounding brass, or a tinkling cymbal . . . though I have all faith, so that I could remove mountains, and have not charity, I am nothing . . . Charity . . . rejoiceth not in iniquity, but rejoiceth in the truth; Beareth all things, believeth all things, hopeth all things, endureth all things . . .'

After that, everybody stood up and with full hearts sang 'Jerusalem'.

The eulogy was spoken by some London buddy of poor Larry's. It went on for too long, but it gave Gerry the opportunity to sit down at the side of the altar and survey the scene. The spirit presiding in the church today was, he thought, love, but love unrequited: the love of God, Who so loved the world that He gave His only begotten Son to save it; and the world didn't seem to care two hoots. Certainly the London crowd, which had entered the church all smiles, gaily greeting old friends as if summoned to a wedding rather than a funeral, were not thinking much about the love of God. And there stood Lizzie bravely acting out the part she had donned like a garment of grief nobly borne, a Jackie Kennedy figure mourning her assassinated husband as she placed one hand calmly on the shoulder of her boy, Lizzie hopelessly in love with the image of a dead man, her thirst for him impossible now ever to slake. There was Dr James, lonely and longing for the touch of love which he had not felt since his prim Scottish Mary died; and there was poor Melanie lurking in the shadows at the back, hoping for a smile from Maisie which Maisie didn't want to give. There too, though Gerry didn't know the truth of it, was Liam Tiernan, also unrequited, disappointed and angry that he'd been unable to persuade Amanda to come with him today, and even more angry and disappointed that in spite of all his attempts to comfort and please her he was still rejected. Liam stared up at the Pre-Raphaelite angel, its wings the colour of sunrise, transillumined still by morning light, and imagined some message was being brought personally to himself. 'That's it,' he thought. 'I've just been barking up the wrong tree. Amanda's never going to love me. So infatuated she was with Larry it's going to be years and years before she gets over that affair.' There too, if only in imagination, was Amanda, grown thin with sleepless misery and guilt, sick with desire for Larry which now could never be assuaged.

Liam had been shocked by the change in her appearance the previous evening, when he tried to persuade her to attend the service.

'No!' she cried. 'Of course I won't come! I want to forget Fossbury and all that part of my life. and I don't

118

want to see you again either, because you remind me of it.'

'Well, I can't help that, can I? There's no need to be nasty to me for something that wasn't my fault. It's just my bad luck to be tarred with the black of that bad day.'

'I'm trying to forget. Only I can't.' She began to cry. She sat down on her sofa and covered her face with both hands.

'As a matter of fact you should be grateful to me, Amanda.'

'Grateful to you?'

'Yes, indeed. What would you have done if I hadn't turned up?'

'Don't, don't!' she begged, turning and twisting on the sofa as if trying to extricate herself from barbed wire. He sat down beside her and put his arms round her shoulders.

'Ah, come now Amanda darling, my beautiful, golden girl. A girl like you wasn't made for grief like this. Of course you've done wrong,' he argued softly. 'You've sinned all right. But who hasn't? Most of us get away with it. You were just unlucky. But that shouldn't be the end of you. You've got to go on living.'

'I've lost him. That's what matters.' She dried her

eyes with the back of a hand. 'And I've hurt Lizzie – unforgivably. That's what I can't face. And that boy . . . I've often wished Timothy was mine, you know,' she added, irrelevantly it seemed to Liam.

'It would be a kindness to both of them if you came to his memorial service. It would do her good to see you there,' he pursued. But she pushed his arms away, and stood up.

'No!' she said fiercely. 'I can't face her. Not yet. She'd read the truth in my eyes. And that she must never know. Not till we're old and don't care any more.'

Liam thought he'd never met a more obstinate woman.

When the eulogy ended at last Gerry returned to face the altar and pray for the soul of departed: 'Eternal rest give unto him O Lord, and let perpetual light shine upon him. Then there was the hymn he'd chosen for everybody to sing together, 'Abide with me', the familiar words Gerry hoped, echoing in every heart: 'fast falls the eventide . . . Help of the helpless, O abide with me . . . Where is death's sting? where, grave, thy victory? . . . if Thou abide with me.'

Subdued into acceptance of inevitability the whole congregation fell meekly to their knees for the Lord's Prayer, after which they began shuffling a bit, thinking about getting out, while Thomas embarked gaily on 'Jesu joy of man's desiring', which he hoped would see them off promptly. When it was all over he thanked his Fossbury choir for their singing, which had pleased him, and then issued Elena's invitation to have lunch at the Barn. It was such small diplomacies which soothed any egos ruffled by preferment of London voices, that helped him to get his own way and still maintain his place as a well liked person in local life. He was of course aware that as a relatively new resident, having lived in Fossbury a mere twenty years, he was still regarded as a foreigner. 'Can't help his Welsh name, can he?' as old Mrs Sims put it.

Thank God that's over at last! Lizzie thought as Elena put a steadying hand on her shoulder and they left the pew. The reception at the Barn was still to come.

Dr James knew he'd have to sacrifice some of his lunch hour to his visiting list as he'd used up an hour of working time to attend Larry's memorial service, but he thought he might just pop into the Barn for ten minutes to please Lizzie, snatch a sandwich and a glass of wine, have a word with Timothy, and tell Maisie how sexy she looked. He also wanted to talk to Liam Tiernan; but Liam was elusive. Each time James tried to catch his eye above the mob of guests serving themselves from the lunch buffet Liam moved away. It was almost as if Liam was trying to avoid him, which was exactly what he was doing. Liam didn't want to talk about the day they last met, or even to be reminded of it. He didn't really want to talk to Lizzie either; but that he knew he could not avoid. He didn't know what he'd say, he knew he'd have to curb his natural garrulity, watch his easy-wagging tongue. But as soon as he saw her small figure emerge from her sitting-room, as if hesitating – hesitating? In her own house? – and her wan face, shadowed even more than usual by her plain black dress, as soon as she looked at him with those large eyes as pleading as a hungry urchin's Liam's kind heart overcame his fears and all his resolutions to be prudent. He immediately put down his plate and glass and advanced towards her with arms outstretched.

'Oh, Lizzie my lovely. It's good to see you,' he murmured as he embraced her tightly, feeling with some alarm how thin she'd grown.

'I'm so glad you've come,' she gasped, disengaging herself from his squeeze. 'I've so wanted to see you – to talk to you.' She pulled him towards her own sitting-room. 'Let's leave the others. They seem to be looking after themselves all right.' She gazed around in a detached sort of way. 'Only a little light Niersteiner and they're happy already! At least they're making some noise. I suppose it's a jolly occasion for them,' she added sarcastically. She was in fact somewhat surprised by the noise. She had always supposed that the ease with which their parties (Larry's and hers) took off was due to his personality, that his warm expansive presence ignited the party spirit, making it glow; but here was this noise around her, and real pleasure in coming together was being expressed by all these people, this time in Larry's absence. It never occurred to her that perhaps the rooms themselves, the generosity of her table and the artistry she had put into its laying out, what Larry used to call 'Lizzie's cornucopia', might have been part of the reason for success. Instead she could only suppose that in some mysterious way Larry himself was still there, still presiding in the house as in her soul.

'They want to remember Larry as he was in life, Lizzie dear. Large and laughing.'

'Bring your plate and glass with you, Liam.'

He followed her, and she shut the door behind him. Feeling trapped and very ill at ease, he sat down in an armchair and placed his plate on a small table beside him. She was sure to want to know everything about that dreadful day in Amanda's house, and he knew he must not divulge any of the facts. He had promised Amanda: a solemn promise to keep her secret for ever.

'You've lost weight tender-loving-careful-angelica,' he said. 'Are you not sleeping at all? And I see you're eating nothing.'

'No. It's difficult. But James is a great help – a tower of strength. And he gives me a few sleeping tablets – just a few at a time.' She laughed. 'He's very conscientious.' She sat down opposite him in a high-backed chair, tense and anxious, smoothing with a forefinger the skirt of her dress over one knee, slowly, deliberately, as if, he thought, she were writing her will. 'Of course I'd never do myself in. There's Timothy to think of anyway.'

'So there is,' said Liam guardedly.

'Why hasn't Amanda come?' she asked, looking up at him. 'I've been longing to see her. She hasn't written, and I can't seem to get her on the phone. Her nasty Ansafone always answers instead. What's the matter with her?'

'She's not been at all well, Lizzie. She's taken it all rather badly.'

'I suppose that's to be expected, especially as he – as it happened in her house. But she couldn't help that, could she? He died of a massive coronary, James told me. It might have happened any time, anywhere.'

'I'll tell her that. It'll be some comfort to her, I know.'

'But why didn't she come to his memorial service today? She might at least have done that. I think it's rather beastly of her – such an old friend.' She spoke angrily.

He remained silent. He looked around the room, and his gaze came to rest on that favourite watercolour of his: the twenties girl sitting spattered with sunshine on a garden seat.

'I suppose you're still wanting that Margaret Tiller-Mount?'

She smiled sadly. 'Well, you may be lucky yet. It looks as if I'm going to have to sell a lot of things.'

He glanced at her quickly, took a large gulp of wine, then put down his glass. 'How come?' he asked.

'Larry's left a lot of debts. It seems he entered into a partnership with a developer, and what they've built they haven't been able to sell. He had to give the Barn as part security for a bank loan. I knew about that, of course, because we talked about it a couple of years ago. I had to give my consent, being part-owner of the house.'

'Oh Lizzie, I am sorry!'

'It was rather a shock, I must admit. I had no idea he was so much in debt. Larry never brought his business worries home to me. They belonged in one of his other lives.'

'But when the houses are finally sold you'll get the money back, won't you?'

'I don't know. The interest on the bridging loan seems so enormous. And there are other debts as well. I really can't imagine how he was able to borrow so much. But then I'm no financier. Not even very good at organising my own small amount of money . . . .'

'But a genius at other things,' he chipped in cheerfully. 'Such as feeding the nearly 5,000!'

'I'm going to plant twelve cherry trees along the borders of the garden to commemorate our twelve years of happy marriage,' she said dreamily.

'You do that.'

'But I can't do it till the autumn when the soil will be damp enough, and the baby trees hibernating. In the meantime I just remember Larry. That's what I'm doing: keeping him alive in my mind. In that way he's not really dead, you see.'

It's a desperate game she's playing, he thought, a last gamble with death. He wondered what she would do when at last she was forced to admit the chips were really down.

'I've written a poem,' she said. Going to her desk she raised the lid and picked up a slip of paper. 'Can you read it? There are a lot of crossings out. Sorry about that. I've been trying to remember that first journey we made, Larry and I, to the Hebrides.'

He took it from her gingerly. She was like a child in her innocent confiding; but he felt like a peeping Tom as he read:

> Bright in memory is
> That Hebridean journey,
> That crossing from Oban, and the sea
> Breathing like a wrestler asleep
> After a long fight.
>
> I remember your cool fingers, can hear
> The withered bracken crack,
> And see the ruined village where
> We felt like ghosts
> Relinquishing an old forgotten world.
>
> Like mourners we were filled
> With the sadness of that grey
> Depopulated island, and
> The erosion of Time foreshadowed
> But not yet marking us.

He glanced up, met her solemn eyes and thought: it is now. Time is marking her now, all right. And what will she do when she admits it has rubbed him out? He said, 'It's awfully good, Lizzie. I didn't know you wrote poetry.'

'Now and again. Mostly dull verse,' she said severely. 'An occasional good phrase perhaps . . . .'

'It is good,' he insisted. 'And what's more it's real.'

'It is to me. But in spite of everything I'll have to sell the house next spring.'

'Oh no!'

'Oh yes. And Timothy's leaving his prep school and starting at the local comprehensive next week. Poor Timothy! I hope he'll be all right.'

'Of course he'll be all right,' he reassured her. 'In this day and age he'll be more than all right if he learns to meet and deal with all sorts and conditions of men – which he wouldn't do in the socially protected atmosphere of his prep school.' Liam remembered the harsh discipline and rough justice of his own old school in Ireland, and the rough Christian Brothers who meted it out. How glad he'd been to flee from it to the relatively soft and self-indulgent but no more wily world of London art dealers! It was a world in which he'd started at the bottom, had cheated and been cheated, had learned a lot the hard way, as he gradually crawled up the ladder of success to a position on a middle rung where he now balanced precariously.

'I hope you're right,' said Lizzie.

They sat silent till Liam suddenly said, 'Let me get you a drink, Lizzie. You certainly need one.'

'Not now, thank you,' she said. 'I drink every evening with James. He comes in after his surgery to eat with me and hold my hand.'

'Does he now? Well hasn't he the luck of the devil?'

'I don't suppose he thinks so. I'm not very good company.'

'Lizzie . . .' Liam spoke tentatively, 'is there anything I can do to help?'

'You could get me a good price for the Volvo,' she replied promptly. 'I've got to sell that quickly. And perhaps later we'll talk about some of my mother's pictures. There's that oil by Laura Knight of circus clowns. It's worth quite a lot, I think.'

'It is indeed. Well don't sell to anyone else till we've talked about it now, will you?'

'No. I promise you. And please will you give Amanda my love when you see her, and tell her I miss her – dreadfully.'

'I'll do that.' He didn't say that after this buffet lunch he intended visiting Amanda's empty house in Frenny Hinton and clearing out all her watercolours along with a few other possessions she wanted him to bring up to her in Pettigrew Place. He didn't tell

Lizzie, and nobody else, he believed, would know. But he had not accounted for the curiosity of country neighbours, nor for the fact that Amanda's front door, painted such a startling yellow, could not remain invisible.

'And now,' said Lizzie, 'I suppose I must go and face the hyenas.'

In the big drawing-room the noise abated here and there as she moved among her guests, greeting them: Edward Bolton, Larry's building partner in black suit with black tie, Miss Brockway, always erect and so correct, and others she hardly knew. She was glad to see Elena seated in one corner surrounded by members of the Fossbury choir as well as her own singers from London, and Thomas Parry literally at her feet, crosslegged on the floor, entranced, his shortsighted eyes bulging behind thick spectacles, glass in hand, his mouth slightly open. He looked, she thought, like a hypnotised goldfish. Elena was no doubt entertaining them all with tales of her thousand and one Chinese nights. Lizzie couldn't help feeling a pang of jealousy, not of Elena's social prowess, but because Larry had been snatched from the mainstream of existence while his mother still swam strongly in it, so old and yet as large as life. It was almost as if for every tale she told, like the original Scheherazade, Elena won an extra day and so postponed her inevitable end. Lizzie knew only too well how those tales would percolate through Fossbury, chiefly through Lorna Dawson, Mrs Sims's daughter, first soprano in St Aldhelm's church choir, who sat tensely on a small chair, a full glass of wine held tightly in both hands above her pinched-up knees, her eyes popping and her ears avid for gossip. She would carry back to her mother a big bagful of gossip crumbs left over from this funeral feast and old Mrs Sims would certainly add a few malicious twists in her retelling. Lizzie was cynical about the kind intentions of mourners.

But in Thomas Verdi Parry's mind and heart were no reservations or criticisms. A Russian lady's soul had called across history and continents to his Welsh *hwyl*, and he sat entranced.

'I am no longer a performing member of our choral society myself,' she was saying. 'My voice is not what it was. But once, long ago, I sang with Chaliapin.'

A stunned silence greeted this piece of information. Was it possible? Had this old lady really met and sung with that great Russian bass whose voice had now passed into musical myth?

'It was in the early or mid-thirties – anyway, before the war – he stopped off in Shanghai. He must have been on one of his last world concert tours. He was very old, I know. White-haired. My singing teacher, you see, who was Russian, had been a pupil of Chaliapin's in the old days before the Bolsheviks; and when the great singer came to Shanghai my teacher, Boris, gave a party for him, to which I was invited. I was a Bright Young Thing then.' A murmur of adulation rose from Thomas's lips, but Elena inserted a modest parenthesis: 'I was never a beauty, you know; but young then. Youth alone can obliterate deficiencies, can't it? Well, after the party some of us went on to a nightclub where they played good jazz.'

'Oh, did you dance, Mrs Weston?' Lorna Dawson interrupted eagerly. 'I often watch old-time dancing on telly.'

'Well yes . . . We used to dance half the night away, night after night,' Elena admitted. 'It was the quick-step I liked best. The band-leader, who was Hungarian, used to announce the dances: "Ziz is zee gwig-step" and the slow foxtrot was "le mouvement slow de foxe". The dancers used to take him seriously, and some of them I swear began to look like foxes slinking over the floor with furtive expressions, slowly swishing their behinds to the rhythm. The only things missing were their bushy tails.'

Thomas laughed delightedly, encouraging her to go on.

'Well, on this particular night as our party came in they were playing a very gwig gwig-step indeed – "You're driving me crazy!" – and everybody was dancing like mad. That tune came out when Amy Johnson flew solo to Australia. It was all the rage.'

Nobody in her audience, not even Thomas, could remember who Amy Johnson was.

'As soon as we came in the manager led us to a reserved table: Chaliapin, Boris and some acolyte whose name I've forgotten, and little me. We sat down to more champagne. I can't remember what we ate. There were some real musicians in that band. Usually when it was late and the crowd had thinned a bit they would play Hungarian folk songs; but this night, as soon as they knew Chaliapin was with us they broke into opera. It was Saint-Saëns's *Samson and Delilah*. The talking stopped, and everybody was looking at Chaliapin. He leaned across the table and spoke to me in Russian: "This is for you, little girl." I think I blushed to the roots of my hair (quite blonde in those days) and stammered, "Oh! but . . ." in English. But Boris held my wrist firmly and said: "It is for you. It is an honour." So I stood up. I was nervous; but I took some deep, steadying breaths, and then I sang that gorgeous and seductive aria: "Softly awakes my heart". And at the end Chaliapin, still sitting at the table, joined in the duet as easily as if he were holding a conversation. Such a voice . . .' A little of the great star's glamour fell on her as she told the story, and a reverential silence greeted the end of it. Thomas grabbed her hand out of her lap and kissed it.

Sandra would have liked to stay on for the party, because, as she put it, let's face it, that's what it was: a wake to remember the deceased with happy thoughts and to try to cheer the poor widow up a bit. She could have helped Mum and Mrs Bassett a lot, and taken a good look at everything as well; but instead she had to rush back home to Clematis Close to relieve Mrs Pratt next door who was keeping an eye on Wilf and the boys. It would have been nice, Sandra thought sadly, to be able to tell Vince all the gas, when they were at last in bed after the boys had stopped quarrelling and fallen asleep, and poor Dad had been turned off like a light by his sleeper tablet but was at least safely tucked up. Vince wasn't much interested in people's clothes, not like she was, although he'd be quite surprised to know that the vicar's wife in black and pearls looked a bit of a sexpot; but he'd be interested in the food served up at the Barn. She'd be able to tell him something about that because she'd slipped in there before the service to join Mum, so they could go to church together; and Mrs Bassett had said, 'Come and look at the table, Sandra, and see if it's all right.' All right? I should think it was. What a spread! Smoked trout fillets bought from the trout farm up beyond Frenny Hinton, and all those pâtés with foreign names, and strange salad mixtures you'd never dream of. There was one made with cucumber cubes and black grapes done in a sauce made of yoghurt spiked with mustard. Spiked was the word she used. Sandra could hear Vince's voice as she hurried home: 'Spiked was it? I wonder poor little Mrs Bassett wasn't spiked herself with all that work!' And her own explaining: 'She had help, of course. Her old ma-in-law, Elena that is, the fatty with the peroxide coiffewer, drove into Swinester to Sainsbury's and brought back the pâtés, and of course Mum was helping all the way. But yes, she do work at her cooking. I suppose it occupies her mind.'

When Sandra opened the garden gate and walked towards her front door she noticed broken glass on the path. Looking up at Wilf's window in alarm, she saw a great hole smashed through it.

'Oh my Gawd!' she moaned. She pushed open the front door and came face to face with Wilf sitting on the bottom stairs with Darren and Chris on either side on the step above. 'What the 'ell's 'appened?' she shrieked. Poor Wilf's arm was swathed in a teacloth from which blood oozed, and his head was wrapped in towels through which emerged his bloody nose and swollen bleeding lips. Sandra took a deep breath and tried to calm down. 'Are you all right, Dad?' she asked, then went on, 'No. Of course not. His poor old face is all slashed and sloshed with blood. You do look a mess. Here! Let me wash it off.'

'It's best to leave it alone, Mum – the blood, I mean,' said Darren. 'We learned that in First Aid. Blood's as good a cleaner as disinfectant.'

'Well, we must try to stop the bleeding. We ought to bandage his face. But how?'

'Monday,' mumbled Dad from between the towels.

'I tried to bandage him with his scarf, but he pulled it off,' offered Chris.

'Course he did, stupid! Couldn't breathe with it across his face, could he?'

Mrs Pratt came bustling into the hall from the kitchen, where she'd been making a cup of restorative tea.

'The ambulance is on its way,' she said. 'He'll have to have stitches. Anyone can see that.' She was calm and in control, with a cup of tea ready in her hand for Dad.

'I called the ambulance first,' Chris claimed proudly, till Darren laughed at him, 'He dialled 909!'

and Chris had to defend himself: 'Well, I got it nearly right, didn't I?'

'He won't be able to drink a cup of tea with that mouth,' said Sandra. 'Have we got a straw somewhere?' And here Chris was of use. He pulled out of his pocket a crumpled but still functional straw from the top of an old fruit-drink pack.

Sandra tried to insert it between Dad's swollen lips, but he pushed her hand away with his undamaged arm, muttering, 'Bloody racket!'

'He doesn't want it,' said Darren.

'What happened?' asked Sandra. 'How'd he do it, Darren?'

'He fell against his bedroom window and broke the glass.'

'He must 'ave been trying to throw out his geriatric pad, I suppose,' said Sandra.

'And cut his nose. And cheek. Bled like anything, it did!' Chris was excited.

Sandra looked at Darren. 'Were you there when he did it? Did you . . . ? Darren, you didn't . . . ?'

'Oh no, Mum! I never!'

'He pushed hisself,' Chris said.

'He fell, stupid!' Darren corrected him. 'He didn't push hisself. He fell against the window. Must have been trying to open it. He shouted for us; but by the time we ran upstairs he was on the floor by the window. And the pad was too.'

'Nice. Nice,' was Dad's comment.

'He doesn't seem to be in pain,' said Sandra. 'However did you get him downstairs?'

'We dragged him,' Chris explained.

'I held him under the arms,' said Darren.

'And I pulled 'is feet,' said Chris.

'He slid down easy,' said Darren. 'Hardly any bumps at all.'

'Oh, my Gawd,' Sandra sighed. And Dad added, 'Monday.'

'They heard the ambulance siren wailing in the distance, approaching. When the ambulance stopped outside the garden gate there was silence in the kitchen while they all waited, Mrs Pratt still holding the undrunk cup of tea. In no time at all the ambulance men had wheeled Dad out and laid him on a bunk inside the van with cheerful, soothing words, and Sandra was sitting beside him. She rose just before they set off for the hospital, to give orders to Darren.

'You must see your dad gets his tea when he comes home from work.'

'Don't you worry your little head no more,' Mrs Pratt intervened. 'I'll see he gets his tea all right. And the boys too.'

'Thank you, Mrs Pratt.' Sandra relaxed in recognition of her competence. 'You're a real friend.' Mrs Pratt smiled suddenly, almost tenderly.

It took Mrs Roxby and Lizzie a couple of hours to clear up after the funeral feast while Elana, tired by this time, put her feet up and reclined on the big sofa in the drawing-room reading the local *Gazette*.

'Did the press attend the service today?' she called out. 'I expect it'll all be in this rag next week.' But in the kitchen they couldn't hear her.

When Mrs Roxby got home, ready to put her own feet up, her landlady Mrs Evans ran up the street eagerly. Mrs Roxby's house was not her own; she rented it from Mrs Evans, whose mother's house it had once been. The reason Mrs Evans hadn't sold the house when her mother died was this: for many years Mrs Roxby had rented a bedsit there. She redecorated and refurnished it with loving care to suit her own taste and to her landlady's amazed admiration. Over the years tenant and landlady became firm friends. When the old woman had a stroke Mrs Roxby helped to look after her; and when she died her will expressed the wish that Mrs Roxby be left tenant of the property during her lifetime. So Mrs Evans's possession of her mother's house was postponed, but in the meantime she collected the rent. Mrs Roxby was happy with this arrangement. 'Better than living down among all them climbers,' was what she said. She referred, not to the yuppie gentrification of Cotswold villages, but to the vegetation clinging to the street names of the Fossbury council estate from Wistaria Way and Clematis Close right up to what she called Honeysuckle Heavenue. Mrs Roxby felt weary by now, but not too weary for a gossip with her landlady.

'Come in, Merle,' Mrs Roxby said. 'And let's 'ave us a cup of tea. It'll all be in the *Gazette* next week. I saw that young reporter there standing at the back of the church. But no photos. He had enough respect to take no photos.' Though if the truth were told Myra Roxby quite fancied the idea of being photographed along with the main persons in today's drama, perhaps with a caption naming her and describing her function as the chief pillar and support behind today's reception at the Barn. Merle, however, seemed less interested in what had been going on at the Barn than in her own story.

'This man,' she said excitedly, as soon as they were in the kitchen. 'He had a big car. And he went up to her door as bold as brass. You know her door?'

'Whose door?'

'Why, Miss Amanda Burton's door. The yellow one. You can't miss it. It's nearly opposite mine, anyway. And as I was just looking out of the window, idle like, I sees this man with the big car. Opened up the boot he did, and went to the door. Didn't knock, so he must have knowed the place was empty. And he had a key. Well, there was no cars parked there this afternoon, so I could see as plain as plain across the road. And then he came out with a lot of picture frames and piles them into the back of the car. Estate car it was. I took the number in case the police needed it. But he did have a key to the house!'

Myra Roxby, who was nothing if not observant, guessed the man that Mrs Evans was talking about must be Liam Tiernan. He was a picture dealer, wasn't he? And always hanging about Amanda when they were down at the Barn at weekends in the old days before . . . before poor Mr Bassett –

'I think I knows who it was,' she said. 'Was it a grey Volvo?' So Amanda needed to sell some of her pictures . . . So what? she asked herself as her friend nodded. But why had Amanda not come down to Frenny Hinton herself for the paintings? And why had she not come to the memorial service when she must know that poor little Lizzie was cut to the heart at not seeing her there? It was all a bit rum.

'I think it was Mr Tiernan,' she said aloud. 'He's a dealer in art pictures. And he was at the Barn today.' But silently she made up her mind to say nothing about this to Lizzie. She would keep her mouth shut for the present, till she knew which way the wind was blowing.

Supremo, big, black, beautiful and menacing, jumped up on her sofa and lifted his head expectantly. She sat down beside him, and stroked his arched back and tickled his pointed ears. 'Do you know what, Merle my dear?' she said. 'I'd rather have a cat than a man any day of the week.' And Mrs Evans, who was herself still happily married, smiled indulgently. She had noticed that women often seemed to love their pets more than their husbands.

Five

Though he wouldn't admit it Timothy was scared on his first day at Chippersley Comprehensive, formerly Dorothy, Lady Chippersley's Grammar School for the sons of Gloucestershire Yeomen. Originally the dozen or so sons were housed in a building next to the Town Hall. Only the foundations of the old school remained, and on the site now stood a bakery. In the course of time the school was moved to larger and larger premises, the latest being a brick building erected after the war beyond the East End of Fossbury where Horse Street petered out into Fox Lane. During the First World War, when the Yeomen owned up to having daughters as well as sons, the school became coed. By the 1990s it held nearly a thousand boys and girls.

'I'll walk with you to school today,' Lizzie said over breakfast. She seemed to know how he felt without being told. 'The exercise will do me good, and I can call at the butcher's on my way back.' Since Larry's death she herself had dreaded going into the town, having to smile at familiar faces, and make the remarks expected of her. Timothy's anxiety lessened so that he was able to swallow his Weetabix without too much difficulty. Darren had promised to wait for him at the school gate, so he hoped he wouldn't have to face a crowd of strangers there quite alone.

Fossbury's few streets stretched over approximately a mile laid out in the shape of a Z, the wide Main Street with its ancient market cross in the middle being the long backbone of the letter which ran from north-east to south-west: Windy Alley the locals called it when they scurried along on cold winter mornings. The transverse southern arm, Frenny Road, marked the boundary of the rich residential area of big houses and large well kept lawns and hedges. This was where Owl House and the Barn were situated. Beyond the northern transverse arm of the Z lay the council estate bordering on industrial sites: the packaging factory where Sandra's husband, Vince Parsons worked, and the beginning of the dugout made by the huge quarry from which roadstone was blasted daily, producing a dust-cloud, soon dispersed when southwesterly winds prevailed, but cursed by housewives when the wind was in the north-east often in hot dry weather when they most needed to keep their windows wide open.

The curses were under the breath, because the quarry had given work to so many of their men in the past and still, in spite of increasing mechanisation and productivity, employed a few.

In twentieth-century terms Fossbury was really only big enough to be called a village; but in the Middle Ages it was important as a centre for wool growing and weaving, and also as a crossing of two roads, one from the West Country to Oxford, the other an ancient packhorse salt route from the Midlands to the south of England. A royal charter was granted in the fourteenth century to hold a market in Main Street. The Town Hall originally was part of buildings belonging to a religious house catering for pilgrims on their way to Oxford; but the priests were thrown out by Henry VIII's Dissolution programme and the buildings sold. At a later date the Bailiff and Burgesses bought it for the town, and so it became the Town Hall. Only one fifteenth-century house now remained. Most of the houses lining Main Street were of the seventeenth century, with dormer windows blinking from their rooflines, but a few eighteenth-century houses had somehow slipped in here and there between the older dwellings. There were still a few gaps in the solid frontage too, holes wide enough once for carriages or waggons to enter on their way to stable, backyard, workshop or smithy, and now a welcome hiding place for cars. Two larger Georgian homes graced the West End; and James's partner, Dr Doynton, lived in one of these.

Timothy and Lizzie walked past the old stone houses, some with bow windows pouting out on to the pavement, some with windowboxes full of petunias wilting after that summer's heatwave, past the banks, enlarged and modernised with façades in keeping with Fossbury's strict planning regulations, past the Bell on the north side and the Cross Keys on the south, past the pair of clipped yews marking the path to the church, the solicitors' and accountants' offices, and the small old-fashioned shops with shoppers' cars inevitably parked outside. This annoyed Lizzie. There was a perfectly good carpark behind the church. Why didn't people use it instead of littering Main Street's handsome frontage with heavy metal, so obstructing traffic and the view?

As Timothy and his mother approached the school gates they could see on a distant ridge beyond Fox Lane huge conical piles of stone which had been ground down into chips for road-surfacing; and Timothy thought they were exciting, like mountains of the moon. Darren was nowhere to be seen, so Lizzie had to let Timothy make his way alone through the crowd of children swarming towards the entrance, a lonely little boy, but stalwart, she thought. He didn't look back. She waited till he had disappeared. He was a strong boy, she knew, valiant and cheerful like his father. He made friends easily. He would plunge into the tide and swim with it if anyone could.

Darren had forgotten his promise to wait for Timothy at the school gates, but unabashed met him cheerily in Mr Harris's form, and sat beside him in class. When a loud buzzer sounded half-way through the morning to announce it was time for break Timothy, who sat near the door, politely opened it for the teacher. Immediately the whole class of thirty rushed out like a herd of stampeding cattle, leaving Timothy and Mr Harris staring at each other across the empty space. Timothy was so surprised he couldn't speak; but Mr Harris laughed, and placing his arm across Timothy's shoulders led him out into the corridor, where he caught sight of Barry Mogg.

'Hey Barry!' he called out. 'You take care of Timothy – show him the ropes, will you?' He knew Barry belonged to Darren's gang.

Barry Mogg was a thin boy, small for his age. Timothy could see simply by watching his face that Barry had been told that this new boy's father had recently died, and that his mother was left with no money to

147

pay the fees of his former private school. Timothy flushed with embarrassment, but at the same time was grateful to Barry, who directed him wordlessly through the hordes of rushing, shouting children to a far corner of the playground, a territory claimed by Darren's gang.

'Timothy lives next door to our doctor,' said Darren. 'And we play croquet on our doctor's lawn. It's not a sissy game! It's brill!'

The others took this introduction silently; but Timothy sensed that in spite of being new and a bit posh, he had somehow been made acceptable by Darren. At dinnertime many of the older pupils raced into Main Street to buy chips from the Chinese takeaway or buns at the bakery; the juniors ate in the school canteen, those like Darren, who brought their own packed lunches, at special tables set aside for them. Timothy joined Darren's gang again. Lizzie had made him some egg sandwiches and packed them into a plastic box with an apple and a small bottle of milk.

'Ugh!' said Darren. 'Milk for bonny babies!' He took a swig from his own can of Coke; and Timothy understood that he'd have to tell Mum that milk was out and Coke was in.

The afternoon moved slowly on through a French lesson given by a young woman whom Timothy found difficult to understand, her French accent being so different from what he'd heard in French lessons before, then through a session of running about the football field and trying to get near enough to the ball to kick it. By half-past three Timothy, his schoolbag slung from his shoulder and his shirt tucked half in and half out of his new long black trousers, was walking home along Main Street.

In her little porch enjoying the sun sat Mrs Sims like a spider in her corner web waiting for flies. Mrs Sims didn't want to eat people; she only wanted to devour their lives. She had been a frugal housekeeper of necessity when young; as the years went by she developed a passion for saving and gradually became first mean then miserly. Her husband had walked out of her home in middle age without explanation and leaving no address, and had not been heard of since. All her children left home, one by one, as soon as they were old enough to realise they could eat better and have more fun without her. Now only Lorna remained in Fossbury, and that was because she was married to Dawson the butcher. Mrs Sims depended on Lorna, not only for cheap offcuts and unsold offal but also for essential supplies of gossip. Old and alone, Mrs Sims found very little to exercise her still healthy body, and not much to occupy her busy brain either, so she had taken up the hobby of collecting, as many people do, in her case collecting other people's lives. It was this vicarious living which excited and fulfilled her and kept her going.

'She should have been a novelist, don't you think?' Lizzie had once asked Mrs Roxby, but Mrs Roxby had replied tartly, 'Her generation left school at twelve, you know. Not enough education to write books.' And Lizzie felt humbled and ashamed.

Mrs Sims saw Timothy coming. She stood up and smiled as he passed, and Timothy politely returned her greeting with a 'Good afternoon.' So she joined him on the pavement, walking beside him and pestering him with statements that were also questions so that he felt bewildered and uncomfortable. First day at school, was it? A bit rough, was it? Not too many little gentlemen there, she'd bet! Well, it'd be nice to stay 'ome with Mum, wouldn't it? And cost her a lot less too, she supposed. Her voice was high and excited, her eyes bright. She was feeling the pleasure of the underdog in seeing the fortunate brought low. She didn't mention Timothy's dead father, but he feared she might any minute.

Thomas Verdi Parry, who lived a few doors away from Mrs Sims and on the same side of the street, happened to leave his house just as they approached.

He recognised at once the look of the hunted on Timothy's face, and guessed the reason why. He smiled broadly at Timothy, greeting him loudly, and pulled him inside his doorway. 'Hullo, old chap! Back from school already? Have a bit of butterscotch.' He closed the door behind them and dropped his voice to a whisper inside the narrow hall. 'Don't take any notice of Mrs Sims. She's mad.'

Though it was most improbable that she could hear their voices outside in the noisy street, even if she applied her ear to the door, Timothy found himself whispering too: 'Who is that lady?'

'She's no lady,' said Thomas loudly as they entered his parlour, where his piano stood. 'She's a poisonous old reptile!' He burst out laughing with sudden relief of tension, and Timothy laughed too. 'Now any time you're passing by, if you're in trouble from her or anybody else, you just knock on my door and pretend you've got a music lesson with me. That's a good idea, isn't it?'

Timothy agreed. As he went out again he looked at the black knocker on the white-painted door. It was a black iron ring grasped by a black hand. Thomas nodded happily when he saw Timothy touch it as if for luck. 'It's an antique,' he explained. 'It's the Clifton Ring. I brought it with me from our house in Bristol.'

He glanced quickly left and right. 'The old rattle-snake's gone,' he said, and added, 'My regards to your grandmother,' as if it was an afterthought, although the sentimental old organist had been dreaming about Elena on and off all day, almost as often, he was surprised to find, as about Maisie in her little black dress and pearl necklace.

'She's gone back to London,' said Timothy. And Thomas smiled and nodded, disappointed though he was.

Sandra and her mum managed to drag the mattress off Wilf's bed and then pull and push it downstairs. A mattress is an awkward thing to handle in a narrow space, and the effort made Mum short of breath.

'Hang on a mo',' she pleaded. 'I'll have to pack it in.'

'What? The mattress?'

'Smoking.'

'Oh that. I seem to have heard that one before.'

The boys were at school, and Vince at work, so they had the house to themselves.

'Where are we going to burn it, Sandra?' asked Mum.

'Backyard.'

Mrs Roxby advised against that. It was too small a space for a bonfire, which might get out of control and set the whole house alight.

'It'll have to be the front garden then – whatever the neighbours say,' said Sandra.

The smelly thing, rolled up and tied with a rope, was at last bundled through the front door and placed in the middle of the lawn.

'We'll have to burn his chair as well,' said Sandra.

'Bed first,' Mum advised. So they climbed the stairs and stood looking at it.

'One leg is broken anyway,' said Sandra. 'Vince propped it up on a brick that corner.'

'It's had its day,' said her mother. 'Like the old man. Dust to dust. Ashes to ashes.'

'It's the bed we're putting on the fire, Mum. Not Dad.'

'Not yet. All in good time,' said Mrs Roxby.

Sandra was shocked. 'You shouldn't say such things. It's wicked, you know.'

'Why?' Mrs Roxby was unabashed. 'The kids can't hear me, can they? And anyway, it's my belief the blighters took a hand in that accident he had.'

'Oh no, Mum. They never! You get me all upset when you say such things!'

'OK. I believe you.'

They began dislocating the bed into its component parts.

'Darren told me he never. And Chris did too.' Sandra spoke in an injured tone.

'OK, OK,' said Mum. 'I *believe* you. Mind the corner of the door.'

The base of the bed was easier to move than the mattress. It slid downstairs aided only by gravity. Then there were the ends of the bed to add to the pile in the garden, and lastly Wilf's battered chair from the living-room.

'I've brought a packet of firelighters,' said Mrs Roxby. She stuffed them in here and there between all the junk, and then she struck the first match. They stood back in solemn silence to watch, and when the bonfire was blazing steadily they went into the house.

'I'll just sit here on the stairs and have a quick drag,' said Mrs Roxby, 'while you brew up the tea.'

Vince, returning unexpectedly early from work, walked in through the back door and found her sitting there.

'Hello, Myra,' he greeted her. 'What you doing sitting on the stairs?' And when she made no reply apart from a nod he went on, 'Poisoning yourself again, I see. Cancer weeds! They'll kill you, you know.'

'I heard you.'

'Why are you sitting on the stairs anyway? There's comfortable chairs in the house.'

'I'm smoking on the stairs so I won't puff poison over your kitchen.'

'That's thoughtful of you, Myra. Very kind. Not like you at all. What's come over you?' It was then he smelt the smoke and heard the crackle from the bonfire. He opened the front door. 'What the 'ell's going on?' he shouted in alarm. 'Myra, what've you been up to?'

Sandra came into the hall. 'It's only Granpa's bed and things, Vince. His bed and mattress.'

'In the interests of hygiene,' added Myra.

'But he's going to need it when he comes out of hospital. Suppose they discharge him tomorrow.' Vince was worried. 'He's only being kept in for a few investigations, you said. Until they take the stitches out.'

'They're looking after him now,' said Sandra calmly.

Vince ran out into the garden to watch the fire burn. It was too late to save anything now, so he fetched a rake and with it tipped back into the central blaze whatever fell out.

'Thank you, Mum,' said Sandra, as they sipped tea

at the kitchen table. 'I could never 'ave managed it without you.'

'That's for sure,' said Myra.

On Saturday Darren had his birthday party, which was much enjoyed by all, especially the cake Sandra had made for him. On Monday she rang up the hospital. Ward Six.

'Ward Six. Sister speaking. Can I help you?' The words were helpful, but the tone guarded.

'It's about my dad,' Sandra began breathlessly. 'I'm Sandra Parsons. How is he? He's Wilfred Roxby.'

'Oh yes. I'm glad you rang, Mrs Parsons. We've been hoping to see you. Your dad's quite well, really. It's good news. No skull fracture when he fell downstairs, but he's rather restless. I think he wants to go home.'

'What makes you think that, Sister?'

'He keeps saying Monday, which it is today.'

'It's just one of his words. Darren says he only knows ten.'

'Who's Darren?'

'That's my son. He was twelve last week. We had a lovely birthday party.'

'Yes. Well, Mr Roxby's stitches are due to come out this afternoon. You can fetch him any time after that.'

'I'm afraid I can't do that.'

'What do you mean?' Sister sounded sharp.

'I'm afraid I haven't a bed for him.'

'You had one when he came into the ward. What's happened to it?'

'I'm afraid it's burnt to a cinder – well, almost. Gone up in smoke. We had a fire.'

'Oh dear, that's unfortunate! We only kept him in for a few investigations. There's nothing more we can do for him. He's fit for discharge now.'

'I'm very grateful for all you've done, Sister,' said Sandra sweetly, but her heartfelt gratitude couldn't banish that little bit of desperation from Sister's voice: 'We can't keep him in Ward Six. We need the bed.'

'Can he go anywhere else?'

'We'll have to see what we can do. Will you be visiting tomorrow? No? I suppose you must have a lot on your hands what with the fire and everything. No one hurt, I hope?'

'No. We're all OK. Only his bed . . .'

'I'll have to see what I can do. I may be able to borrow a camp-bed from the Helping-in-the-Community Service and send it with him in the ambulance. But please phone tomorrow, will you?'

'Yes, Sister. Thank you, Sister.' Sandra sounded very meek.

Timothy had not been invited to Darren's birthday party. He accepted that exclusion because he was new. You couldn't expect to belong immediately, could you? He had to think of some way in which he could win what in ancient times, before the invention of the internal combustion engine, might have been called his spurs. So one afternoon when school was over for the day, and he should have been going home to tea, he suggested to Darren and Barry Mogg an expedition to the moon.

'A moon landing,' he said.

'Go on!' mocked Darren.

Timothy pointed to the distant man-made hills. 'It's like an alien planet,' he said.

'There's notices up there against trespassing. All over,' warned Barry, whose Dad worked in the quarry, but they followed Timothy to the end of Fox Lane, into a patch of scrubby woodland and up a steep slope studded with fallen rocks and overgrown with brambles. At the top was barbed wire and a notice in big red letters: DANGER. KEEP OUT. They crouched down. Timothy put his ear to the ground as Red Indians do. They waited.

'There's no one about,' whispered Timothy.

'They'll be hiding,' said Barry. 'Waiting for us. Enemy aliens.'

One by one they crawled through the wire, carefully holding up the strands for each other. Then they walked to the edge of a great pile of coarse rubble and climbed up on it. Further on were mounds of grit of variously sized pieces. The last one in the row was composed of very small fragments like fine shingle.

'Come on,' said Barry. 'I'm goin' to the top!' He ran up, but as he ran his feet sank in the loose sandy stuff, and within a few seconds the top he was trying to reach began to fold over and crumble, and very soon he was knocked sideways and rolled over by an avalanche. The other two boys saw him being engulfed, but Timothy was able to grab hold of one of his legs. A second later Darren was helping him to tug, and together they managed to pull Barry out as a great wave of stone gathering speed and noise slid down and spread itself around the base of the heap.

Barry fell out on to his shoulders and knees. His eyes, ears, nostrils and mouth were full of dust and gravel, which made him cough and spit, and when his friends patted his back, clouds of dust rose from his school blazer. They heard voices, and a man shouted. Without a word they fled towards the perimeter fence. This time they were not careful but scrambled through the wire as best they could, tearing clothes, arms and legs in their hasty exit. When they reached the bottom of the bramble-tangled slope, they hid behind a group of elder trees, whose leaves were already beginning to yellow in the September sun.

'It was an avalanche!' said Timothy.

'You saved my life,' said Barry. He took from the pocket of his blazer a dusty tube of Smarties and offered them round. Each boy took one and sucked it solemnly.

'Got to be secret, this,' said Darren.

'Swear,' breathed Timothy, holding out his wrist, where a large scratch was still bleeding. The others crossed their wrists over it, mingling their blood with his. It was a blood brotherhood they were solemnising. And Barry, his eyelids still encrusted with roadstone dust, whispered: 'Never tell!'

When Timothy got home late for tea Lizzie met him at the back door.

'What on earth have you been up to?' she demanded, seeing with horror the state of his torn clothes, and knowing how long it would take to mend them. He revealed his bleeding wrist to mollify her anger.

'Oh my goodness!' she cried at once. 'That needs a plaster. What happened?'

'We went a little way down Fox Lane. And I fell into a bank of blackberry bushes,' he explained as they went indoors. He couldn't help wondering what the others would tell their mothers.

Barry Mogg didn't exactly break his promise, but he was unable to keep the secret. He was the smallest and youngest of five children; his father was a rough man with a quick temper and flying fists, and Barry was afraid of him. His mother knew at once where he'd been. Since her husband worked as a quarryman she recognised the sight and smell of grit.

'Barry,' she accused him as soon as he arrived home. 'You never 'ave bin' playin' around them rubble dumps? Your Dad'll 'alf kill you!'

The prospect of being half-killed by his father after so nearly escaping death from an avalanche of grit so unnerved Barry that he threw himself speechless against his mother's ample chest, and sobbed. She covered him with protective arms, thankful it was not a Saturday, when her husband spent the morning in the Fleece in Horse Street and afterwards came home to his dinner ready to hit anybody. She made Barry strip off all his clothes, and threw them in the washing machine. Then she rummaged in a box containing clothes outgrown by his elder brother and found some black trousers and a shirt that would have to do. When he was washed and his hair brushed, and he was sitting quietly at the kitchen table eating baked beans on toast and drinking sugared tea she spoke to him in measured tones: 'Don't 'ee never go near that quarry dirt no more,' she said. She watched him fondly, remembering those awful months when as a baby he contracted whooping cough, and the guilt she carried, which pressed on her like a sack of coal on her back every time the poor mite vomited after coughing, because it was she who (scared by all the talk at the time about brain damage caused by immunisation) had refused to let Doctor give him the jab. The whooping lasted six months, and after that he got a bad chest every winter for several years, so he never seemed to put on the weight and growth of his brothers. What she feared, even more than her husband's fists, was the quarry dust.

'Too much dust up there,' she said, pouring him out a second mug of tea. 'Don't do those lungs of yours no good. Not if any of them big boys tempt you up there again. Never! And we'll say no more about it. Promise me, now.'

Subdued, but safe now, Barry promised: 'OK, Mum. Never, no more.'

Sandra, who had a lot on her mind, accepted Darren's torn trousers, shredded socks and bloodied ankles as all part of the human condition, and simply groaned, 'Oh my Gawd, whatever 'ave you done?' She knew she should have phoned Sister, Ward Six several days ago, but she hadn't. Sister couldn't phone her at Clematis Close because there was no phone in the house, but it was only a matter of time before the hospital got on to Mum, whose phone number she'd provided as next of kin. Sister had in fact been trying all that day to contact Mrs Roxby; but Myra was out at work, so it was not till evening when she was listening to the TV news and asking herself sardonically what lies the politicians were going to tell her tonight, that a persistent ringing broke through the sound of the newscaster's voice.

'Sister, Ward Six here. Is that Mrs Roxby? I've been trying to get you all day.'

'Sorry about that, Sister. Must have been out at work.'

'Yes. Well . . . I'm very sorry to have to tell you it's bad news. It's about Mr Wilfred Roxby – your former husband, I understand?'

'That's right.'

'I'm sorry I was unable to contact your daughter. I believe she's not on the phone?'

'That's right.'

'I asked her to phone, but she hasn't. Not since the beginning of the week. He took a turn for the worse yesterday.'

'Oh yes?'

Sister had mixed feelings about the hopeful tone in Myra Roxby's voice: sorrow that she obviously didn't care what happened to her ex-husband, but relief that the message was going to be easier to deliver.

'I'm very sorry to have to tell you that he passed away yesterday.'

There was a short pause before Myra asked, 'What did he die of, then?'

'It was laryngeal obstruction, actually. Rather unexpected. He'd made a perfect recovery from his fall, and the stitches were taken out on Monday. It was a beautiful scar, well healed. But during his tea yesterday he swallowed a big piece of baked potato which stuck in his throat and choked him.'

'Dear Lord!' gasped Myra.

'We did everything we could. The duty doctor rushed him into intensive care; but it was too late. I'm sorry.'

'He wasn't used to eating solids,' said Myra.

Sister bridled, and her voice was sharp. 'Nobody told me he was on a fluid diet,' she said defensively.

'Had been for years,' said Myra. 'Mostly scrumpy.'

There was a brief silence before Sister said, 'Will someone come to Ward Six to pick up his things? And the death certificate? And you'll have to make arrangements with the undertaker of course.'

'I'll see to that,' said Myra briskly. 'Is he still in Ward Six?'

'No. The body is now in the hospital mortuary.'

'Yes. I suppose it would be. And thank you, Sister, for all you've done. I'm sure you couldn't have done no more.'

Even Vince admitted that Myra was wonderful over the funeral. 'Amazing Grace' was the song she chose for music during the service at the crematorium. Everybody, even the boys, liked it, and Mrs Pratt observed that it was truly heavenly. All the mourners were especially kind to Chris, who was the youngest present, and who asked some difficult questions about what was happening to Wilf. Darren didn't mention Wilf, but he kept asking how hot the furnace was and what temperature was needed to reduce everything to ash. Myra gave a little reception in her house in Frenny Hinton when it was all over. She provided glasses of sherry with small egg and cress sandwiches with the crusts removed, all very refined. There were Mars bars to comfort the boys. Mrs Evans, one of the guests, offered her congratulations as she left.

'Well I don't think congratulations is quite in order for a funeral,' said Myra.

'You know very well I don't mean that,' said Mrs Evans without a flicker of a smile. 'It's the way you did it all: everything just so.'

The phrase tickled Myra. On Sunday when she was watering and spraying her house plants, snipping off a dead leaf here and there, she told them, 'I'm making you just so my prettiest. Just so!' And when black Supremo jumped on to her lap as she was reading her Sunday paper she stroked him behind the ears murmuring, 'You're a bit of just so, Supremo, that's for sure!'

When Sandra conscientiously took Dad's leftover tablets back to the surgery she wanted to see Dr James personally. The receptionist seemed unwilling, and tried to persuade her to see the new young trainee doctor instead; but when she heard it was about a death she reluctantly agreed, if Sandra would wait. Sandra was willing to wait. In fact she was pleased to sit and think for once. She was so unused to having a moment to spare that idleness, even in a queue, seemed to her a pleasure.

'Well, Sandra,' said Dr James when at last she was allowed into his surgery and sat down opposite to him at his desk, with the newfangled computer they were all using now blinking at his side. 'It looks as if poor Wilf is home and dry at last in Part Four Accommodation.'

'Part Four Accommodation, Doctor. What's that?'

'Six foot underground.'

Sandra couldn't help laughing, but she put him right.

'Oh no, Doctor! It wasn't burial at all. It was cremation. He went up in smoke.'

'Then he's got himself a bed in the celestial highrise.'

'I suppose so, Doctor. He's built himself a castle in the air, perhaps. Any rate I do believe he's better off where he is – even if it was a baked potato put him there in the end.'

Dr James hadn't heard about the baked potato, so she told him the story. He didn't seem to find it quite as funny as Mum had.

'Well, Sandra,' he said, 'whatever way he went and wherever he is he should be grateful to you. Everybody should be more grateful to you than they probably are. Not many daughters are as good as you were to your old dad.' Then Sandra began to cry, so he pulled out a tissue from a box on the top of his desk, and handed her one.

That night Sandra and Vince talked lovingly to each other for the first time in months. They were in bed. Vince had just set the alarm for 6 a.m. as he was on early shift next day.

'I'm afraid I wasn't much help to you with your old dad,' he said, and as Sandra made no comment he added, 'It's nice being on our own again, isn't it?'

Sandra agreed it was, but that somehow she felt a bit guilty.

'What d'you mean, Sandra? Guilty for what? It wasn't your fault they choked him with a baked potato. What you deserve is the MBE for Magnificent Bloody Endeavour. You should get a medal for what you did. Nobody could have done no more.'

'That's what Dr James said. "He's gone up in smoke," I says. "Built himself a castle in the air," says I.'

'Your dad never built anything. It's you who's always building dreams.'

'Mm . . . mm . . .' murmured Sandra, who was beginning to feel sleepy.

'What are you going to do with the ashes, Sandra?' Vince pursued. 'I don't like to see them sitting there on the kitchen dresser. It puts me off my food thinking of the poor old bugger crumbled up inside that plastic pot.'

'It's a funeral urn.'

'Whatever it is, I hope you're not going to keep it there too long.'

'I'm going to plant a rose in the lawn where we burnt his bed,' she said dreamily. 'And I'm going to put ashes round the roots. New Dawn. I saw it in a catalogue. Pink. Lovely, it is.'

'I believe it's a climber, Sandra. My gran used to have one climbing over her porch.'

'Well then you'll have to build a pillar for it, won't you, Vince?' and although he made no reply because he was feeling sleepy too, she mumbled, 'Dad always did need something to lean on.'

Six

September's gales brought rain to the summer-parched garden, and by October Lizzie was able to work the soil once more. She was able to dig up and burn the three-year-old strawberry plants which had completed what she considered their best fruiting life. Like humans, plants grow old and tired and lose their immunity to disease, so in August she pegged down into pots new suckers which in autumn she planted out into fresh soil. In this way she kept her strawberry bed strong and healthy as it crept down a few feet each year towards the river. The river was, of course, very useful to her in times of drought.

She supposed people would think it odd taking so much trouble in the garden when she would be leaving it next spring, but to Lizzie the garden was not something you could abandon any more than you could a child. Soil was sacred, and had to be worked and cared for, whoever derived the benefits of such effort.

Raspberry canes had already after fruiting, been thinned, and new strong suckers tied back into their wire frames. She suspected that the raspberry stock, originally grown in a cool virus-free Scottish climate, might be getting a bit sick, but she hoped that it would last another year or two. By the end of October, when the wild cherry saplings ordered from Westerleigh Trees arrived, each in its tubular packing, the soil was moist yet not too heavy, the atmosphere cool but not yet threatening frosts, several bags of farmyard manure had been dumped by her farming neighbour at her back gate, and everything seemed perfect for carrying out her plan. So on Saturday morning she organised a planting party with Timothy and his friends. They had all been told to wear old clothes and wellies, and be prepared to deal with muck.

First they had to dig holes, six on the south and six near the north boundaries of the garden, a series of holes each twelve feet apart from the next. Timothy and Darren dug on the south while she and Barry Mogg dug on the north side. Little Chris, who was too young not to pester his brother and disrupt his work, she kept with her. She gave him a tape measure and set him to mark out with stones all the twelve spaces. When the holes were dug Timothy and Darren attacked with spades the oldest and most mature of her compost heaps, and piled the crumbly stuff into a wheelbarrow, from which the others filled buckets.

'Only fill them half full,' advised Lizzie, 'or they'll be too heavy to carry.' Some of this, which Lizzie kept saying was 'lovely! delicious!', was dropped into the bottom of each hole. Then they stood around watching her unpack the little trees, spread out their roots inside the holes, and hold them steady while Timothy and Darren dribbled more compost, mixed with garden earth, on top. Barry Mogg held a rake with which he levelled off the surface. The boys were then allowed to tread it down.

'But not too heavily,' implored Lizzie. 'Anyone would think you were a herd of elephants trumpeting and trampling on the African bushveld!'

'What's a bush felt?' asked Barry. 'Is it a sun-hat?'

'You tell him, Timothy,' said Lizzie as she went into the house to fetch mugs and a jug of orange juice, which they drank as they sat crosslegged on the grass.

Lizzie lay down, her arms folded behind her head; and for the first time since Larry's death she felt a little peace steal over her, a certain satisfaction in physical work and a job done. Then she realised she hadn't staked the trees, but she held her tongue and decided to do the staking alone, after the boys had gone home.

'It's manure now,' she said. 'Lovely filthy stuff!'

There were the usual retching noises and laughs, faces pulled and noses held, all the acting boys go through at the mention of shit; but they managed with spades and buckets and a wheelbarrow to work their way along the lines of saplings, spreading a layer round each.

Lizzie imagined, as she surveyed the scene, what it would look like in eight or ten years' time. I would plant bulbs – Anemone blanda – blues – under them, she thought. It would be a heavenly sight. She did not really mind that she wouldn't be there to see it. A thing of beauty is a joy for ever, whoever makes it and whoever enjoys it. It would be her own private memorial to Larry. It was fitting that he, her prince among men, should grow into these trees, so beautiful in their grace and vigour when they bloomed each spring. He would in a very real way be part of them, would thrust his vitality and joy in living into their branches and their flowering, because they would be fed by his ashes. In a drawer in her bedroom Lizzie had hidden the plastic casket of ashes. She intended, when she was alone with Timothy later that evening, to scatter a little of that ash round every root.

'Watering now,' she commanded, and Chris and Barry raced for the watering cans and the outdoor tap.

Watering was what they'd been looking forward to most of all.

When the work was finished, and they were all floppy and weary from their exertions, she made them remove their wellies and wash their hands before coming into the kitchen for a lunch of baked beans and sausages with chips, and a few Brussels sprouts sneaked on to each plate. Lizzie promised ice-cream for each clean plate, so even the sprouts were swept up and swallowed. Into each palm she dropped two pound coins. 'Wages for a gardener's assistants,' she said.

'Thank you, Mrs Bassett,' said Barry solemnly. 'It was great.' Lizzie smiled and ruffled his hair affectionately. He was a small boy with an anxious expression which tugged at her heart.

In the evening she and Timothy scattered the ashes. They didn't talk much; but when it was finished they sat on the step of the terrace and looked down towards the river.

'It's funny,' said Timothy, 'to think that we're all made of the same stuff.'

'Same as other animals,' said Lizzie. 'And plants too. Same as the earth itself, really. But it does make you understand we're all brothers under the skin, doesn't it?'

'But not the same while we're living – are we?'

'Very different. And yet the same,' said Lizzie.

'I do wish Daddy was here, and we could talk about it with him.'

'Yes. So do I.'

'That night after his bath Timothy crept into his mother's bed. He was reading when she came up to say goodnight.

'Jim-Jams didn't come for supper tonight,' he said.

'No. It's his weekend off duty. So he's gone over the Severn Bridge into Wales to spend the weekend with his brother's family.'

'Is he going to climb that mountain?'

'Plynlimon? It's not much of a mountain, really. And quite a gradual grassy climb. Daddy and I once did it together.' She decided to go down to Larry's workshop and find a map to show Timothy. On the shelf above the maps she saw that engagement diary she'd found in the Volvo and neglected to work through. With a sigh she pulled it out and carried it upstairs with the map.

'If you find the Black Mountains, and then go north-west towards Aberystwyth, you'll see Plynlimon,' she said; and while Timothy was studying the map she flicked over the pages of the diary. It was too late now to write to anyone mentioned in it; and anyway Miss

Brockway had almost certainly dealt with all that weeks ago. Lizzie was glad she'd written to Miss Brockway before she left, thanking her for all her years of work and dedication, and glad, too, that she didn't have to meet the unlucky draughtsmen, some young trainees among them, who'd lost their jobs along with her. She noticed the entry for June (one Thursday) which read: *Cottesloe Theatre. A.* She couldn't remember Larry telling her about that visit, but perhaps it had been a dull play. She turned over the page; on the following Thursday there was an entry which simply said: *7 p.m. P.P.* Did that mean Pettigrew Place? She thumbed through a few more pages to discover that Thursday evenings were given either to P.P. or to A. Had he been seeing Amanda somewhere regularly every Thursday evening?

'Here it is,' said Timothy. 'And there are some big lakes too.'

'Let's have a look,' said Lizzie. 'It's probably the Elan Valley reservoir. A wonderful sight when it's full and the dam lets water fall over it . . . Daddy used to say it was a marvellous piece of nineteenth-century engineering.'

Unexpectedly Timothy began to cry. His distress pushed all other thoughts from her mind as she sat on the bed and put her arms round him. When he dried his tears and lay down to hug his pillow she felt so exhausted by the emotional demands of the day as well as the physical exercise that she decided to go to bed early herself; and when she climbed in beside Timothy she fell asleep at once.

Dr James had often noticed that after a brief holiday, or even a change of scene, he returned to work with his clinical sense enhanced. Clinical sense was a funny thing, he thought – a sixth sense that makes a doctor aware, simply by seeing a patient walk into the room, whether he is ill or not. It could be an awkward gift to possess, too, if you suddenly saw a stranger in a crowded street whom you knew was sick, perhaps even diagnosed at a glance his disease, and wondered if he was getting the appropriate help. It was, he thought, rather like the skill of the antiquarian, who just by handling a piece of porcelain could date it – by its feel, by its colours and style of decoration, could place its manufacture and say whether it was rare or not. So when Mrs Pewsey, a stout middle-aged far-mer's wife, came into his surgery, breathing a little faster than the effort warranted, and sat down opposite him smiling cheerfully out of her lemony pale face, he knew at once she was ill. The computer screen revealed nothing of importance in her past history, and her slim file told him she was not a frequent attender at surgery.

'I'm afraid I'm a bit of a fraud really, Doctor,' she said, 'taking up your time like this when you're so busy. But my 'usband says: "What's ailing you, girl? You used to be able to lift a sack of potatoes on to your back as easy as stirring your tea with a spoon, and now it makes you pant like a frog out of water." '

'Short of breath, are you, Mrs Pewsey?'

'I suppose that's what it is.'

James looked at his watch. Time and motion studies recently worked out for the new efficiently-to-be-run NHS showed that he could give each patient no more than seven to ten minutes without running very late, but Mrs Pewsey, he knew, would need a great deal more time than that. She needed a full examination. 'Dyspnoea,' he wrote on her notes. 'How long have you noticed it?' he asked.

'I can't rightly say, Doctor. Six months maybe. But they do tell me as I'm paler than I was. I used to be ruddy. Cheeks always red. We put it down to the cold winds up on our land. It's that bit higher than Fossbury Main Street. And we all know Fossbury's cold enough. "Pewsey's Wold where the wind blows cold", Jack used to say of our farm. But my cheeks is that pale nowadays my daughter says to me – must have been last Christmas, because we were getting ready to take her to a Young Farmers' dance – she says, "Why don't you use a blusher, Mum?" Well I never heard of such a thing! Using rouge at my age? Near on a year it must be.'

Without interrupting the flow of her talk James had persuaded her to remove her coat, and was taking her blood pressure, which proved normal. He noticed the jugular veins in her neck were too full, and with his fingers he felt a firm rubbery lump above one collar-bone. 'I'd like to examine you on the couch, Mrs Pewsey,' he said.

'Nothing wrong, is there, Doctor?' She was alarmed. 'It's not my heart, is it? My father died of heart.'

He listened to her lungs. Under his fingertips he could feel peculiar ridges in the skin of her chest, like the surface of a sandy beach pressed down and rippled by a receding tide. When he felt her belly he found a large firm swelling coming from the splenic region.

'No. It's not your heart, but your heart is having a hard time trying to keep up with you because it's not getting enough oxygen. I think you're pretty anaemic.'

'How can that be, Doctor?' She was indignant. 'I eat

well. None of this newfangled vegetarian stuff. I eat plenty of good meat as well as greens.'

'I'll have to take some blood to find out what kind of anaemia it is,' he said. He took a sample of blood from the vein above the crook of her right elbow, then pressed it out through the needle into a tiny tube ready for analysis. All this he did in silence. He was thinking: it must be leukaemia. And next week when I get the report I shall have the unpleasant job of telling her and her husband. If it's the lymphatic type, which it probably is, she'll be lucky, because that has a better prognosis, and can be treated nowadays. He hadn't seen a case for several years. He must look it up in the books when he got home. He was afraid, though, that that queer skin of hers, the like of which he'd never seen before, was probably a bad omen.

'Will you make an appointment for Tuesday next week, Mrs Pewsey? I'll have the results by then.' He prescribed a mild diuretic tablet to be taken each morning. 'It'll clear your lungs a bit of fluid,' he explained. 'And help the breathing.'

'Thank you, Doctor. Will you be watching the fireworks next week in Pewsey's field? Jack lent the field for the town bonfire. Let's hope it's dry. That way there won't be too much mud, nor too many cars stuck in it.'

The Pewseys often lent that field for fêtes in aid of charity, and twice a year, in March and September, they let it to the travelling fair. They were short of cash, he knew, since subsidies had been cut and their milk quota reduced. He wondered how Jack would cope without his wife's free labour. She was certainly too ill for heavy work, although she'd probably survive a few years yet. He supposed the 'developers' who had been pressing Pewsey to sell his fields for housing would at last persuade him to do so, and that bit of countryside to the north-east of Fossbury, where planning regulations would be less strict than among Main Street's listed buildings, would be smothered with ugly little red houses like a measles rash.

He thought Timothy would like to know about the bonfire, so he brought the subject up at supper that evening at the Barn. But Timothy was more interested in what Jim-Jams could tell him about Plynlimon.

'It's not Everest, you know,' said James. 'Anyone can do it.'

Lizzie announced that she would have to travel to London early next week to visit Larry's solicitor, and probably his bank manager as well.

'I think I'll have to see Liam too,' she said. 'He seems to have sold the Volvo, and I need the cash. I'll probably have to stay overnight in Surbiton with

Elena. That's easy; but I was wondering about Timothy . . . .' She looked uncertainly from one to the other.

'No problem,' said James. 'He can stay with me. Would you like that, Timothy? Two old bachelors together? I'll see he gets off in the morning in time for school.'

'Oh brill!' said Timothy. 'Brill!'

On the day his mother parked her Mini at Swinester station and caught the Inter-City to London, Timothy went straight from school to Owl House. After tea he sat down dutifully to do his homework in James's study, where the doctor had to leave him in order to attend to evening surgery. At about seven o'clock Darren and Barry came to the back door, and after hurried conference in the kitchen they left the house. It was dark in the garden, and in the road outside, but Main Street was brightly lit. By the yew trees at the church gate Darren said, 'We'd better go through the cemetery. That way nobody'll see us.' They crept along in single file, keeping close to the hedge and hoping it would hide their shadows, and soon reached the vicarage garden where the big chestnut tree grew. Their feet made crunchy noises on the crisp, new-fallen leaves, and it was fun kicking them about.

'Ssh!' said Darren. 'There's a dog in there.' But no dog barked.

Barry began to feel among the leaves for smooth-skinned conkers, which he stuffed into his pockets. Darren had brought a plastic carrier to fill. They wanted as many conkers as they could find to throw handfuls into Pewsey's bonfire on 5 November to make them explode and sound like gunfire, and so give everybody standing near a fright. Darren picked up a stick and began hitting a branch above his head, when Timothy hissed, 'Ssh!' He had seen another figure, someone tall wearing a long coat, creeping along the hedge as they had done. They crouched down behind the trunk of the great tree and watched silently. At first they thought it was a burglar, till they heard footsteps on the gravel by the house. It didn't sound like the tread of a man's flat shoes. Were there women burglars? The intruder picked up a handful of gravel and threw it at a lighted window on the first floor. All the windows on the ground floor were black.

The boys didn't know that Mr Foster was not at home – it was his evening for his study course in archaeology at the Swinester Tech – but Melanie had discovered this. She threw a second handful of pebbles and waited below the window. After a pause it was opened by Maisie, who called out in alarm: 'Who is it? What's up?'

The boys could see Melanie silhouetted against the light from the open window as Maisie leaned out; they could hear every word in the quiet garden.

'Oh, it's you. Well, go away – why don't you?'

'I just want to talk to you, Maisie. And you never let me. You keep avoiding me.' Melanie's voice was quiet but plaintive and aggrieved.

'I don't want to talk to you. That's why. You pester me. Go away!' shouted Maisie, her anger rising uncontrollably. 'Go away, will you?' Then she screamed shrilly, 'I like men, I like men!' and shut the window with a bang.

Immediately a light appeared downstairs and the french windows burst open as Maisie's elder daughter, a plump girl of fourteen or so, still in her school skirt and blouse, ran out.

'Get out, you toad!' she shouted. 'My mum doesn't ever want to see you. So don't come back – ever – or we'll call the police!'

Melanie turned and fled without a word. All the lights at the back of the house went out.

Timothy felt rather sorry for the fleeing figure. It wasn't very nice to be called a toad. Did she look like one? He hadn't been able to see her face. Mr Thomas

Parry looked like a frog, but nobody called him a toad. In Timothy's opinion the strange woman seemed more like a bat in her long black coat, which billowed out behind her as she ran.

'Well I never!' said Barry in a hoarse whisper. 'She likes men! She likes men!'

'Who'd 'a thought it?' said Darren aloud. 'A vicar's wife, too!'

They scampered back across the garden to the cemetery, and ran out into Main Street. Timothy was safely back inside Owl House before James returned from work. They watched TV happily together till after the *Nine O'Clock News*, when Timothy was pushed off to bed in a small room which used to be a dressing-room in the days when James and Mary shared the big double bedroom next to it. James couldn't help remembering sadly that Mary had prepared the little dressing-room as a nursery. The pale blue wallpaper was still there, and the blue curtains she had stitched still hung in the window. He noticed as he pulled them together that the edges where they met had faded. The room had never been used for that baby because poor Mary miscarried at four months. 'There's no sense in greetin', Jamie.' He could hear her voice. 'We're still young. We'll try again.' But they were unlucky. And there were no babies.

Seven years ago she had skidded on an icy patch of road on the M4 coming home after a weekend reunion in London with some of her old schoolfriends – what she called 'a bit of a giggle'. It was on 7 February. The day was clear but cold. Her car slewed across the central reservation and overturned several times. She was dead when the ambulance arrived. One of the blessings remembered from the debris of that black day was that no other car had been involved in the crash. A sweet, honourable girl, he would have trusted her with his life. At first it wasn't worth living without her; and he was thankful then that there weren't any babies. Motherless babies were a problem.

The big bonfire in Pewsey's field was piled high with rubbish: dead branches, rags, broken wooden crates, rotting mattresses, a few bales of mouldy hay, an odd shoe or two, and an unhinged painted door; someone had even added a twisted bicycle frame without its wheels. Pewsey had doused the base with paraffin a few hours before dark to encourage the blaze. Two members of the Frostbiters (a charitable all-male club founded after the war to help the poor of Fossbury to keep warm in winter, but now working for wider charitable aims) collected money at the gate: 20p. for each person on foot, £1 for each car. Other responsible citizens of the town, all with their own supplies of fireworks, stood ready in strategic positions on the field.

When at last the bonfire finally burst into flames a roar went up from the crowd; and then rockets exploded and Catherine wheels began to whirl, shooting out sparks. Excited cries greeted the rise of the rockets, and their shining coloured rain fell to an accompaniment of subdued moans.

It was strange how the spectacle of fire and fireworks excited almost everybody, thought Dr James as he passed the field in his Peugeot. He was on his way to visit a farmer in Easton Malreward, three miles away, who had fallen out of a hayloft and had, by the sound of his wife's tale told over the phone, almost certainly dislocated his shoulder, probably fracturing a bone as well.

Gerry Foster, who was watching the display with his two daughters, considered the phenomenon of man's delight in fire further. This Guy Fawkes fun was originally a celebration of anti-Papist feeling centred on hatred of the Catholic Gunpowder Plotters; but the festival of fire in autumn was much older than that. Before the Reformation, it had been the feast of All Souls, when the dead were remembered with prayers and the lighting of candles to help them on their way through Purgatory. Before Christianity it was probably a festival to mark the dying of the year, and the hope of a renewed soil fertility after the winter. Such festivals were held all over the world. The Japanese, he'd read, went out into the countryside with lanterns to celebrate on an evening in late autumn. And ancient Egyptians, he had recently learned from his archaeology course at the Swinester Tech, held a festival following the inundation of the Nile delta. They made little boats of papyrus leaves, and loaded them with lights and offerings of food, and pushed the frail cargoes out on to flood waters hoping to help their dead as they groped their passage through the dark underworld. He remembered, too, that they made straw dollies of Osiris, which they buried in the mud. In spring, when the effigies were dug up and found to be sprouting corn, they were seen as promises of resurrection, of new life to come after death. Man's primeval desire to be in touch with his dead had very little part in Guy Fawkes night jollity, but he supposed that all the raucous shouting and the thrill of watching the fire was a useful release of high spirits; and it did seem to bond the community together in a peculiar way.

He was standing next to Barry Mogg's mother and could hear her talking to her friend while she held

Barry's hand tightly: Her gran told her, and her gran's gran told her gran, that in the olden days they used to watch bull-baiting on Guy Fawkes day. The poor beast was tethered in Main Street, and the dog-fanciers all sat around under the Market Cross. The bull got that excited by all the noise and lights, snorting and tossing his head, and the bulldogs raring to go . . . Quite a few of them were killed and injured by the bull tossing them, mind; but some got their teeth into the poor beast's neck, and maybe his windpipe too. Betting and gambling on their chances, that's what the men did.

Gerry could picture the scene: gore galore, dogs barking and howling and the enraged bull bellowing. That's what people liked: blood and fire and lots of noise. It was not so very different from Roman circuses. The appetite for cruelty was held in check nowadays, but it was there, hidden underneath all that harmless hatred of the guy. He saw Barry beside his mother, his solemn eyes glowing with an exultation that seemed almost holy. It was not, unfortunately, a look you often saw in church. Moving away from the bonfire he bumped into Timothy with Lizzie muffled up in anorak and scarf.

'Did you hear the conkers exploding?' asked Timothy.

Among so many other noises Gerry had not distinguished the explosion of conkers, but he nodded amiably. Such a small white lie was excusable, especially as tonight seemed to be bringing out a smile in Lizzie.

After Pewsey's bonfire night November sank into its usual uneventfulness, when nothing much happened and people were not yet ready for Christmas. Lizzie liked November in spite of its dull foggy days and its hoar frost settling at night on grass and dead vegetation. October was her favourite month with its flamboyant colours and fruitfulness; but she also liked the occasional streaking of thin sunlight through banks of fog, the diamond brilliance of wet cobwebs in hedges and on the grass, and the raking of her thick harvest of leaves to cover tender roots against the fiercer cold to come.

James and his partners held a practice meeting to decide where they would hold the Christmas lunch for the staff this year, and how they would carve up the duty rota for Christmas. Dr Julia Orchard, whose ancestral name had once been Baumgarten, would be in Vienna for Christmas. Julia was a friend of Lizzie's, who sometimes visited her after evening surgery, when they drank a glass of sherry together and looked at Lizzie's pictures. Julia was probably the only inhabitant of Fossbury apart from Lizzie and James who had any interest in art. The general opinion was once expressed to James by Pewsey: 'Paintings . . . ? Oh arr . . . Art. . . . Well, I like to see a nicely painted door. And I can understand a neat bit of shearing on the sign above the Fleece in Horse Street; but Art . . . well, what's it for?' The fact that some folk paid thousands, millions even, for a painting was a matter for disbelief, or wonder, or simply a confirmation of his view that half the world was mad.

James came to be on duty over Christmas. He didn't mind much because he had no family of his own apart from his brother in Aberystwyth, who didn't really want him around again so soon. The true joys of Christmas were for children. It was the feast of the Christ Child; and it was for children, who alone could light a renewal of hope in the cynical, disappointed old heart of the world. He had no children through whose innocent eyes he could glimpse this hope, and no wife either. Christmas was often, he knew, a horrible time for single people, who while their friends and neighbours rejoiced or quarrelled in the bosom of their families, felt most alone. So he preferred to occupy his mind with work at this time, and would take a day off immediately afterwards.

Lizzie had arranged to take Timothy to his grandmother's house for the holiday, where they were to be joined by Larry's sister, her husband and their children.

'I'd be awfully grateful, James, if you'd keep an eye on the Barn while we're away,' she said. 'Just pop in now and again. Turn a few lights on and off.'

'It'll do you good to get away,' he said. 'Good for Timothy, too, to have company of his own age.'

'I'll leave the Mini in the station car park and go by Inter-City. Timothy likes the train.' The Volvo had been sold for less than she'd hoped for from Liam's London connections, but considering the recession a fair price. A local garage owner, who dealt in second-hand cars, had paid her and driven the Volvo away. 'I've left some nice grub for you in my fridge,' she added.

'No need, Lizzie my angel. Dr Doynton has very kindly invited me to Christmas dinner so I shall be very well fed in the traditional manner, ending up with port in his study. No doubt I shall have to listen to his tales of general practice before the Ark, and be suitably horrified by stories of the progress of AIDS in Zambia from his grandson, who will join the men for the port. So I shan't be as lonely as I expected after all.'

'Aren't you going to be on duty?'

'Yes. And I might be called out with my mouth still

full of turkey. But patients are very considerate on Christmas Day. They hardly ever call you out. It's Christmas Eve and Boxing Day when I shall be busy.'

'With your mouth still full of turkey!' Timothy called out of the window as they drove away. He thought that very funny. As he adjusted his seatbelt he said, 'Do you know, when I stayed with Jim-Jams that last time you went to London he said we were two old bachelors together.'

'Did he?'

'Do you think he's lonely at Owl House?'

'I expect he is sometimes. But he loves his work. That seems to take up most of his time and energy.'

'I hope he has a happy Christmas,' said Timothy doubtfully.

Christmas Eve was just as James had predicted. All surgeries were full and his list of home visits was long. In a lull after 7 p.m. he walked across the gardens to the Barn and let himself in. He turned lights on in the sitting-room and pulled curtains; he went into the kitchen and opened the fridge. There were meals for him in dishes covered in aluminium foil, all labelled with dates in Lizzie's neat handwriting. Needless to say, he had no intention of sticking to her programme;

he would help himself at random, or perhaps peep under their dainty veils and pick and choose among the tasty snacks. He endured enough ordering of his days already without having his meals meticulously planned! All the same he couldn't help admiring her. He heaved a sigh, thinking what a wonderful wife she must have been to Larry. The lucky sod! For his short lifespan anyway, poor man . . . He put a dish under Lizzie's grill and ate supper at her kitchen table, trying to recall the exact words of that hymn of praise in the Bible for an excellent woman. Her price is beyond rubies, he remembered. Her children would rise up and call her blessed. He'd have to go easy on the drink, he was on duty.

When he was leaving the house he left a light on in the sitting-room. He'd come back later and turn that off.

The bleep soon called him out to a semi-conscious teenager whose mother suspected he'd been sniffing glue; but he was only very drunk. It would not be a happy Christmas Day for him tomorrow, thought James: he'll have one hell of a hangover – worth suffering if it taught him some discretion. Then it was the usual mixed bag of sore throats and swollen eardrums in children, and an unexpected hypersensitivity rash in a girl who'd been persuaded by an advert in a women's magazine to take some herbal remedy of unknown source and strength to cure her acne. Her mum thought she'd swallowed poison. He tried to reassure them both, and promised a cure in six months after a course of tetracycline.

'Can't do it in time for New Year,' he said. 'But by next Christmas I promise you'll be the Belle of the Ball!'

At 3 a.m. on Christmas morning he fell into bed and slept. No more calls disturbed him; and at noon he rose, had a bath and shaved before driving up to Dr Doynton's house, where he enjoyed a wonderful traditional English Christmas dinner cooked and served by Dorothy, Dr Doynton's white-haired, once-beautiful, but rather silent wife. Besides his host and hostess there were seated at the table their son Patrick, a successful accountant, his wife, and their two children, the younger a girl still at school, the elder, Mark, a medical student, tanned from his recent sojourn in the tropics.

After the dinner Mrs Doynton shooed the men off into the doctor's study, and steered her daughter-in-law and granddaughter into the kitchen to help with the washing up.

'It's not very arduous work,' she said. 'Simply loading the dishwasher. But we'll have to clear the table first.'

In the study the men sat in easy chairs and sipped port. James felt rather sleepy; but he knew his senior partner liked to talk about the past when he got the chance, and realised that the return he'd have to make for his good dinner was to egg him on and listen.

'I bet doctors weren't half so busy in the days when the welfare state didn't pay the bill,' he said.

'My dear fellow, in the days when doctors were paid directly by patients they had great difficulty being paid at all. My father employed a debt-collector who went round the houses of the poor with a notebook in which he entered the sixpence a week they paid off and so on. In those days the health of women and children of the working class was largely neglected. It was only the man of the family, the wage-earner who could afford a medical consultation.' They sipped in silence, giving him time to pause for breath. 'It was also the man, on whose work the family depended for survival, who ate the meat and drank the milk they could afford,' he went on. 'Anyone who thinks a return to private medicine would be good for the nation's health needs his head examined. I know what it was like before the NHS from my own experience, and even more from my father's. In his day the women of the poor who lost blood in repeated pregnancies, or in heavy menstruation, and whose diet was too meagre to make up for the iron lost, used to be chronically anaemic. How often do you see the spoon-shaped nails of iron-deficiency anaemia today?' He leaned over to Mark. 'I don't suppose you ever look for them – do you? – but immediately reach for the syringe and a blood sample to send away for analysis.'

'Not in Africa,' said Mark, and laughed. A shadow passed over the room: the silence of an angel passing – the Angel of Death, as each thought of AIDS and the danger of the needle loaded with contaminated blood. The silence was broken by Dr Doynton.

'In my day we never enjoyed these so-called "electives" to study tropical diseases in far-off glamorous places. The furthest we got away from medical school was a few weeks in a fever hospital; but we did at least learn to tell the difference between a measles and a scarlet fever rash.'

'When did you first come to Fossbury, Grandad?' asked Mark.

'I came in the fifties as a young man when the NHS was just beginning to take over. But my father was here before me, in the twenties, as a very poorly paid young assistant to Dr Page.' He laughed. 'There's nobody like Dr Page around these days. I believe he was unique even then. He worked single-handed before my father joined him. Hunting was his passion, not medicine; and that's why he wanted another pair of hands – to take over the practice on the two days a week he hunted.'

'He was killed, wasn't he? While out hunting?' put in Patrick, with some satisfaction, as if this served the doctor right.

'Fell at a jump and broke his neck,' said his father. 'That's how my father came to take over the practice, and the house as well.' He paused. 'Yes. Hunting was indeed his passion. Every Wednesday morning at 9 a.m. precisely he walked sedately up Main Street on his chestnut hunter, a good strong sixteen hands of well-groomed horseflesh. A fine figure of a man, Dad used to say, in his hunting jacket, hand-stitched for him by Creevey, the little hump-backed tailor who used to hang out in Horse Street next door to the Fleece – now of course, long departed – a white stock under his chin, and with his wide ginger moustache looking quite foxy himself, so I'm told. When he came to that first bow window on the north side he'd rein in and without dismounting he'd tap on the glass with his crop. There was an old woman sitting there with her bandaged leg propped up on a stool, and as soon as she saw him she'd unwind the bandages to reveal her varicose ulcer. He'd nod when he'd seen it, then the old woman would bind it all up again as he passed on along the street. Nobody criticised him. Everybody thought it quite the proper way for a hunting doctor to behave.'

Mark laughed aloud, but James, who was finding it difficult to keep awake, simply smiled.

'Tell Mark about the night of the horsehair stitching,' he prompted, when Patrick made his getaway, leaving the room to help prepare the coffee.

'Dr Page kept his horse in a stable at the back of the house, you see. He employed a young lad as a groom. My father's bedroom was at the back overlooking the stable. One night – it must have been a Saturday night because that was always drinkers' night – long after midnight, they were both woken by shouting and loud knocking on the front door. It was Dad's job to do the nightwork; but as Dr Page slept at the front of the house he was woken first. He got up and leaned out of the window in his pyjamas, searching below in the darkness with his flashlight and shouting, 'What the hell are you waking up the neighbourhood for?' Below there were two men standing unsteadily supporting each other. Even in that grudging light he could see blood all over one man's head and shirt. 'All right. I'll come down,' he grumbled. By this time Dad, also in his pyjamas, was on his way down to the surgery with a box of matches. No electricity then, but there was gas. You had to keep a box of matches in a pocket of every jacket in those days! He lit the gas mantle in the surgery and let it flare up. 'Better let the bugger in,' said Dr Page. My father was searching for horsehair sutures, but couldn't find any. No nylon in those days, Mark. We used sterilised horsehair for stitching skin wounds. 'Bring him in! Bring him in!' said Dr Page. So Dad let him in by the surgery entrance at the back, and began cleaning the wound, cutting the hair of the scalp round the gash. Someone had hit him with a broken bottle. But no sutures could be found anywhere. Failure of administration there, James, what? "Tell you what, Doynton," said Dr Page, and pulling him away into the stable he confided: "There's a perfectly good suture in the horse's tail, what?" and gave a laugh. So he plucked out a long hair, and Dad swished it about in a jar of surgical spirit; then he used it to stitch the wound. A week later the stitches came out. Perfect scar. Healed by first intention. No complications.'

'What about tetanus?' asked Mark, aghast.

'I take it that horse just didn't keep any spores in his gut,' said his grandfather.

The bleep in James's pocket suddenly summoned him as Patrick put his head round the door.

'Don't rush off,' said the old doctor. 'There's no particular urgency, is there? Time for the coffee Patrick's just made, I'm sure.' They rose and moved into the sitting-room where the women were already drinking coffee round a coal fire.

'Can I come with you?' asked Mark, when James decided to go. He was an eager student. As he sat down in the passenger seat of James's Peugeot and fastened his seat belt he commented: 'He's a funny old stick, my grandfather.'

'But a very good doctor,' said James. 'He doesn't miss much. Out of date, of course, but who isn't? The rate at which medicine's moving leaves us all behind. And leaves some very valuable things as well.' He started the engine and drove through the empty town, through the uncharacteristically quiet council estate, south to the village of Malmsford.

'Your grandfather learned his craft in an era when the most important tools were his five senses and that sixth, clinical sense, which he had to acquire. He had his stethoscope, of course, and his auriscope and ophthalmoscope, when he'd learned how to use them; he could get an X-ray taken, but the electrocardiogram was in its infancy, and biochemistry, apart from estimating sugar and one or two other things in blood, virtually unknown.'

'Antibiotics didn't come in till after the war, did they?'

'Before the war there were usually four or five infant deaths from pneumonia every winter in Fossbury. People forget that.' He frowned over the steering wheel. 'It's a baby we're visiting. I don't delay visiting a baby. They can die so quickly. They can also recover amazingly quickly, often against the odds. Nothing so surprising as medical practice.'

They had to slow down behind a herd of Friesians crossing the road on the way to evening milking. The farmer saluted James, and his dog, a wily Welsh collie, sloped by close to the ground, glancing quickly this way and that, his pointed nose ordering the slow obedient cows.

'There are some things the past tells us which even a high-tech age mustn't forget. New discoveries that appear to be random are always built on past ones. Remember Pasteur's dictum: "Chance favours the prepared mind." And then there's *Ars longa, vita brevis*, and all that . . . The Hippocratic lessons: very old truths, but absolutely basic. They never change. The art takes long to learn, life is short, experience fallible and judgement difficult. In other words keep your eyes open, be critical of yourself, and don't believe in every hasty generalisation!'

They stopped at a roadside cottage whose door was opened by a corpulent young man swinging a beer can. It was, after all, Christmas Day.

'I have a young doctor with me,' said James. 'May we both come in?'

In the sitting-room on a crimson carpet heavily stained with old spills of food and drink two small children were playing with their Christmas toys. A baby's bottle, half full of milk and its teat haloed with carpet-fluff, rolled about on the floor between them. A little dog, which had trotted out to the door with its master, jumped up on the settee. On a chair by the fire sat a young mother crouched in soundless misery over her whimpering baby, a child of about ten months. The toddlers stared unblinkingly at Mark while James knelt before the baby and spoke quietly to the mother. How long had the baby been vomiting, how many stools had he passed that day, had the other kids been ill too? He examined the baby and then told her what to do: no solid food, and no milk, for twenty-four hours, but little drinks of water every half-hour until the vomiting ceased. He picked up the feeding bottle from the floor and took it into the kitchen, where he emptied it into the sink and rinsed it out.

'I was ever so careful with sterilising it when he was tiny,' the mother said defensively.

'Yes, of course,' said James. 'He wouldn't be a big strong boy now if you hadn't been; but he's still a bit delicate to infections that wouldn't hurt you or me. And make everybody in the house wash hands after using the toilet paper, now, won't you?'

As they left the cottage, he said to Mark, 'D. and V. The African babykiller. The age-old babykiller everywhere.' He sighed. 'Health education is uphill work even today, even in Britain. But what can you expect? And where do you begin? Three kids under five are more than she can cope with; and although they can afford wall-to-wall carpeting and an expensive three-piece suite they don't understand that a baby's bottle must be kept sterilised and away from the patter of little puppies' paws. But the child'll be all right. She's very anxious, like all good mothers when their kids are ill. She'll stay awake all night to drip water into him. I just hope she won't try to feed him bacon and eggs for breakfast.' He wrote the name down in his diary for a visit next day.

On the way back they stopped at the Health Centre on the corner of Wistaria Way, as James wanted to write some notes into the records of patients he'd seen the day before.

'I'll walk,' said Mark. 'The exercise will do me good. Thanks a lot.' He slammed the car door, and sauntered off with the easy, nonchalant stride of the young. James, swinging his stethoscope, thoughtfully watched him go.

It was dark by the time he got home. He parked the car in his drive and walked across to the Barn for the routine turning-on of lights. A red Metro was parked inside the gate, and as he stood holding Lizzie's bunch of keys and looking at the strange car somebody came across the terrace from the back of the house. He couldn't see who it was, but guessed by the footsteps that it was a woman. She stopped when she caught sight of him, hesitated, then asked, 'James?'

'Why, Amanda!' he cried with outstretched arms. 'Amanda, is it really you? You've made my Christmas day for me. What a lovely surprise!'

The warmth of his greeting rather surprised her. She was hoping to see Lizzie, had come down to her cottage in Frenny Hinton for Christmas and didn't know that Lizzie was away.

'She's with her ma-in-law and other relatives in Surbiton,' Dr James explained, opening the door. 'Caretaker is all I am.'

'I was hoping she'd put me up for the night,' she said.

'What's wrong with your own house?'

'Christmas is lonely when you're alone like me,' she said. 'And somehow I couldn't face sleeping there. Not after . . . not after what happened.'

He nodded.

'I'm going to sell the place, you know,' she went on. 'I came down partly to start packing and clearing up.'

An unreasonable feeling of anger swept over him. 'Oh no, Amanda! You can't leave us. Why must you go? Lizzie's missed you, you know – badly.' And so, he thought, shall I.

She moved about the kitchen uncertainly. 'Shall I make a cup of tea?'

He stood watching her. He was swinging the house keys, and thinking suddenly that it might irritate her he popped them into a trouser pocket. The whole place seemed different, pervaded with a dreamlike quality. No longer an empty house he was looking after, it was a sacred grove in which, if you sat still and listened, you would hear mysterious voices echoing, which would soon divulge a secret you had long desired to know. He knew he must look silly standing there gaping. He thought perhaps he was drunk, certainly weak at the knees. He sat down quickly.

'We ought to open a bottle of champagne,' he said, 'to celebrate your return. But sadly I'm on duty, so I'd best be sober. Yes, tea would be nice.' She turned, smiling, holding the kettle. The way she moved was like music, he thought, a paean of praise sung by some great choir would not be more exhilarating. 'It's all such a surprise,' he said as they faced each other across the kitchen table over very hot tea. 'I mean, to find you here. To find you lonely on Christmas Day – a girl like you – '

'Christmas can be really horrible for single people,' she said.

'Yes, I know.'

'But at least you have your work.'

'Why do you want to sell your house?' he asked abruptly.

'I can't put it down to hard times, can I? Accountants are about the only people doing well out of the recession. We're inundated with bankruptcies. But – is it so surprising? I can't bear to be in it alone. It's an unlucky house.'

He scrutinised her, noticing the changes in her since he had last seen her on that day of the party. Her eyes seemed larger, more sombre, and her beautiful hair was longer. He imagined it must be soft and fragrant too, but wasn't near enough to touch it and smell it.

'Have you eaten today?' he asked. 'I've eaten too much. But Lizzie's left lots of stuff, so if you're hungry – ' He swore as the bleep buzzed in his pocket. She helped herself to food from the fridge while he wrote down the message.

'I'll have to go,' he said. 'Just my luck.'

'Do you think – ' she asked timidly, 'do you think Lizzie'd mind if I slept here tonight?'

'Why should she? I know she'll be very disappointed not to see you. You know your way around the house. I won't show you up to the bedroom, or I might overstay my welcome.'

She laughed at that, a delightful, frivolous, flirtatious laugh; and James was so filled with joy that his luck no longer seemed quite so bad.

'I'll have to lock up,' he said. 'I only have this one set of keys. So I'll have to lock you in too.'

'Quite an ogre, aren't you?'

'It may be the only way for an ogre to make sure of seeing you again before you disappear from Fossbury.'

She walked with him to the door and kissed him lightly on the cheek, dismissing him; but he swung round and held her for a moment in a tight embrace. And then he touched her hair with his lips. This time he could feel and smell it. As he walked towards his own house his step was springy, and he felt alert. He thought: it must be like this when you're floating along in the basket of a hot-air balloon and a sudden burst of flame makes you shoot up in the sky. He felt the exultation people feel on the first full clear day of spring, as if he could see all the bulbs in Lizzie's garden bursting into a dazzle of bloom, when in fact not one single snowdrop had yet pierced the soil. It struck him like a revelation: I have been asleep for years, and now I am awake. He felt slightly unsteady, but he wasn't drunk. Nor was he ill in any way. He'd never felt better in his life. What was happening to him? Was it the world around him that was reeling? He opened his front door and walked into the sitting-room. My God! he thought. Am I falling in love? He sat down in front of a blank television set and asked himself: can this be love? He wondered what Mary would have said to all this; but Mary didn't say a word.

Seven

Requests for home visits began to come in early on Boxing Day. James let them accumulate for a while, sorting them out into groups according to geographical area. He dressed and made his breakfast: tea and toast and bitter marmalade. Then he took a stroll around his garden where a few gleams of winter sunshine made the decay of what used to be a herbaceous border more obvious. He stood and viewed with gloom the invasion by brambles of the shrubbery between him and the Barn. He was letting the minutes pass. He didn't want to ring Amanda too early, although he was afraid if he left it too late he might miss her.

She answered the phone immediately, so he guessed she was down in the kitchen.

'Did you sleep all right?' he asked.

'Like a top. Does a top sleep? Anyway, well.'

'Good. What will you do today?'

'I must pack up all the things I want to take back

with me to town, and heap them into the Metro. I'll have to do a bit of cleaning as well. There's mould growing in places. It's been empty too long.'

'Look Amanda, I've got to work today, but I finish at six. Will you let me take you out to dinner? I know a very nice little country restaurant in Malmsford. I could book a table.'

'That sounds marvellous, James. Thank you. But don't go away now without letting me out. You locked me up. Remember?'

'Oh yes! OK. I'll be over with the keys.'

She was having breakfast when he arrived. She was dressed in what must have been an old dressing-gown of Lizzie's, a woolly garment which was too short for her. Her feet were bare, and her hair unbrushed. He was aware of a sudden desire to brush it for her, slowly and lingeringly. Seeing her without her armour of glamour, he couldn't help wondering if she was unconcerned about her appearance because she'd always been so confident of her own beauty she had no need to bother about how she looked, or if he was of so little importance to her that she didn't care. If so she misjudged the situation. He was not put off; it rather turned him on because it made him feel she was just that bit more accessible. He handed her Lizzie's bunch of keys.

'Till six then?' she said.

'Give me time to bath and make myself pretty for you.'

She laughed. 'Till seven?'

When he phoned Troubleful House in Malmsford he was told that they were holding a houseparty for the Christmas period; but yes, they could let him have the table for two by the fire at 7.30. then he set off on his rounds, calling first on a teenage girl in Azalea Crescent who had produced a finely speckled rash all over her face and chest. She was not very ill, but had a few enlarged glands in her neck. 'Rubella,' he said. 'Weren't you immunised for German measles, then?'

She hung her head. 'I was scared of the needle.' Her mother defended her: 'She never could take the needle, Doctor. Screamed the place down when you gave her the baby jabs. Don't you remember?' He didn't, for the simple reason that it was not he but Dr Orchard who ran the immunisation clinic. 'It'll break her heart, if she can't go dancing tonight, Doctor – but I reckon she can't. There's a crowd of them going to the disco in Swinester in a minibus. But not with that spotty face . . . .'

'Oh no, Mum! I couldn't. Not with my face like this!' She cringed, and covering her face with her hands, cried with vexation at the unfairness of life.

'Certainly not,' said James firmly. 'You're highly infectious. But lucky too, as a matter of fact – lucky to get this now. If you got it when you were pregnant your baby might be born deaf or blind.' She looked so thoroughly frightened then that he added, patting her arm, 'But you'll be all right now. You won't get it again.'

His next case was more serious: a quarryman of sixty-odd years, and a heavy smoker, who had been coughing for a long time and thought nothing of it until the previous night, when he had laughed unrestrainedly over a joke his brother told him and suddenly coughed up blood. 'Enough to stain the carpet,' he said. James examined his chest, told him he needed an X-ray, and then said he'd better see a chest specialist. He and his wife didn't ask any questions. They sat side by side very quietly on the settee. The brother who had told the bloodletting joke went out into the garden during the doctor's visit and lit a fag; but as James left the house he caught him up at the gate.

'Not too serious, is it, Doctor?'

'I'm afraid it may be, but we'll see what the X-ray says. And I'll make sure he gets the best treatment available.'

The man stood on the pavement as James threw his

medical bag on the passenger seat and then went round to the driver's side.

'That's what comes of telling jokes,' he said moodily. 'I'll have to give them up for the New Year.'

'It's smoking you want to give up,' said James over the roof of the car. 'Not jokes.' Cigarette in hand, the man watched James drive away; when he was out of sight he threw the fag on the pavement and ground the life out of it with his shoe.

The rest of the day James spent dealing with minor ailments which hardly warranted a doctor's visit on a Bank Holiday; but he knew they were all anxious people who called him out. Anxiety is a great magnifier of distress. He had never been so glad as when at last 6 p.m. approached, never so grateful to anyone as when he handed over his list of cases and the bleep to Tom Barton, the young trainee.

'I've left the bleep at the Health Centre for you to pick up, Tom. And the best of luck!' he almost sang out over the phone. 'I'm off now for two nights and a whole day. Isn't that great? It is for me.' Tom Barton thought as he replaced the receiver that James was surprisingly cheerful after his spate of Christmas duty. And he hadn't even had time yet to stoke up on whisky!

In his bath James sang snatches of arias from Handel's

"Messiah". As he dried himself he reflected that in all probability neither Handel nor the Messiah would approve of his desires and intentions for this evening. He laughed, forgiving himself. He put on a clean white shirt and his dark grey suit; he carefully fixed his tie, which he considered rather daringly modern with its splashes and spirals of blue and red, and as he surveyed himself in the mirror he thought: I look a city gent. I expect that's what she likes.

Amanda experienced a qualm of apprehension when she saw how formally dressed he was. A well mannered and kind-hearted girl, she could suffer fools gladly if they made her laugh; but stuffed shirts and bores she found hard to take. She was beginning to be afraid the evening might turn out to be a stuffy and sticky one.

James had no such qualms, though he was surprised she was dressed so simply. She wore no jewellery, and didn't need to. She was wearing what appeared to him to be a long silk shirt open at the neck. He couldn't make up his mind whether it was green or blue; it shimmered and changed colour as she moved, but whatever colour it was it threw up the glow of sapphires in her eyes, and the gleam of her hair was like a gold setting to a fabulous jewel. He was being too romantic, he knew, carried away by the glamour of the moment. 'That colour suits you,' he said.

'It's Thai silk. Rather nice, don't you think?'

'It's more than nice. It's like yourself – elusive and lovely.'

She was glad as she got into his car that at least he was articulate. As she struggled with her seat-belt, and he leaned over to help her, she caught the faintest whiff of – was it whisky? He hadn't offered her one in the house, but he'd had one himself to give himself Dutch courage. That must mean he was a little bit afraid of her. She smiled up at him encouragingly, and his eyes met hers in a soft, blissful look. She turned away quickly then, thinking: Oh no! Not love! Love is so painful. . . . She remembered that French saying about there always being one who is loved and another who does the loving. She was afraid this nice man was going to fall in love with her and get hurt because she could not return his love. How could she love anyone after Larry? Oh Larry! Larry. . . . And her spirits drooped.

They revived with a glow of happy expectation as soon as she entered Troubleful House. It was just the sort of place she liked: a very old inn which had not been glossed and glitzed out of all recognition. From the low ceilings and heavy blackened oak beams hung swags of evergreen entwined with scarlet ribbons, with plenty of glossy leaves, red berries and satiny surfaces to catch the glimmer of light from shaded lamps and the flickering fire. The fireplace was enormous, spreading, except for an alcove on one side of it, over the whole width of the end wall. A massive square-cut oak beam supported the chimney, and on the stone hearth great logs of wood burned leisurely, their red embers greeting Amanda's nylon-clad legs with welcoming warmth as she drew near. Their table was in the alcove. White fans of crisp linen stood in each place; and on the centre of the table was an old-fashioned silver-plated ice-bucket containing a bottle of champagne leaning among cubes of ice.

'Oh James!'

'It's a very special day, Amanda. We're celebrating Christmas together, aren't we? A little late perhaps, but none the worse for that.'

The waiter hovered over them. Did they want a traditional turkey dinner, or would they prefer something just that bit different? There was watercress soup and pheasant *à la Georgienne*, which turned out to mean cooked with garlic and yoghurt and orange sauce with chopped walnuts.

'Sounds too good to be true!' cried Amanda.

'Wait and see. My mother used to say to me when I

was impatient for my birthday and its promised bicycle, "Everything comes to those who wait." Perhaps it's coming true for me tonight.'

They were silent as the cork popped and the tall glasses were filled with rising bubbles.

'To the New Year,' she said.

'To us,' he murmured.

They clinked glasses across the table, their fingers round the stems touching briefly, and as they did so he moved his ring finger and tickled hers. He's not wasting much time, she thought, but said, 'It's a heavenly old place, James. And what a strange name. Is there a story to it?'

'Of course. Every stone in England is steeped in history, isn't it? And that usually means blood. History is merely a tale of fighting and savagery.'

'Well, I don't know,' she tempered his statement. 'Here in the Cotswolds a few centuries of peaceful progress and good living do seem to have emerged.' He had no intention of spoiling her enjoyment of dinner by telling her about the hunger of the rural poor till very recent times, so he didn't interrupt. 'But what happened here?' she asked.

'It was during the Civil War. The last battle was fought at Stow-on-the-Wold, you know, and a wretched Royalist fleeing from the field took refuge in the cellar here among the beer barrels. He was betrayed to the Parliamentary soldiers by a maid-servant, for reasons of her own, whatever they were. They dragged him out and tied him to a tree. But the innkeeper defended him loudly, and bravely too, I think, pointing out that the battle was won, and if they were the true Christian men they claimed to be they would show mercy. So they trussed him up as well, and tied him to the tree beside the first prisoner, and left them out there in the open all night. At dawn they were both shot where they stood. The innkeeper's wife and daughter were made to dig the grave beneath the tree, while the soldiers lounged about in the yard till the dead were buried. They say it was an oak tree, and that it lived two hundred years, fed by the bodies of those two men. But it's gone now.'

They were silent over the delicious soup.

'I wonder they don't haunt the place,' she remarked.

'I believe there was some ghost story once; but that was long ago. The ghosts departed when the tree fell.' After another pause he asked, 'How come you're alone at Christmas, Amanda? No family?'

She shook her head. 'Not now.'

'And no love either?' He looked at her boldly.

She dropped her eyes and stared at the soup. 'I'm

rather scared of love,' she said. 'It can be a painful experience.'

'That's sad, Amanda,' he said, rejoicing secretly that perhaps the field was clear for him. 'Probably that's because you're beautiful. Men regard beauty as a glittering prize, don't they? And that attracts the predators. Perhaps you've been unlucky.' She said nothing. After a moment he ploughed on doggedly, 'I'm not a predator. As a matter of fact I'm rather timid with women, though I'm not timid in other ways. I was a keen rugby player once, and tackled with ferocity I'm told.'

'I don't think I like the prospect of being tackled,' she said, 'with or without ferocity.' They both laughed.

'Do you see anything of Liam Tiernan these days?' he asked. He had suspected, that day in August when they were all three together in her cottage, that Liam might have been more than a friend to her.

'Now and then,' she said. 'He's gone back to Ireland for Christmas. He still has people over there.'

The Christmas house-party guests left the dining-room after they had eaten and moved to another, from which could be heard sounds of music, voices and laughter, and chairs being dragged across a stone floor. They seemed to be playing some sort of game. James and Amanda left the table and sat facing the fire as they drank coffee. They didn't talk much, but stared at the embers, now and again exchanging a trivial comment and a smile. James was filled with joy and gratitude for Amanda's presence, for his freedom from the burdens of work, for all the good food and wine he'd enjoyed, and Amanda, relaxed and happy, felt her guilt and worries slip away from her as she gazed at the hypnotic flickering of flames, and for the first time in months she felt at ease.

They drove back in silence, rather slowly because banks of fog were falling into dips along the way. Suddenly caught in the car's headlights, a large dog-fox, sauntering across the road with the swagger of a prize athlete, stood for a moment to stare at them, and then with a swish of his splendid tail slid into the hedge.

'Oh, what a beauty!' gasped Amanda. 'What a wonderful animal.'

'But a predator,' said James grimly, remembering some childhood Sunday dinnertime at home. When they were all in the kitchen eating, a fox, in broad daylight, in twenty minutes had killed two of his mother's hens and left another three mortally wounded in the orchard grass. 'Cruel, and wasteful in cruelty.'

'I suppose that's his nature,' she found herself pleading for him.

'Nature is red in tooth and claw, and no mistake,' said James shortly.

She was aware at once of the first sharp difference between them. He was a countryman, nearer to the basic realities of life than she was; and she wondered if he would despise her as a sentimental city dweller. But when they drew up inside the gate of the Barn, and she began fishing in her bag for her keys, he put his arms round her and spoke in a low urgent voice: 'Don't leave me, Amanda. Come into my bed. You won't be lonely there.'

She was overcome with tenderness for him when he kissed her very lightly on the lips, and to her own surprise she clung to him. When they opened the doors and tumbled out he forgot to lock the car. Nor did he bother to lock the door of his own house behind them.

She stood and watched in amazement as he stripped off his clothes with speed but no formality at all, and threw them about, some on a chair, some on the floor. When he was naked before her, and began with a trembling hand to unbutton her shirt-dress, she did not resist, but took his hands and kissed them, first one, then the other.

'You have the most beautiful breasts,' he said quietly, 'with nipples like wild strawberries.' He put his lips round them and licked them. When they lay together on his bed they touched each other's faces, looking long, smiling and searching, as if trying to learn what lay deep beneath the skin, smiling and searching with the happy receptivity of children probing rock pools for wonders on a summer seashore. They abandoned their bodies to the delight of soft caressing and the electric excitement of exploring fingers; and after the joy and exhilaration of sex achieved they lay quietly together and slept the untroubled sleep of cradled babes.

Amanda woke before it was light. She sat on the edge of the bed and shook out her hair, remembering his tenderness. In lovemaking he was loving. No amount of experience, of studied effort, of sophistication in erotic techniques can make up for the real thing. Love makes you love; and he had made her love him last night.

She went into the bathroom and turned on the light to reveal its full horror. Strange that it hadn't struck her last night . . . the bathroom suite in denture pink, the lavatory bowl and seat waiting with its gaping gums to bite her bum as she sat down. She giggled soundlessly as she peed, looking at the white tiles sprigged with pink flowers not seen in any field. Could this be James's taste? Perhaps his wife's? She stood in the bath, pulled the frightful pink curtains of pink plastic (blue flowers this time) around her, and turned on the shower. That at least was efficient, and hot too.

James waking up found himself alone in bed, and for a moment suffered a pang of desolation thinking himself deserted already. Then he heard water running and a humming noise in a more or less soprano register. Amanda singing? He lay back smiling on his pillow. What a marvellous girl she was! Could she, was it possible that she might love him a little? A girl like her? He didn't know much about her and love, everybody says, is blind. That she'd had many lovers was almost certain; but he hoped, since she'd spoken of herself as single, that he was her only lover now. It was foolish to have too high expectations. The gods of love were jealous gods and would thwart high hopes. He would be grateful for the happiness which had come his way; of the future he must not ask too much.

Fog had frozen overnight on bare trees and hedges, transforming them into weird crystal shapes, and where pale winter sunlight struck the branches ice melted and fell with a soft plop on the road. They

224

drove north out of Fossbury towards Harper's Edge where James knew of beech woods to walk in and a spectacular valley if mists cleared later in the morning.

They didn't talk much in the woods. They enjoyed the rhythmic movement of all their limbs as they walked, and the soft crips crunch of beech leaves underfoot. It was quiet here on this Cotswold ridge, far away from traffic, and even the winter birds were silent, though once a male pheasant, with a startled raucous scream from his burnished blue throat, flew up before them. Amanda clutched her own throat and cried out, 'Oh look, James! Look!'

When they reached the end of the wood and looked down on James's promised valley it seemed enclosed in a bowl of hills. It was filled with low-lying fog, and the village in the bottom was half submerged as if inundated by dammed-up lake waters on which a few tall black skeleton trees floated. 'It doesn't look real,' said Amanda. 'It's like a dream.' James, putting an arm around her waist, was silent. They descended the hill towards the drowned village and found a pub, where they ate sandwiches and drank beer before the return walk.

'Lizzie's going to sell the Barn, you know. She's decided to live with Elena for a time.'

'I thought she might have to.'

'How did it happen, Amanda, that Larry left his affairs in such a mess?'

'It was awful bad luck, really. He was tied up with developers building flats and offices. They had to borrow money. And then the recession hit them, Larry had to borrow money to keep his end of the business going, and he was being paid nothing. Apart from that he was always a big spender – didn't know the meaning of the word thrift.'

'Lizzie doesn't seem to have had any idea of what went on.'

'No. He didn't talk to her about business. But it was bad luck his dying like that suddenly. I think if he'd lived, and been able just to hang on by the skin of his teeth till the recession ended and money began to flow in again, he'd have been – all right.'

'Strange he didn't share these anxieties with her. He must have been anxious, wasn't he?'

'He used to say, "Lizzie lives in a different world. I like to keep it that way." He was a bit of a gambler, too, James. He rather liked walking along a razor's edge.'

They had come out of the woods again and were gazing at a field of winter wheat. Leaning over a five-barred gate they watched three magpies swoop over a piece of carrion, and chase each other, squawking.

'Lizzie's old-fashioned, isn't she?' he said. 'Not a feminist at all.'

'Oh yes she is. All women are, now that we've woken up to it. But feminism is a word with many meanings. Lizzie does it in her own way. She's very strong, I sometimes think – very much her own woman. But not money-wise, that's all.'

'And you? Are you a feminist?'

'Of course. But I'm not aggressive. At least I hope not. That's self-defeating.'

'You avoid confrontation?'

'Yes, if I can. I hold out the velvet glove; but there's sometimes steel inside.'

'I suppose that's the way successful professional women work. I notice Julia is always very conciliatory in committee meetings, but she seems to get her own way somehow.'

'Who's Julia?'

'She's my female partner.'

'Is she a good doctor?'

'Yes. In her own line.' As they turned away from the gate James said, 'I was worried about Lizzie at first. Thought she might crack up. But just before Christmas she seemed to be showing signs of new life.'

It was dark by the time they got back.

'Too tired for dressing up and dining out,' said

Amanda. 'Let's just have tea by the fire.' So while she went into the kitchen to make tea James went next door to raid Lizzie's fridge, where he found a spaghetti Bolognese quite big enough for two.

'Needs warming up. Parmesan cheese in cupboard to left of stove.' He presented the dish to Amanda and retreated to the sitting-room where warmth from the wood-burning stove greeted him and dismay at the frowsty appearance of his home struck him: books and papers piled on tables and chairs and floor, and his bottle of whisky with the empty glass on a small table by his fireside chair. He made an effort to tidy up the place, hiding the whisky and its glass in a corner cupboard. Then he went down to the cellar to find a good bottle of Wine Society claret, which he uncorked and placed near the stove.

'I believe in letting things breathe,' he said when he saw Amanda glance at the bottle as she came in with a tray. He took it from her and placed it on the hearth between two chairs. 'Do you find me old-fashioned?' he asked as she knelt down to pour the tea.

'Well, yes, I suppose you are a bit.' She handed him a cup. 'But don't change, James. I like it.'

They enjoyed a leisurely meal, tea and supper rolled into one; and when Amanda leaned back on her chair, letting her neck rest on her interlocked fingers and sighed with contentment, 'What a lovely walk it was!' James felt his cup of happiness brimming over.

'We could have lots of lovely walks if you stayed in Fossbury,' he said. 'And the practice could employ you as business manager and accountant. You'd be perfect for the job. Doctors aren't much good at that sort of thing; and anyway we haven't the time for it. That's what the new NHS is demanding of us.'

'So it's arithmetic you want, not me?'

'Oh, honey child! You know what you are to me. After all these years spent in a loveless desert you're my manna from heaven. Milk and honey. The promised land.'

'You're very biblical, James.'

'My grandfather was a Welsh preacher, so I'm dyed in biblical wool, so to speak.'

She laughed to see him lock the front door with pompous ceremony, reminding him that he'd forgotten all the locks last night. When she sat naked on the bed, her long legs crossed in nearly-yoga position, her hands hiding that lovely crisp, crinkly pubic hair of hers, so like a gold filigree setting for a fabulous jewel, he walked to the bedroom door and locked that too. Then he threw himself on the end of the bed, and seized her by the thighs.

'Oh! Rugby tackle tonight, is it?' she asked. They were laughing as they kissed.

The clock radio woke them at 7 a.m. Over breakfast James groaned, 'I've got to work today, Amanda. And tomorrow, and tomorrow, and tomorrow.' He sighed.

'Well, so have I.'

'When can I see you again?'

'When can you?'

'New Year's Eve, after surgery. And I shall have New Year's Day off.'

'Well, come up to my place, James. After surgery – or when you like.'

'Till then, honey child.'

'Till then.'

They strolled out to the cars without speaking; but when Amanda was seated at her steering wheel she turned to him as he stood at the window. 'I've had such a lovely Christmas with you, James – the happiest Christmas since I was a child.' She smiled up at him, and still smiling reversed her Metro out into the road.

At 9 a.m. Mrs Roxby let herself in to clear up the doctor's house. He was already in the surgery and Amanda, in her Metro loaded with pictures, china and linen, was driving up the M4 eastwards. Mrs Roxby saw the tray of dirty crocks and cutlery by the stove, the empty red-stained glasses on the small tables by the hearth, and she noted the two used breakfast cups on the kitchen table. Merle Evans had revealed to her on Boxing Day when she came in for a glass of sherry that the yellow door opposite had been open, and that 'that Amanda' came down the stairs wearing jeans and a thick, loose jersey, and piled stuff into the boot of the Metro parked a few doors away. Mrs Roxby had seen no sign of the Metro either at the Barn or at Owl House; but she did just wonder. . . . When she found two damp bath towels on the floor of the pink bath-room her wondering changed to suspicion, and when she stripped the bed, to 90 per cent certainty. 'Who'd 'a' thought it? That Amanda!' she said aloud. She clicked her tongue. 'Poor little Mrs Bassett will be sorry to miss her, though.' Then she smiled. 'Well I wish him luck!' She was fond of Dr James.

The last two days of December crept on with very slow tomorrows for James. New Year's Eve seemed the longest day. Days before bank holidays were always hectic, with patients asking for last-minute visits and prescriptions before they went away or ran out of tablets and could foresee closed chemists' shops. He was thankful to hand over to Julia, who was back from Vienna and blooming with health and vigour.

After the evening surgery he felt in need of rest; but the thought of seeing Amanda again helped him to revive after a bath, a toasted cheese sandwich and a strong cup of tea. The weather was cold, clear and crisp, and driving conditions on the motorway, in spite of heavier traffic than he'd expected so late in the evening, were good. But it took him some time to find Pettigrew Place and to park his car, so it was nearly midnight when he climbed to the first floor and heard sounds of saxophone blues billowing from under the door of Amanda's flat. The noise of party-goers with a moderately high blood alcohol level deadened the sound of his ringing. He had to press the doorbell more than once before Amanda let him in. She was wearing a scarlet silk shirt loose over black pants. He could see with the appraising eye of the sober that she was slightly the worse for drink, but she murmured as she pulled him inside, 'Don't worry, James. They'll all go soon after midnight.'

Several young couples lounged about on sofa, chairs and floor, all slightly drunk and waiting, glass in hand, to greet the New Year, as well as two men who were probably lovers, one with a well-shaped pretty profile and that smooth, soft, ageless and slightly dusty skin he'd learned to associate with the third sex. The voice of Billie Holliday was singing on disc, the rhythm and sadness both tugging for your attention, even if you couldn't catch the words, bidding you look down, Man, and see the mess we've made of things. Bells clanged suddenly from a nearby church, and James heard cheering outside. Everybody in the room staggered upright and kissed everybody else and, laughing, toasted the innocent newborn year.

It seemed a long time before they all found their coats, said their goodbyes and after more kissing of Amanda finally made their way downstairs, leaving her sitting on the floor in the position in which he'd last seen her naked on his bed.

'Looking back on the old year is bloody awful, isn't it?' In spite of all the celebrating she was in the mood for sombre nostalgia; maudlin, an unkind observer would have called it. She shook her hair as if trying to wake up from a bad dream, and said, 'Help yourself to more wine, James. You're very sober tonight.'

He refilled his glass and sat down on the carpet opposite her.

'It seems ages since Christmas,' she said. 'How've you been?'

'Just longing to see you again.'

'It's been a bad old year, James. Bad, bad. . . .'

He took one of her hands and kissed it. 'Was it so bad for you, Amanda? What's been happening?'

She pulled her hand out of his and wiped away the tears that were forming. 'How long can you go on loving a man who's dead, for heaven's sake?' she demanded.

'You had a lover who died?'

'Larry,' she said. 'We were lovers. The great love of my life – if you want to know. He died in my bed. That time you came to my house in Frenny Hinton we pretended, Liam and I, that he'd fallen at the front door. It was Liam's idea to do it: dress him and drag him downstairs. It was to save us all, but chiefly for Lizzie's sake. I don't think she had any idea – about Larry and me.'

'How long did this affair go on?' he asked.

'One year, seven months and twelve days.'

'And you love him still?'

'He's dead, James, for heaven's sake! But yes, in a way I do. He casts a long shadow.' Then her head dropped on to his shoulder, and she wept uncontrollably. He stroked her hair, he kissed her neck, he put his arms round her and held her tight; but he felt stunned and helpless. She blew her nose loudly on the grey silk handkerchief he offered from the breast pocket of his jacket. 'And then there's this awful guilt I have towards Lizzie. What have I done to her? At first I simply couldn't face her. And then at Christmas when I'd made up my mind to go and see her, she wasn't there. I made Liam promise, swear, he would never let her know the truth. It doesn't get easier to bear, you know. Time and all that don't seem to have healed it yet. Every day I still think of that ghastly scene on the stairs. It's a haunting. But there's no tree I can cut down to lay my ghosts.' For the first time that evening she smiled at him.

'Perhaps,' he said, helping her to her feet, 'perhaps the New Year will bury them.' He pushed her into the bedroom, then watched her take off her shirt and trousers and fall into bed, still wearing her pants and bra.

'Will you ever forgive me?' she asked, peeping at him over the top of the duvet she'd pulled up over her nose.

He leaned over and kissed her forehead.

'Goodnight, sweet James,' she said. 'Confession makes you sleepy.'

It wasn't only confession that was making her sleepy. She'll have one hell of a hangover tomorrow, he thought grimly as he undressed and got into bed beside her. She was already asleep; but he lay awake thinking, imagining and thinking. It was not a happy night.

In the early hours he rose, and padding about her

kitchenette in bare feet he found kettle, tea and teapot, and made tea. She opened her eyes unwillingly as he came into the bedroom with a tray.

'Terrible head,' she groaned.

'Yes, I know,' he said. 'But I've got two aspirins here for you.'

'You know what you are, James? You're an angel.' She swallowed the pills, drank some more tea and lay back on her pillow. He stood over her, stroking her forehead. Once she opened her eyes and, he thought, looked lovingly at him.

'Healing hands,' she murmured.

'Healing eyes,' he said as she closed them.

He decided the best thing to do was to let her sleep, so he dressed. Before leaving he surveyed the post-party chaos in the living-room and the dirty glasses and dishes and thought: whatever stage of feminism she is at she can clean up her own mess. He was not quite angel enough to do it for her. He scribbled a note for her on the pad by the phone: 'Ring me when you feel better. It's going to be a good New Year. Love always.' He went out, found his car and drove out of London to the M4, then westwards home to Fossbury and his shabby old Owl House. He sat down before the cold grate and opened a bottle of whisky. He had landed up in a troubleful house indeed. On the first day and half the night of the New Year he sat up drinking and trying to think, then drinking and trying not to think. Man is born unto trouble as the sparks fly upward. Job, he remembered.

Eight

Doreen, who had protective feelings towards Dr
James, saw him looking rather the worse for wear at
morning surgery and judged he'd gone over the top a
bit at the New Year. She left the pile of patients'
records on his desk and whisked herself to the door
with a brief greeting: 'Happy New Year, Doctor!' He
lifted dull eyes at her departing figure and muttered,
'Happy New Year, Doreen.' But when a week passed
and he still wore a hopeless expression and no longer
exchanged the cheerful teasing she was used to, she got
worried.

'I've made my New Year's resolution, Doctor,' she
said one morning as soon as he arrived and threw his
medical bag on the desk. 'And do you know what it
is?'

'Morning, Doreen. What New Year resolution?'

'I'm going to put on a happy face for morning surgery no matter how many patients are waiting. What's yours?'

'What do you suggest?'

'I think you should look after your own health for once, Doctor.'

'You think I'm getting old, Doreen? Going to seed?'

'I wouldn't say that, Doctor. But I think you're overdoing things – looking worn out.'

Dr James walked over to the small mirror above the hand-basin, and glancing at his face in it saw time passing, saw himself being carried along with it and missing so much on the way.

'You're absolutely right, Doreen. I'm putting on weight, drinking too much, and not taking enough exercise. So here's my New Year resolution: I shall run round my garden ten times every morning before breakfast – unless it's snowing.'

'Good for you, Doctor! I'll pray for snow.' And she whisked out.

He persisted for a whole week in running as fast as he could back and forth across the lawn and up and down the garden paths. He applauded himself and felt minimally healthier. His concentration and energy during working hours was fairly good, but at times when he was alone, driving his car from patient to patient, or in the evenings after he left Lizzie and returned home, his thoughts always circled round Amanda and all the details of their last encounter. Certain of her phrases were branded on his memory, and each time he remembered them he felt a fresh searing pain. Her admission that she still loved Larry, and her words, 'He casts a long shadow,' hurt. The sinking sun casts a long shadow. So Larry was her sun, the source of all her joy, of all her desire for life. The affair had lasted 'one year seven months and twelve days'; even now she was still counting her glorious days with him. And Larry – the sod! People had a superstitious dread of speaking ill of the dead, but nobody could stop him, or blame him, for thinking of the evil Larry had done. What sort of man was he who, besides casting this long shadow over Amanda's life, left an adoring wife and son virtually penniless? It was (according to Amanda) probably bad luck rather than self-indulgent squandering of capital, bad manage-ment or folly that had made him bankrupt; but hadn't he deceived one if not two women in love? How did he come to hold such power over these two lovely women that he could enslave them both from beyond the grave? James was bitterly angry and jealous, though he told himself it was absurd to try to battle with a ghost, crazy to be jealous of one; and yet that's exactly what he was. He knew that even if time healed Amanda's aching heart he could never hope to be more than a second-best. Hadn't she said Larry was the great love of her life?

It was then that he heard for the first time in weeks Mary's calm, sensible, rational voice: 'She'd have to come to terms with someone, too, you know.'

He hit his head with his fist. Of course she would! What an egotist he was, seeing this problem from his point of view alone. If she was ever to love him more than casually she would think, perhaps already had thought, of Mary. If ever – and it seemed now a wildly improbable dream – she agreed to marry him and come to live in Owl House she would be aware of Mary, whose house it had been, all day and every day. Undoubtedly they would both be haunted by their own and each other's past. This idea consoled him a little; the possibility of mutual suffering eased his pain. Then he remembered that other thing she'd said, when they were dining at Troubleful House: 'Love can be painful.' So Larry hadn't brought her unmitigated joy. And to see a lover, an adulterous lover, dying in your bed must be the worst of terrible experiences. No wonder she'd wept so bitterly that day he was called to her house in Frenny Hinton! At the time he'd thought her emotion a bit excessive, but considering the circumstances he now knew, he saw that her grief must

241

have been unbelievable; moreover the burden of guilt that fell on her that day, and which she would have to carry for years to come, was awful to contemplate. It was this realisation that pushed him into writing to her.

'Amanda, my Golden Girl, what you told me makes no difference to my feelings for you. At first I was despondent, imagining I could never compete in that high-stakes sort of affair you had with Larry, that I could never be more than a poor second-best to you. But as each day passes I know, common sense tells me, that my chances of success get better. I am alive and he is not. I love you still, powerfully, passionately and without alteration. Love is not love which alters when it alteration finds, as the Bard told us long ago. I believe I could make you happy, happier than Larry did, because I would give you all of myself, while he only gave you half, as you well know, throughout that one year, seven months and twelve days. What happened to you was a terrible thing to happen to anybody; to you who loved so much it must have been unbearable agony. I know you are unhappy, my darling, and that makes my heart ache for you. But we had a lovely Christmas, didn't we? So I want you to give us a chance together. If you think you might, give me a ring any evening after nine. I shall be hovering near the phone like an adolescent girl. James.'

Amanda's secret was a torment in another way: it lay like a barbed wire entanglement between him and Lizzie. He could no longer feel free and easy with her when always in the dark recesses of his mind there lurked these dangerous spikes on which unguarded words might catch, might thrust and tear into the tender new optimism he saw beginning to emerge in her. So, hoping she wouldn't notice the change in him, he was very careful in his talk.

Lizzie had other preoccupations. Christmas in Surbiton with Elena had done her good. Timothy enjoyed the company of his cousins and soaked up his grandmother's worship with the complacency of a cat licking cream. They all played games, during which Lizzie joined in the quick laughter of the young; they went for walks together, they ate companionable meals, slept well, and returned home happier. It was when she found Amanda's letter on her desk that Lizzie felt the first twinge of uneasiness: 'Lizzie dear, so sorry to miss you on Christmas Day. Had hoped to meet and talk. Can we, perhaps, in the New Year? Sorry, too, to squat in the Barn. Will you forgive? Enjoyed your spaghetti Bolognese with James. A big thank you for stolen hospitality. Love Amanda.'

She had heard about the spaghetti Bolognese from James, and was happy that it had been eaten in his sitting-room with a bottle of claret; but she was bitterly disappointed that Amanda had at last visited her, only to find the Barn deserted. She wondered why Amanda had been unwilling to sleep in her own house – because the death had occurred there? It seemed a rather surprising reaction for her. In fact, all Amanda's reactions to Larry's death had been strange. Lizzie, walking through her bedrooms, saw that the bed in the spare room had not been used. Had she slept in Timothy's bed, or Lizzie's, or under a duvet on the drawing-room sofa? Imagining Amanda alone in her house, perhaps in her bed, worried her.

But as the January days passed, exceptionally mild that year, and the first snowdrops appeared in her garden she felt a little lifting of her heart. One evening in February, when the days were perceptibly lengthening, during the last bright minutes before darkness fell, she stood suddenly rapt to see her witch-hazel in bloom. Ah God, what miraculous fire in the dead wood! Delicate gold flowers like tiny chrysanthemums bursting from black branches, like tongues of flame: a burning bush. . . . At the same moment a misselthrush above her head began to sing, and looking up to search for him she saw between the bare branches of his tree a paper-white crescent moon. A shock of unexpected joy ran through her as she stood there. It is paradise, she thought. Missel-thrushes sing early in the year; they're getting rare these days. That Hammamelis must be more than ten years old; it's never bloomed like that before.

Next day she tried to write her feelings into a poem, which with many corrections and crossings-out James saw on her desk.

> Witch-hazel is in flower,
> The moon a waxen chip,
> When from his dark tower
> A thrush lets music slip:
> Molten music, golden shower
> Splintering the cold glass hour,
> Making the torpid shadows hum
> With prophecy of days to come.
> And I like Lazarus winter-bound
> Awake, and tremble at the sound.

'Why Lizzie dear,' he said, 'what a lovely little poem.'

He poured her a glass of Vouvray.

'I've read a lot of poetry, James. Brought up on it, really. I was once a BA Hons in Eng. Lit., you know.'

'Whatever you once were, Lizzie dear, this means to

me that you're coming back to life – a sort of resurrection.'

She smiled, and touched his arm in passing as she handed him a helping of cheese soufflé. 'So difficult to get it right,' she said. 'Cheese soufflé, I mean.'

'It's just right. Perfect,' said James, balancing a piece of the fluffy stuff on his fork, and wondering how Larry could have deceived her so. How *could* he?

They sipped in silence, smiling across the rims of their glasses, and savouring the wine.

'That Amanda was down at Christmas, I hear,' said Mrs Roxby as she scrubbed out the kitchen sink. 'Mrs Evans, my friend what lives opposite her yellow door, saw it open and Amanda going up and down the stairs half the day.'

A sharp image hit Lizzie: a door opening straight into the narrow hall of a terraced house to reveal steep stairs, and Amanda descending.

'What was she doing?'

'Loading up her car with stuff – picture frames, china, cushions and what not. Is she moving or what?'

'I haven't heard anything,' said Lizzie.

A few days later Mrs Roxby reported that a FOR SALE notice now stood at Amanda's gate. So she was selling up and moving out, leaving the area without a word of explanation to any of her friends. James had not heard of it, and seemed more upset by the news than she was.

That night Lizzie woke in terror, shaking and sweating. Sleep fled from her as the threatening visions of her nightmare stood around her bed. She lay awake in the dark trying to fathom its meaning. Amanda was coming down a narrow staircase. She wore a long white nightdress, and over one shoulder a tartan plaid shawl. In her hand was a bloodstained dagger from which red blood dripped on to her clothes. At the bottom of the stairs Larry was curled up, gagged and bound. Lizzie couldn't be sure whether he was dead or alive. Was Amanda going to loosen his bonds with her knife, or was she going to murder him? And what had she already done upstairs? Lizzie felt an uncomfortable contraction in her stomach as if she herself had been struck. What was this horrible dream trying to tell her?

Lizzie trusted her subconscious self, though she often suppressed its fears and rages. She believed that dreams, though irrational, often revealed some truth, which like a persevering little mole burrowing through subterranean tunnels of darkness emerged now and again into the light of day. Scientific truth is ferreted

247

out by reason and added to by painstaking accumulation of observed facts; psychological truth has a different, mythic quality, which can be grasped sometimes in symbols by the imagination: the creative Big Bang, or the revelation on the road to Damascus, seen in a flash – but only in a glass darkly. It was this sort of truth that dreams revealed. So what was her own little mole bringing to the surface?

Amanda appeared as Lucia di Lammermoor in Donizetti's opera. Elena had once taken Lizzie with Larry, before they were married, to see it performed at Covent Garden. She remembered the wide staircase to the foyer, built by thoughtful Victorians, wide enough, as Larry explained to her, to enable ladies with full crinolines to mount two abreast, like swans unruffled in their majestic onward swim. It was on the staircase during the interval that they had met again after a long separation, she and Amanda, that time. How excited they had been to see each other suddenly and unexpectedly like that. Lizzie recalled that she had cried during the mad scene, and Larry had held her hand when poor Lucia, in bloodstained bridal gown, sang of how she'd killed the bridegroom her brothers forced her to marry when all her heart was given to a lover. Then Lizzie remembered another image which might have triggered off her nightmare:

that vivid passage in *Madame Bovary* where Emma unexpectedly meets her lover Leon at the opera – *Lucia di Lammermoor* again – and Emma is carried away by pathetic longings for the great romantic lover she imagines the tenor must be when she hears him sing.

Lizzie got out of bed and, quietly in order not to wake Timothy, slipped downstairs to the sitting-room. It took her a few seconds to find Flaubert's novel, and a few more to locate the passage and begin to read of Emma's anxieties about how to conform to her own *petit bourgeois* image of how to look and behave correctly in such a situation; and oh! her irritation and shame at the solecisms her husband, poor clumsy, stupid Charles, committed with every move he made and every word he uttered. Her excitement and adoration of the tenor's 'splendid pallor of the sort that lends a marmoreal majesty to the ardent races of the south', and the final sentence of that paragraph: 'A fine voice, imperturbable self-possession, more personality than intelligence and more power than poetry, went to complete the armoury of this admirable mountebank-type, with its ingredients of the hairdresser and the toreador.' What a marvellous brief portrait Flaubert drew!

She read several pages, then learned that Emma and

Charles left the theatre with Leon during the third act, and the mad bride's dramatic aria was not described. So these images had certainly not come to her from her reading of *Madame Bovary*.

An unpleasant, irrational fancy caught her then that Amanda (the unreal nightmare Amanda) had plunged that knife into Lizzie as she lay asleep, and then went downstairs to loosen Larry's bonds. Lizzie sat down in her armchair. She was trembling. After a minute she felt very cold, so she rose and went into the kitchen to heat water for a hot-water bottle, which she hugged as she mounted the stairs again and climbed back into bed. She lay still, trying to control the wild fancies and feelings which were whirling about inside her head, trying to order them with fences of remembered facts.

Amanda and Larry were certainly meeting regularly and frequently all last spring and summer, sometimes at Pettigrew Place. That was recorded in Larry's engagement diary for the period. Amanda was certainly an exceptionally beautiful woman, whom many men desired. And Larry? Amanda was an old schoolfriend. She and Lizzie were intimate and told each other some things they told no one else; but you couldn't expect even an old schoolfriend to tell you she's having an affair with your husband, could you? So was Amanda deceiving her all last year? And why had she avoided her so entirely since Larry's death until Christmas Day, when she had arrived unannounced and unexpected, unless it was guilt that kept her away? Of course, if she was loaded with unendurable guilt she would naturally want to leave behind her the place where Larry had died so suddenly, to cut herself off from a past so full of unhappy memories. Was that why she was putting her house up for sale? Then Lizzie thought of Larry, who had been father, husband, brother, friend and lover to her, in whose arms and in the house he'd built for her, she felt so safe. It was impossible. As daylight grew her image of Larry brightened and strengthened her once more. By the time she woke Timothy and went down again to the kitchen to prepare his breakfast she had convinced herself that all she had seen during the night was nothing but a bad dream, full of fears and fancies but of no particular significance.

The February days moved on, lengthening, brightening, and still so uncannily mild that the newcomers in Fossbury were saying these were the first signs of global warming, of a climatic shift, and where was all the expected rain going? while the old-timers shook their heads agreeing with each other: 'Arr. But February 'tain't out yet!'

Maisie dropped into Larry's kitchen for coffee, and to beg for items for the coming jumble sale.

'How's your lady-love these days, Maisie?'

'Good news. She doesn't love me any more. I saw her sitting in the caff at the bus centre with a woman friend.'

'That *is* good news!' Lizzie seemed enthusiastic.

'They were drinking out of paper cups and eating hamburgers.'

'Oh better still. That should be enough to kill off any remaining yearnings!' Maisie shot a quick glance across the table, thinking Lizzie was quite herself again. 'I'll go through Larry's things, Maisie, and bring you a boxful to the church hall.'

Lizzie had not opened his wardrobe since that fatal day. It had been too painful to touch, even to contemplate his clothes; but now she forced herself to bring his suits out of the cupboard and lay them on the bed. They would have to be cleaned, so pockets had to be emptied, a couple of handkerchiefs, a few coins and a pencil stub removed. Larry hadn't left much behind him here. He was a tidy man and liked his clothes to hang well without bulges; but in the breast pocket of his cream-coloured lightweight summer jacket, the one he'd been wearing on the day before the party, there were two or three folded papers, bills she presumed. When Lizzie dropped them on the bed a piece of heavier paper slipped out sideways, revealing handwriting. She picked it up, and read: 'Darling, I am so terribly sorry for what happened last night. His visit was quite unexpected. I certainly never invited him. So I hope you'll forgive and understand. Till next week – ' No signature. No date. But she knew that handwriting. It was Amanda's. Unmistakably.

She sat down on the bed clutching the paper in her shaking fingers. Quite different people did sometimes have similar handwriting, didn't they? She couldn't be absolutely certain Amanda had written it. It was a love letter of a sort; but was Amanda the lover? All the small niggling anxieties she had felt and suppressed before her bad dream and all the terrors of that nightmare flooded back in an unstoppable rising tide. She carried the scrap of paper down to the sitting-room, opened her desk and found Amanda's Christmas note. She smoothed out both pieces of paper and compared the writing, carefully examining the crossings of the Ts and the linking of the Ss. She had to admit there were differences, which might indicate they were not written by the same hand or might, she supposed, be due to the fact that the Christmas note was scribbled in pencil, with Lizzie's own pencil attached by a string to a hook by the phone, whereas the note from Larry's pocket was written in biro.

She was thrown into an agony of alternate suspicions and disbelief in her suspicions, feelings so violent that after a few hours she was exhausted. I must do something, she thought. Activity will numb these feelings. So she put on her wellies and armed with a garden fork began to search for weeds. It was still too early in the year for the annual crop, but she dug out the few she found with vicious jabs. But soon she realised that no amount of weeding, nor of any kind of gardening nor, she believed, anything else in her whole life was going to solve this problem. It was essential to find out the truth. If only she could be absolutely sure of Larry's betrayal she might perhaps know what to do. If your house has been razed to the ground the options are, after all, simplified, was what in the bitterness of her soul she told herself. I must know. I must know.

'Are you all right, Lizzie? Has something happened?' asked James that evening; and Timothy looked up from his homework spread out over the kitchen table.

'A bit too much gardening today, I think,' she said, finding it astonishing that she could go on automatically preparing food and answering questions when she had to make such an effort of will to move, even to speak, when she could almost hear her whole world sliding slowly, rumbling into ruin around her. 'I won't be here tomorrow evening, James. I have to go to London about some unfinished business of Larry's. I shall be back late. But I've asked Mrs Roxby to give Timothy his tea, and perhaps you and Timothy will help yourselves to supper.'

Next day she parked her Mini at Swinester station, and feeling rather sick caught the Inter-City to Paddington. It would be useless arriving in the morning when Amanda would be at work, but Lizzie reckoned that on a weekday she would get back to her flat between 5 and 6 p.m. Lizzie intended arriving unexpected and uninvited like the mysterious man in the letter, like Amanda herself at Christmas. She would confront Amanda and demand to know the facts. Even the appalling truth she feared would be easier to bear than this paralysing uncertainty.

She arrived at Paddington with time to spare, so she walked through the station entrance of the Great Western Hotel, a vast Victorian hotel built by Brunel in which travellers could collect themselves and their luggage, dine well and rest comfortably before taking his Great Western Railway to Bristol and embarkation for the long, swaying voyage across the Atlantic to America. The marble-pillared lobby, now a tearoom, was filled with a heterogeneous assembly of people of various ethnic origins. Lizzie was glad to sit down. You could at least get a decent cup of tea here, served by a waitress undoubtedly less subservient than in Brunel's day, but willing enough, and you could drink it out of a clean china cup. The Underground, when she got there, was filled with fast-moving strangers, and although nothing like as crowded as she knew it would be in the rush hour, it made her feel depersonalised, as she poured herself in and out of the glass tubes of carriages on the Circle Line, like a bubble of steam escaping during some gigantic chemical experiment.

There was no reply to her ring on Amanda's doorbell, so she waited in the hall on the ground floor of the block of flats.

'Why, what a surprise, Lizzie!' cried Amanda as she finally came through the main door. She kissed Lizzie on both cheeks. 'Come up and let me give you a cup of tea.'

As the lift rose, Lizzie said, 'Sorry to dump myself on you like this, Amanda, but I wanted to talk. And you did say in your note – '

'Are you staying in town?' Amanda interrupted. Lizzie could see she was nervous.

'Oh no. I've got to get back to Fossbury tonight.

I've left Timothy with Mrs Roxby, and he'll have supper with James.'

'How is dear James?'

'Rather moody these days for some reason.'

Amanda was silent as they emerged from the lift. Lizzie spoke very little while Amanda threw her coat and briefcase on the bed and switched on the kettle; but when they were seated together on the sofa, and Amanda seemed relaxed, warming her hands round a cup of tea, Lizzie came straight to the point.

'Why have you been avoiding me, Amanda?'

'Yes . . . I know it was bad of me. But I couldn't face you, Lizzie – not after what happened – not at first.'

'It wasn't your fault, Amanda. I didn't blame you. He might have had his coronary while in the car and killed you both.'

Amanda drank her tea in silence, glancing once or twice out of the window at other windows across the road.

'I believe you were seeing him quite often, weren't you? I mean, the dates in his diary showed – '

'Yes. That's because we – the firm I work for – acted as accountants for Bolton on the building side of the business. And occasionally there were dinners, or other entertainments laid on. Yes. . . .'

'I began to have this feeling you might be having an affair,' Lizzie forced herself to say. 'I'm sorry, Amanda, if I'm being paranoid, but you see – ' In confusion she opened her handbag and pulled out the crumpled little letter for Amanda to read.

'Oh Lord!' gasped Amanda. She didn't read it; she didn't need to, because she recognised it. She swallowed, then began to speak very fast. 'I loved him, Lizzie. That's really what happened, if you must know.' Her confession poured out unchecked. 'I know it was awful of me – unforgivable, looking back – but I couldn't really help myself. I was simply mad about him. Bowled over. Crazily, passionately in love. Larry wasn't exactly an ordinary sort of man, was he, Lizzie? I needn't tell you that. He was a man in a million, as we both know. I'd never met anyone like him before. I loved him. And his dying like that – in my house – well, it was more than I could bear!' She was hiding her face in her hands and weeping quietly. Then they put their arms round each other, and Lizzie cried while Amanda uttered little moans. After a while Amanda sniffed, blew her nose and asked, 'What do you intend doing, Lizzie?'

'I'll have to sell the house and move. I shall probably live with Elena for a bit. I don't know yet what I'll do myself, but I'll have to earn my living, like you.'

'It's all been terrible for you, I know.'

'But why must you sell your cottage, Amanda? Are you in a mess financially too?'

'For God's sake, Lizzie! I can't ever sleep there again. How could I? He died in my bed.' She regretted it as soon as she'd said it, when she saw Lizzie recoil as if hit. There was a long silence. Amanda slid off the sofa and walked to the window, where she stared at the rain that was beginning to fall.

'Does Dr James know, then?' asked Lizzie.

'Liam Tiernan came – to offer me a lift back to town, or something – he helped me get Larry downstairs. We called James later. We decided to deceive him. It was for your sake as much as mine.'

I wanted the truth, thought Lizzie; and now I've had it.

'I think of it all the time,' said Amanda. 'It doesn't seem to get any easier. I suppose I shall have to go on living with it for the rest of my life. I can't see any way out – no future – ' She began to cry again.

Lizzie spoke automatically, like a soldier drilled for combat, years of practice in looking on the bright side by her often penniless and sometimes drunken, but always optimistic mother coming to her aid: 'We'll have to start again, Amanda. Put all this behind us . . . start again.' She did not, however, add: 'We'll keep in touch.' She remembered she had a train to catch, and a child waiting for her at the other end of a train journey.

'It's pouring with rain, Lizzie. I'd better call a taxi for you.'

They kissed before Lizzie entered the lift, thinking: It's I who should have stabbed her with a knife. And as the lift doors closed Amanda said to herself: I feel like Judas.

Lizzie sat by a window in the Inter-City streaking west through the wet darkness, and watched the rain sliding down the outside of the glass. It had come at last: the February rain. February Filldyke. She thought of Othello when he was convinced of Desdemona's adultery: 'But I do love thee! and when I love thee not / Chaos is come again.' Blossom was what Larry had called her before he'd left her on that last day. It was his private endearment for her. But now that beautiful flower had fallen to the ground, its petals shrivelled and brown, smelling not of honey but of death and decay. She shivered in the overheated carriage. An old woman opposite her pulled open a plastic carrier-bag on to the table between them and made crackling noises inside it as she searched for biscuits. Lizzie stared blankly at her thinking: And when I love thee not, Chaos is come again.

Nine

The partners usually met in March to discuss policy, finance, staffing changes if any, and holiday leave for the next financial year. Julia suggested a meeting in her house, and promised them all a dinner and drinks to make the meeting more leisurely and comfortable. Besides, she had a personal announcement to make. Julia lived in Easton Malreward, in what had once been the head gardener's cottage on the large estate of a Victorian banker. The estate, somewhat reduced in size since the war by the selling of land to neighbouring farmers, was now owned by a developer, absentee apart from the few times a year when he filled his mansion with house parties for weekends in the country. There was no resident gardener now. Julia had bought the cottage when she joined the Fossbury practice, enlarged the front parlour by adding a glassed-in extension, where she kept tender plants in pots, and

261

modernised the house. Through a decade of pottering she had improved the garden.

After the warm February and the heavy rain at the end of it March came in with a fierce frost, which to Lizzie's distress shrivelled her beautiful witch-hazel flowers and struck viciously at tentatively emerging green shoots of clematis. James was in sombre mood. Although he had almost given up hope he still waited every evening for the phone to ring and Amanda's voice to come tripping joyfully down the wire to him; but she had not phoned. He had received a note from her in January: 'Thank you, dear James, for your lovely letter. Bless you! Will ring you when I have thought about it more.' That kept hope flickering in his breast; but common sense told him that as it was now two months since he'd last seen her it was increasingly unlikely that she would ring at all. What with disappointment and the gruelling demands winter ailments make on all GPs, James felt sad and tired. He decided he would take his leave early this year, if the others agreed, take the car over to France and make a leisurely journey along the Loire, admiring the romantic châteaux, visiting vineyards, tasting wines and perhaps buying some to bring home. Spring comes a little earlier to the Loire region than to Fossbury, and the thought of that spring sunshine and the blossoming of plum and cherry orchards lifted his spirits a little.

Over sherry in Julia's parlour the partners talked about Dr Doynton's impending retirement. His wife Dorothy said they'd just bought a small house near Ludlow, near her sister's family, while the old doctor grumbled about putting his Fossbury house on the market at a time of recession and falling house prices.

'Good time to buy, of course,' he said, 'but not to sell.'

The trainee, Tom Barton, whom they all liked and considered a good, reliable, hard-working doctor, had been asked to join the practice as junior partner. So he was present at the dinner with his wife Belinda, who was expecting their first baby. James would move up to the senior partner position. Over soup, Julia announced she was going to be married. There was an immediate happy chorus of congratulations and good wishes; but James looked up in horror.

'Not leaving us I hope?' he asked.

'Oh no, not leaving Fossbury. No. Peter will be joining me here when he retires from his school at the end of July. He has two grown-up daughters who visit him quite often, so we'll be looking for a bigger house.'

'Ah!' exclaimed the Doyntons in unison.

Tom Barton began to wonder if he and Belinda could afford to buy Julia's cottage.

'Peter's mad on growing things,' said Julia. 'He wants to try organic gardening without pesticides and with natural fertilisers. So I think he'll need a bit of land.'

'Oh,' said the Doyntons, disappointed, because their house, although large and elegant, had only a small garden at the back of Main Street.

Julia was wondering about the Barn. 'Lizzie's going to sell up and move out, isn't she?'

James told them that Lizzie was about to put the Barn into a local estate agent's hands, and that it would be advertised immediately.

'Perhaps I'd better talk to her at once,' said Julia. 'She could save agency fees if we could agree on a price.'

As they ate Julia's roast duck with fresh orange salad, holidays were discussed. James would begin his in the middle of March, Julia hers in August after her marriage at the end of July.

'Will you be married in Fossbury?' asked Dorothy Doynton hopefully.

'In white?' asked Belinda. It was the only thing she said all evening. James noted her prettiness with pleasure, but deplored her inability to speak.

'Neither,' said Julia. 'Sorry! It'll be a Registry Office wedding. And I'm too old for virginal white. But I'll certainly give a party when we've bought our new house. And you'll certainly all be invited.'

Belinda was silently calculating: by the end of August her baby would be a month old and her figure might be returning to its former shape, so she'd be able to wear a nice dress.

Over the dessert, raspberries out of Julia's deep-freeze served with cream, Dr Doynton suggested a toast to the new financial year.

'It's going to be an eventful one – what with me being pensioned off, Julia being married, and Tom and Belinda here becoming parents – '

'Rather like a children's party game of General Post,' said Tom. 'Everybody moving up or moving house!'

'Except me,' said James gloomily.

Julia rose from the table, and resting one hand on his shoulder refilled his glass; and Tom said, 'But you're going to be my senior partner – *sir*!' Everybody, even James, laughed good-humouredly.

After Timothy had fallen asleep Lizzie put on a coat and gloves and walked out on to the terrace, then down to the stream which shone like a ribbon of steel in the bright moonlight. It was bitterly cold; but the water was still running: only here and there by the banks were there pockets of thin ice. High in the south-west the three jewels of Orion's belt shone out bold and bright in the night sky. Lizzie remembered that time in Nigeria, that hot tropical night when she wore a dress of midnight blue streaked with spangles of silver thread, and a silver buckled belt. A supremely handsome black man whom Larry had addressed as Othello took her hand and bowed low over it, calling her Queen of the Night; and later Larry told her she was his heaventree of stars. The memory of it all was ashes in her mouth. She turned and walked back to the house. Knowing she'd be unable to sleep she went into the sitting-room, which was still warm, and sat down. Blossom . . . she kept repeating the word in her head, and each time it seemed to wither more.

She knew that very soon she must take steps towards earning some sort of a living, get a job, as Elena put it, 'go out to work in the world', or in more up-to-date phraseology 'the market-place'. To Lizzie that meant a noisy, squalid area full of people shouting and shoving in an atmosphere smelling of pollution and dishonesty. But that, she thought, she could face, must face, in order to keep herself and Timothy alive.

What was more difficult to come to terms with was the desolation of her inner world. That heaventree of stars with Larry locked in her arms was now an image streaked with dirt, with shreds of old plastic shopping-bags stuck to it, and empty tin cans and fag-ends of damp cigarettes thrown at it, ripped up and moulder-ing like a disused billboard. Larry had done this. Together Larry and Amanda had desecrated her most holy temple.

She stirred in her chair. She thought of the warmth of her bed, of her hot-water bottle, remembered being teased by Larry for what he called an old-fashioned addiction to it, when the electric blanket was so much more efficient a bed-warmer. It was, she supposed as she climbed the stairs, rather like Timothy's attach-ment to his teddy bear. She went into his room, and in the light from the corridor saw him lying on his side with one arm flung over his face, so beautiful in sleep that it made her heart ache to see him. She pulled his arm gently down and covered it with the duvet. Before getting into bed she drew back the curtains. From where she lay she could see Orion's belt. Stars unchanging through thousands, through millions of years . . . the same stars that Sappho saw, surviving human hearts that alter, that grow old and cold and die, surviving Sappho, only fragments of whose poems have come down to us. She murmured Sappho's lament softly, repeated it like a litany, crooned it like a lullaby, but it didn't help her to sleep: The moon has set and the Pleiades / Time passes, passes / And I lie alone. She groaned aloud. She was alone at last with the appalling truth from which there was no hiding place.

When at last James did receive a phone call from Pettigrew Place it was not Amanda's voice he heard but Liam Tiernan's.

'Could you possibly come up and see her, James? I don't understand these things too well myself, but it seems to me she's cracking up. She hasn't been to work for a week, she's not eating enough to keep a bird alive, and she says she can't sleep at night. I tried to persuade her to go to her own doctor here, but she's as obstinate as a mule, and will not. The only doctor she'll see, she says, is yourself.' After which monologue there was a pause, while James at the other end did some thinking, trying to make plans calmly while his pulse raced and a turmoil of mixed feelings rushed about in his head.

'Tell her I'll be with her tomorrow, early evening,' he said. He was due to finish work at noon next day, and had booked on Brittany Ferries for the afternoon of the day after.

'It's a good thing Liam phoned when he did,' he told Amanda as soon as he saw her. 'One day later and I'd have been on my way to France.'

It didn't take him long to realise she was in need of help, sick with unhappiness and feelings of guilt, listless, without power to direct her own life, and that he must do this for her, at least till she was restored to health.

'Put on your glad rags, girl,' he said. 'We're going to eat, drink and be merry, for tomorrow we sail for France. So put away that misery now. You've had enough of it, and so, as a matter of fact, have I.'

With surprising meekness she did as he told her. They ate dinner at a small Indian restaurant round the corner and drank a bottle of Valpolicella. They didn't talk much, but over the last of the wine she told him about her meeting with Lizzie. Afterwards they went to bed together, drowsily letting the closeness of their bodies comfort them.

'Healing hands . . .' she murmured.

'Healing eyes,' he said. 'Light of my life . . .' And then they made love: happy, grateful love.

They had to rise early next morning in order to pack all that Amanda needed for a month's holiday. James washed up the accumulated dirty dishes and hoovered the flat. Before they left London he phoned Dr Orchard. 'Julia – I'm a bit worried about Lizzie. I've been visiting her daily, as you know. She was coping all right – beginning to come out of her bereavement sadness; but I've just learned that she's had another blow, which might I fear be too much for her. Will you visit her – keep an eye on her? And Julia,' he added, 'we're off to the Loire today!'

'I can tell by your voice, James, that she must be delectable.' Julia caught the fact that he was not travelling alone, and heard his happiness on the phone.

'She says you're delectable,' he said in an aside to Amanda. 'Yes. That's just about what she is. Delectable!'

'Don't worry, James. I'll look in on Lizzie every day,' said Julia. 'And James – have a marvellous, happy time!'

After that he decided to throw all his cares and responsibilities over his shoulders, forget Fossbury, forget the past and concentrate only on Amanda and their journey together up the Loire valley.

'I'm going to make you happy, Amanda,' he said, as soon as they were out of the tangle of London traffic and he put his foot on the accelerator. 'You'll see. I'm going to mend your broken heart.'

*

Timothy walked cheerfully home swinging his school-bag and swiping at things here and there as he passed: a litter bin, greengrocery displayed in trays, a stand with a swinging board advertising aromatherapy. Smells! he thought, and lunged, missing as it swung back. He saw the bent figure of old Mrs Sims engulfed in an anorak several sizes too large creeping ahead of him, and wondered about taking a swipe at her; but prudence prevailed, so he overtook her quickly with averted eyes.

When he got home his tea was ready on the kitchen table: buttered slices of bread and a pot of home-made jam. He threw his bag on the floor and cramming some bread and jam into his mouth wandered off into the other rooms to look for Lizzie. He found her in the sitting-room, slumped sideways over the arm of her chair with her right arm dangling. She had been sick all over the carpet. Her head had fallen forward. Her eyes were shut, and she looked queer.

'Mum?' he said, and then more urgently, 'Mum? What's up, Mum?'

She uttered a soft groan and tried to rise, but staggered and fell on the floor, where she vomited again and lay gasping like a fish. Terror seized him. The memory of his father's sudden death was still bright in his memory; now his mother was ill, perhaps dying

271

like Dad, and there was no one in the house but himself.

Timothy ran as fast as he could to Dr James's house, and hammered on the door till he remembered that Jim-Jams had gone away on holiday the day before. Panic caught at his throat and made him sob. He didn't know what to do. Telephone, he thought. Ambulance. Suddenly he remembered Thomas Parry's Clifton ring, the black hand clutching the black iron ring on his white-painted door. He sprinted up the street till he was out of breath, and threw himself panting against Mr Parry's door knocker.

'My goodness! My gracious!' cried Mr Parry, opening the door. 'Whatever is the matter?' Timothy fell into his arms and was led into the front parlour.

'It's Mum. She's dying. She can't speak – Dr James isn't there – ' Timothy began to weep copiously.

'Sit down, child,' said Thomas. 'Have a piece of butterscotch.' He pulled a wrapped sweet out of a box on the windowsill and pressed it into Timothy's hand, where it remained unwrapped. Then he went to the phone. He was put through to the doctor on duty, who happened to be Dr Orchard.

'Come now, Timothy,' he said. 'We'll go back to your mother, and Dr Orchard will join us there in ten minutes.'

272

In less than half an hour they were both seated inside an ambulance, with Lizzie wrapped in a blanket and laid out on a bunk, speeding towards Swinester, sirens wailing. Dr Orchard must have phoned the casualty officer, because no sooner had they arrived at casualty than Lizzie was wheeled down a long shiny corridor to intensive care, and Timothy and Mr Parry were told to wait. That was the hardest part: waiting and not knowing what was happening to her. Timothy picked up some dog-eared comics that were scattered about a table in the waiting-room, and looked gloomily through the pages, while Thomas made comments he hoped would cheer them both up: she'll be all right, we got her here in time, doctors can do wonders these days, she'll be right as rain, old chap, you wait and see – till even he fell silent remembering the glass rolling on the floor beside Lizzie's chair and the small discarded empty bottle he'd picked up from under the cushion, and wondered how many aspirins she'd swallowed, and how many you had to take to kill yourself.

At last they were allowed to go into Ward 22 and see Lizzie. She looked almost as white as the bed she lay in. Strapped to one arm was a tube attached to a glass bottle, which dripped what looked like drops of water. She didn't speak. She didn't open her eyes; but the nurse let Timothy hold her free hand.

'Come back tomorrow,' said the nurse. 'She'll be better then.' And to Thomas she added, 'She's going to be all right.'

Outside the hospital it was dark. They stood uncertainly in the entrance till a taxi bringing relatives to visit patients pulled up, and Thomas ran towards the driver.

'Expensive,' he said when they were on their way back to Fossbury. 'But there's no other way, is there?'

'I think I ought to phone my grandmother,' said Timothy.

'Of course. You can do that from my house.' Thomas was pleased: this might give him an opportunity to talk to her himself.

Elena picked up the receiver in her hall and heard Timothy's voice: 'Is that you, *babushka*?' Then the voice stopped, and a series of sobs and gasps bounced along the wires to her ear. 'What's happened, darling child?' she cried. She became very agitated. 'What is it? Oh my dear Lord . . . !'

Thomas took the phone gently from Timothy, and spoke as calmly as he could. 'This is Thomas Parry here. You remember me?'

'Yes. Of course I do. For heaven's sake what's going on?'

'It's Lizzie, I'm afraid. We've just taken her to hospital. Yes. Swinester, Ward 22. But she's going to be all right. They say she'll pull through.'

'Oh dear Lord, thank God for that!' Elena gasped. 'I'll come down by train tomorrow morning. Yes. I'll go straight to the hospital. Will you look after Timothy tonight? Yes. I know you will. You're a real chum!'

Thomas made up the bed in his small spare room, and after seeing Timothy eat a bowl of cornflakes and drink a mug of cocoa he tucked him into bed.

'We'll go to the hospital tomorrow,' he said. 'There's a bus mid-morning. Leaves from the market cross about eleven.'

'Thank you, Mr Parry,' said Timothy sedately. 'I think you're brill!' Thomas ruffled the child's hair as he grinned up from his pillow, then closed the door quietly behind him. In his ears there echoed Elena's voice: 'You're a real chum!' making him rejoice. It was a hymn of praise.

Although not medically classified as comatose, Lizzie was not fully aware of what was going on for a day or two. Familiar faces loomed in and out of the dark forgetfulness around her hospital bed: Timothy popping up beside her; someone holding her hands while big tears splashed down on them from Elena's wide, hurt eyes; Thomas Parry staring at her as if he'd just jumped out of Jeremy Fisher's pond, his thick glasses glistening; Gerry Foster hovering; and Maisie offering chocolates. On the third day she woke up, sat up, and found herself looking into the face of Liam Tiernan.

'You've been on a very long journey, Angelica,' he said.

'How did you get here?' she asked, and he replied, 'I came to meet you when you got back.'

She knew she was being uncharacteristically emotional because what he said made her cry. She was glad he didn't say anything else, and grateful simply to hold his hand till the young doctor in charge arrived to look her over, and Liam had to go.

'Is there a bell ringing somewhere?' she asked. 'I hear it all the time.'

'It's the effect of acetylsalicylic acid poisoning on the ear,' he explained.

She made a face. 'Only myself to blame, then.' She looked away.

'It was a near thing. Touch and go, you know.' He made her stand up by the bed and walk a few steps to see if she was still staggering. 'We shall have to keep an eye on you for a bit because of the possibility of bleeding from the stomach.'

Then Julia arrived to talk about practical things:

date of discharge from hospital, and some sessions of what she called 'sorting things out for yourself'.

'I know I've given everybody a lot of trouble,' said Lizzie. 'Terrible selfishness, I know, when I think of Timothy.'

'He needs you,' Julia reminded her. 'Will you do it again?'

'No. I don't think so. I feel as if all that water running into my veins has washed me clean, somehow. In some way a different person from last week.'

'That's good. What about trying your legs?'

So Lizzie got out of bed once more, and putting on a towelling bathrobe and slippers walked with Julia gingerly to the end of the ward and into a little side ward, which was empty except for two chairs.

'Are you warm enough?' asked Julia, sitting down with her.

'I feel such a fool – so ashamed,' Lizzie said.

'Have you ever tried it before?'

'You mean when I was a girl? No. Though I was sometimes desperately unhappy when I was a child. I was about twelve or thirteen when I knew I was unhappy.'

'Tell me about it.'

'My parents were both painters – met at the Slade – quite good they both were, but they seldom sold any of their work, so we were always short of money. I remember being pretty hungry when I was little; but worse than that was the disorder and the mess in the house. My mother was always standing before her easel wearing a dirty old overall . . . paint-stained fingers, and sometimes paint smears on her face too. She never cared what happened in the kitchen. I was very young when I learned that by tidying up and washing up I could earn attention and praise. They used to exchange glances and laugh and call me their little housekeeper. But when I got to be about twelve I remember one day searching for bread and finding only a mouldy half-loaf, and seeing all the dirty dishes piled around the sink and the empty bottles thrown under it, some still dribbling wine dregs on the floorboards. I was suddenly terribly angry. I cut off the mouldy sides of bread and ate the clean middle with some margarine from the fridge. I remember swearing – making a solemn vow – that never would I live like them when I grew up. I suppose that's what must have started me off on what Larry used to call my "perfectionist trail". I wanted things to be tidy, orderly, controlled. I wanted to control them.'

'Something went out of control last week?'

'Yes,' Lizzie admitted; but she wasn't ready to tell Julia yet about Amanda and Larry.

'Suicide is an aggressive act,' said Julia. 'Were you trying to punish someone?' But Lizzie did not reply to that. Instead she pursued her older memories. 'Soon after that my father left us – ran off with a younger woman, deserted me and Mummy for a stranger. I felt betrayed, hurt and bewildered; and Mummy went to pieces then. She changed completely. From being a careless, laughing woman she became shrewish. She drank more and screamed at me – mostly cursing my father and his fancy woman. She used to hurl plates at the wall as well. Sometimes they still had food on them, which I'd cooked for her, and as they smashed the gravy dripped down the wallpaper. It was chaos, really. Then one day deliverance turned up in the shape of an aunt, my father's sister, a square-shaped woman in tweeds and sensible shoes to whom I'm eternally grateful, because she took control of us. She put Mummy in a nursing home to be dried out – dried out more than once as a matter of fact, because she was never cured. She packed me off to boarding school, telling me to "Have a jolly good term!" and she filled my tuck-box with ginger snaps and Cadbury's fruit and nut bars. Things were better after that. Chaos receded and order was restored. Life was bleak, but tolerable.'

'Do you know what the First Commandment is?' asked Julia.

Lizzie looked directly at her, surprised at what seemed an irrelevant interruption. 'Yes. I think so. It's about worshipping one God and not having graven images, isn't it?'

Julia took from the capacious pocket of her jacket an old copy of the King James Bible. 'I've marked the passage in Exodus with a bookmark,' she said. 'Tell me what you think when you see me tomorrow.'

Lizzie took the book back to bed and between nursing attentions and the solicitous interruptions of visitors she read: 'I am the Lord thy God which have brought thee out of the land of Egypt, out of the house of bondage. (Does Julia think that was my mother's house?) Thou shalt have no other gods before me. Thou shalt not make unto thee any graven image, or any likeness of any thing that is in heaven above, or that is in the earth beneath, or that is in the water under the earth: Thou shalt not bow down thyself to them, nor serve them: For I the Lord thy God am a jealous God, visiting the iniquity of the fathers upon the children unto the third and fourth generation of them that hate me.'

What did Julia want me to read into all this? she wondered. That I'm being punished with despair because I don't believe in her jealous God? I suppose in a way a psychiatrist does try to save your soul. Or perhaps to give you one? She remembered the story of the Little Mermaid, so terribly sad it was, but her favourite among all fairy stories in childhood. The Little Mermaid didn't have a soul. It was only when she fell in love with her human Prince that she wanted one, and that was only so that she could be near him. She yearned for the unattainable. Poor Little Mermaid, she had to change her tail for a pair of legs; and then every step she took was as painful as a knife-thrust. All the same she danced before the Prince to please him, while he watched her with his human Princess beside him, in 'laughing dalliance'. She remembered the phrase from her storybook. A shudder ran through her when she thought of Larry and Amanda in laughing dalliance. So it had come to that . . . Once she used to imagine herself in her mother's house as a poor little mermaid, working to keep her parents going. It was their laughing dalliance between the canvases she saw then. She decided to tell Julia about the Little Mermaid connection tomorrow.

But during the night the meaning of that First Commandment was revealed to her. Perhaps she had made Larry into a god? She had certainly adored him, thinking him perfect, her Prince among men; she had endowed him with godlike, not human qualities; and she expected him to have no human failings. Certainly they used to enjoy the fleshpots of Egypt together; but had the Barn really been a house of bondage? Was it a sort of slavery she had sold herself into? Perhaps that was what romantic love was: a bondage of the spirit . . .

Opening her eyes and looking into the darkness of the ward, at the little shaded lamp on the night sister's desk, at her empty chair, and listening to the sounds of breathing and occasional creaking of a bed she thought: I suppose that's what it is: the worshipping of lesser gods.

When she next saw Julia, which was after she got home again, there didn't seem any need to talk about graven images and lesser gods. Julia brought Peter to view the Barn, particularly the garden, and Lizzie was so delighted with his enthusiasm and his know-how about gardens that she had no qualms about handing hers over to him. He promised to take special care of the twelve woodland cherries.

'I could teach English, you know,' she told him as they walked along the stand of little trees. 'I'd have to get something called a PGCE first. That means a postgrad. Cert. of Ed.; but it only takes a year, and I think I might enjoy going back to college. That's what

I care about most: the well of English undefiled, which is getting so polluted along with everything else – that and Timothy. Yes, I think I could persuade a pupil or two, now and again, to love the language and our literature, and even, possibly occasionally, with Milton's help, justify the ways of God to men.'

Timothy laughed when Peter, whom Lizzie had described as Julia's boyfriend, turned out to be an old fogey with grey hair who was the head of a big comprehensive somewhere in Warwickshire. He was quite happy to relinquish the Barn to them because he was going to live with Elena in Surbiton, where there were several schools for him to choose from. Elena he knew would keep him and Lizzie safe. He'd had a nasty dream when Lizzie was in hospital that she'd swallowed some bathwater as she sat in her bath and grew smaller and smaller like Alice in Wonderland, till she suddenly disappeared down the plughole. Elena and Timothy had left their bedroom doors open that night in case they woke and wanted anything; but he didn't cry out. He didn't want to wake her; he knew it was only a dream. All the same he was glad he was not going away to boarding school again. At a day school he'd be able to keep an eye on his mother. And she was going back to school! That was funny too.

To Julia, Lizzie confided, 'It's a funny thing, you

know, but all that drip of whatever the doctors used to wash out my blood seems to have washed me, myself, as well. I'm not quite the same person that I was.'

'It's been a catharsis,' said Julia.

Elena was pleased to share her home with Timothy and Lizzie. They made her life less lonely, and they brought new friends to the house. Thomas Parry came up from Fossbury for a day during the Easter holidays, lunch with Elena and a walk with Timothy afterwards. Elena was of course delighted to have this elderly beau fluttering his heat-seeking wings around her. She hadn't enjoyed this sort of flirtation for a very long time; but all the old love of power over men in this game, even if only transitory, surged up inside her. He played for her on the piano Schubert's *Shepherd on the Rocks*, which he transposed into a lower key so that she could sing some of the easier passages with him.

'An exquisite melody for a lovely lady,' he declared gallantly. She struck him on the cheek with two play-ful fingers. 'Now Thomas, you know I'm much too old for flattery!' she reprimanded him; but he knew she had no very serious objection.

Liam, who was often at a loose end at weekends, took to coming for Sunday lunch, cooked by Lizzie. Usually he found that he had to adjust his speech to the people present: a slight accent was chic – it made them think Irish eyes were smiling – but a thick brogue reminded them of peat bogs beyond the Pale, chickens in the living room and the IRA. With Lizzie he could be himself. One Sunday after lunch he took her to see the hothouses at Kew. After they'd sweated and gasped in the heat and humidity under tropical palms they moved into a cooler glasshouse, where orchids grew.

'Julia thinks I had an unhappy childhood,' Lizzie said, stopping to squeeze a fat bulb with an inquisitive finger and thumb.

'Lizzie!' Liam was nervous of being caught by some official. 'You're not supposed to *touch* the plants.' But she took no notice.

'She thinks it may have warped me a bit – taken some of the bounce out of me. What was your childhood like?'

'Bloody awful,' he replied uncompromisingly. 'My father was often drunk, and sometimes dangerous as well. My poor mother was like the Woman who lived in a Shoe. She had so many kids she didn't know if she was coming or going. But us kids got on together OK. We did a lot of laughing, and that saved us, I think. I've often thought laughter may be as efficacious as prayer in the matter of saving souls.'

Releasing the orchid bulb, she squeezed his arm.

'Really, Liam, there's something wonderful about you. It's the survival factor. So much bounce. . . .' She was admiring a spray of pale pink cymbidium, twenty perfectly shaped flowers on a single arched stem. 'It takes your breath away, doesn't it? So beautiful . . . I think I shall try to grow them in that broken-down conservatory at the back of Elena's drawing-room. They don't need extra heat, you know – only protection from frost. There's a pane of glass needs replacing there, and some rotting wood needs treating. I wondered if perhaps you could . . . ?'

'I could indeed; and I will too. I'm a dab hand at DIY.'

Later, over a cup of tea he said, 'I've found a buyer for that Girl in a Garden. Though you know I like her so much myself I don't want to let her go.'

'I need the money,' she said. 'She'll have to go, Liam. Will you take 20 per cent?'

She was coming on, he thought, growing quite worldly-wise at last. He was glad of that. Any extra thickness of skin which his tender little Angelica could grow to protect herself from further pain would be all to the good.

Lizzie caught his eye across the table and smiled. She thought: I've got a steep and stony path ahead of me and this kind, unpretentious man is trying to help me climb.

'D'you know, Liam, what I'd like best?'

'Tell me.'

'An ice-cream cornet. Timothy's favourite: Cornetto. That's something I can't cook.' Her eyes followed him as he moved to the counter to order one; but she wasn't thinking of him. She was thinking Larry had been wrong about those Russian dolls hiding one inside the other. He thought of them as an image of the chambers of his soul. Inside the innermost one was where she dwelt. That's what he said; but it wasn't true. It couldn't possibly be true, because, as she now knew, in that innermost compartment of ourselves there is nobody with us. We are alone. When people learn this they often feel such panic that they throw themselves at God, beseeching Him to inhabit them. Others, like her mother, try to forget their terror in alcohol or other drugs, and some in their despair take the quicker route to self-destruction.

She regarded the Cornetto with concentration before she licked it. 'It's you who's the angel, Liam, not me,' she said.

'Is that so? Ah well, we can all be angels somewhere, some of the time.'

But the fact is, she told herself, I'm on another trip now. This spiritual journey towards independence is one I've got to make without him.

Ten

From the car park they could see the creamy white castle with its four blue conical turrets. Standing high and four-square on its rock above the river it was visible from anywhere in the town. When they climbed the spiral staircase to the watchtower and looked out they could see for miles around the lush green landscape of the garden of France, the rectangular vineyards with vines planted in straight furrows, the white fuzz of plum orchards in bloom, the blue river winding, and the darker slate blue of hundreds of steep roofs over hundreds of white stone houses in Saumur.

'It's just like a fairy tale castle!' cried Amanda when she saw it.

After wandering through the castle in the wake of a French guide they walked down through gardens into the town towards an open-air market full of noise and coloured stalls, at one of which James stopped to buy a fantastic mask for Timothy while Amanda shopped for lunch. She bought a long *baguette* of crisp bread, and then went into a *charcuterie*. She was examining the sausages and potted meats when a young man in jeans and T-shirt spoke to her.

'You a Brit? Say! What's this "rillettes" stuff thay say is so good?' He spoke English with a slight American twang.

'I'm getting this one,' said Amanda. 'It's minced and pounded duck meat with heaven knows what heavenly flavours added.'

They left the shop with their purchases and found James, who put on his vampire mask to greet them. 'Do you think Timothy will like it?' he asked.

'He'll love it,' said Amanda. 'Especially the plastic fangs.'

The young stranger joined them to walk back to the car park.

'Have you seen Fontevraud?' he asked. 'Amazing! Absolutely . . . Henry II is buried there. He's the one who found Becket troublesome. I'm doing history,' he added.

'We're going there this afternoon,' said Amanda.

They left him unchaining his bike.

'We should have offered him lunch,' said Amanda.

'Far too early. Besides, he's one of the predators,' said James.

'Nonsense!' declared Amanda. 'He's just a poor student. Very young and very enthusiastic.'

'I can see I'm going to suffer the pangs of jealousy,' he grumbled. 'Trouble is, what you need, my girl, is more than one middle-aged GP to ward them off. What you need is a posse of armed security guards!'

'You are a jealous man!'

'I was never jealous with Mary. It wasn't that she was unattractive to men, but she had an air about her that signalled: thus far and no further. She was rather strict.'

Amanda thought: It's I who will be jealous. She took off her sunglasses as she climbed into the passenger seat. 'You mustn't be so possessive, James,' she said.

'Well, I don't want any wasps buzzing round my honeypot.'

'Aren't you a WASP yourself?'

'No. I'm a Welsh hornet.' He caught her hand when she laughed, and held it.

'Anyway,' she said, 'I don't think that young man is a Yank at all. He comes from Clapham, or somewhere like that, and has just put on that twang.'

He adjusted his seat-belt. She was certainly a different girl from the one he'd rescued, crushed with misery and remorse, from her London flat. There was no doubt she was excited by all the new sights and sounds, eager every morning over croissants and coffee for the new things to come, and relaxed and contented in his arms at the end of every day. Sometimes he caught her looking at him speculatively with a trace of surprise, even of wonder, and guessed that she was thinking: I am happy with this man. We are happy together. And if he caught her eye he would wink at her solemnly and tell himself with delight and some feeling of triumph: I'm banishing those Billie Holliday blues.

Fontevraud did indeed prove stunning. The twelfth-century abbey church, almost empty of tourists so early in the year, struck a chill on Amanda's shoulders from the cold stone and the severity of its massive pillars and unadorned arches. In the transept they stared in awed silence at the Plantagenet tombs. There lay Henry II, unmistakably, in spite of the paint flaking off his limestone likeness, a ruthless leader of men, Count of Anjou, King of England and founder of the house of Plantagenet which ruled so much of France for three centuries. Beside him lay his queen, Eleanor of Aquitane, and their son, the legendary Richard Lionheart, all three carved in stone.

Coming out into the warm sunshine again felt like a release. They spread out the map over the bonnet of the car and located Fontevraud near the junction of the river Vienne with the Loire.

'Let's go along the south bank of the Vienne a bit further,' he suggested. 'I rather like this rolling countryside.'

They chose a spot higher up the river for their lunch. Amanda sat down crosslegged on the grass beside the picnic basket. He couldn't see her face, which was shaded by a large straw hat as she stooped to pick up a pebble near her feet and threw it into the water.

'In that hat you look like a painting by Augustus John,' he said.

'Is that a compliment?'

'You don't need any compliments. You just are. A phenomenon. A feast for my eyes, and a glorious uplift of the spirit as well as other parts of me.'

She threw another pebble. He watched it plunge into the current; he watched water flowing swiftly over the place where it had disappeared and thought: I know very little about her. I only know her here and now. I don't know anything about the layers of days accumulated which have made her what she is. 'Were you an only child?' he asked.

'I had a brother, Robert, but he went to Australia in his twenties, and I haven't seen him since.' She would have liked him to talk more about his dead wife, but didn't like to probe. Give him time, she thought. Give him time. . . . 'We were left orphans rather young. A well-to-do aunt took charge of us and sent us both to boarding school – separate, of course. So we only met in the holidays. She left us both her money; but I think he was always her favourite.'

'Was she kind?'

'Oh yes. Kind enough, but a bit eccentric. Wise though, in a sort of Cassandra-like way. . . . She used to warn me about my face! It would *not* be my fortune, she used to say. "Your face will be your undoing if you don't look out." That was when I started flirting with Robert's schoolfriends. My brother was good-looking; but she never said that to him!' She scooped some rillette of duck out of its little pot and spread it on bread, which she handed to him.

'I expect she was worried – your aunt,' James said. 'Beauty is like wealth to the fortune hunter. She foresaw the predators.' He got up and walked down to the river's edge where in a little swirling backwater he'd placed a half-bottle of white Anjou upright between the pebbles to cool. 'Only half measures for drivers,' he explained as he poured it into Amanda's outstretched plastic cup, and drank some from his own before lying down on his back with his arms folded into a pillow behind his neck. Watching big white clouds drifting, he felt they had all the time in the world.

'We never had any children,' he said suddenly. 'Mary had a miscarriage once. It was sad for her – for me too. In the end I believe she came to regard me as her child. She was always telling me what to do, fussing about my clothes, making me eat up my vegetables – nagging me, really.' He laughed.

Amanda threw a third pebble.

'She was like your aunt,' he went on. 'Always warning me of danger. The only one she didn't warn me of was her own. She was killed in a car crash you see, driving back from London on the M4. I missed her of course. Grieved. Terribly at first. Still do, in a way. . . .' He sat up.

'Dear James,' she said. 'I'm so sorry.' They were both silent, sipping the good wine.

When they got back to their hotel James lay on the bed watching Amanda's silhouette blurred by the opaque glass walls of the *cabinet de toilette* as she showered inside; and after a while he joined her. They soaped each others backs and embraced in the narrow space, letting the warm water fall over their faces as they kissed. At dinner they drank sparkling Saumur as an aperitif. James swore it was so good you couldn't tell it from champagne. Amanda drank it with her food: quenelles of pike caught in the Loire, poached in white wine and served with *beurre blanc*.

'This sauce is delicious,' she said. 'I must find out how it's made.'

James ordered a local speciality, *matelot d'anguille*, eel stewed in red wine, and found it necessary to drink the wine of Chinon with it. 'Which reminds me,' he said, 'of Joan of Arc. Do we have to visit that castle tomorrow? I think we're in grave danger of falling sick of a surfeit of castles.'

'There's a forest of Chinon on the map,' said Amanda. 'What about walking there tomorrow?'

'Here's to your blue eyes!' he said. 'Made even more beautiful by the Chinon I'm drinking . . .'

'There's plenty of time to see Chinon,' said Amanda. 'This book says,' she tapped the travel guide on the table beside her plate, 'that the Loire is the longest river in France, 628 miles long, and there are one hundred castles open to the public.'

'No castles tomorrow,' said James firmly. 'Although I wouldn't mind seeing one or two of those caves dug out of the limestone where they hide the wine cellars.'

*

The first days of April fell softly on Chenonceau. The plane trees in the avenue leading to the château shook out their new leaves and shimmered in the morning sunshine. An air of tranquillity pervaded the formal gardens with their neat box hedges trimmed into elaborate designs between paths swept clean and lined with well clipped shrubs and trees. No noisy groups of children being instructed in their glorious heritage invaded the place, and adult tourists were as yet few. Nor was there any mandatory guided tour, so James and Amanda were free to wander at will through the park, the terraced gardens and at last the lovely little palace, the ultimate expression in French Renaissance architecture of the new delight in living of that age.

It was the home of the legendary Diane de Poitiers who was the mistress of two kings and who outlived them both. It was she who built the beautiful bridge over the Cher as an extension to the house, connecting it with woods on the far side of the river where she used to hunt.

'They say she used to swim naked in this river at sunrise,' said Amanda as they stood on the bank waiting while a boy in jeans untied a small rowing boat and pulled it towards them. 'And then she climbed out of the water and on to the back of a white stallion, which galloped away with her into the woods.'

'Read white stallion as code-word for King,' said James.

They climbed into the boat and James took the oars while Amanda sat in the stern in charge of the rudder. They glided across a stretch of calm water, and then under the first of five arches of Diane's bridge.

'Henri was seventeen when he fell in love with Diane. She was a widow of thirty-seven.' Amanda leant over the side of the skiff and let the water dribble through her fingers. 'Same age as me.'

'I dare say you're a reincarnation of her – Diane the Huntress. But I'm afraid I'm not the King.' They emerged from the archway and shot up the river before turning to navigate the second arch.

'Do you think she had any children by Henri? There's no mention of children in the book,' said Amanda.

James, guessing this conversation might lead them into dangerous waters, replied carefully: 'From the obstetric point of view, if she had her first child at thirty-seven, she'd be regarded as an elderly primip. She might even have had difficulty in conceiving, unless of course she'd had children by her husband before that.'

'Elderly primip!' Amanda was indignant. 'At thirty-seven!'

'She was probably like you,' he said as they slipped through the second arch and began to negotiate the third. 'Certainly fertile, and absolutely at the peak of physical health. She was supposed to be ageless, wasn't she?'

'Well, she was adored by Henri till he died. It says in the book that people put down her eternal youth to witchcraft.'

'I dare say all that swimming in the Cher kept her in good shape. And she ate well, didn't she? Grew vegetables in the garden?'

'Artichokes,' said Amanda. 'So you don't think I'd have any difficulty having a baby?'

'Why? Do you want one?'

She was silent, then, till they were entering the fourth arch, when she suddenly said, 'Of course I do, Jamie. Doesn't every woman?' Such a surge of electricity shot through him that he jerked the right oar out of its rowlock, and it fell with a splash and began to float away on the current.

'We'll have to forget the fifth arch,' he said, 'and follow that bloody oar downstream. Don't laugh, Amanda! Steer like mad or we'll lose it.' They caught up with it eventually when the boat and the wayward oar bumped together into a curve on the bank.

'We can go back to the fifth arch now,' said Amanda.

'I think I ought to advise you,' said James after they'd disembarked and tipped the boat-boy, 'medically speaking, that is, that you should not delay your plan too long.'

'What plan?'

'Childbearing.'

'Oh!' And to his surprise Amanda blushed.

'I've got a new goat's cheese for our picnic,' she promised him as they walked back to the car.

They drove north a few kilometres into the forest of Amboise, where they ate their picnic sitting at the base of a giant beech tree. They spent the afternoon walking through woodland, kicking up last autumn's dead leaves and relishing the smells of damp earth underneath, and of small plants pushing their way upward through the leaf mould into new life. Clumps of primroses were emerging from the bank beside the path, and white wood anemones scattered under the trees gleamed like stars. Amanda picked two primroses for James and stuck the stems behind his ears; he stooped and pulled out two anemones, which he threaded through her hair.

'I bet you've never worn primroses behind your ears before!'

'Diane the Huntress crowned with stars. . . .' he told her.

They were standing face to face when she suddenly confessed in a confused rush: 'I could never be an elderly primip, because I got pregnant in my twenties. I had an abortion, you see. An awful wrench it was, too, because I wanted that baby.' He took both her hands and held them firmly. 'It was the eccentric aunt who helped me then. My lover cleared off and left me to it.' When she looked up into his face she saw tears in his eyes. 'Why Jamie dear!' she cried. 'Why should you cry for me now? It was all a long time ago.'

'Because of the waste, Amanda. Because of the loss of what would have been a beautiful baby. Because of all that wasted love of yours.'

She lifted one of his hands and rubbed it slowly across her cheek before kissing it. 'Dear Jamie,' she spoke softly. 'Jamie dear. . . .'

By the time they got back to Le Verger Vert, a small country inn they'd discovered near Chenonceaux, they were tired and hungry; but before they went down to the dining-room Amanda opened their bedroom window and leant out. Below her spread the little orchard, which was being tempted by the mild spring into early flowering. Out of a tangle of black branches a blizzard of white blossom was about to burst. The cherries would be in bloom for Easter.

'It's heaven – or the next-best thing,' she sighed, and smiled at him over her shoulder.

There was no choice on the menu; the lady of the house simply presented her single dish of the day, which was excellent: a chicken fricassée with mushrooms and fried potatoes and a green salad served with a carafe of local red wine. The mushrooms, she explained rapidly and with immense confidence, were grown inside the limestone caves around Saumur, which produced, in a climate and environment perfect for their cultivation, enough mushrooms for the whole of France. They were the best in the world, '*Naturellement!*' She beamed over the steaming dish.

'It's like a honeymoon for me, Amanda.'

'But we're not married.'

'No.'

'Marriage is for children, isn't it?'

They were lying naked side by side on top of the bed, their faces close together; her upper arm round his neck, his hand round her smooth buttock. She closed her eyes, feeling sleepy. 'All that walking . . .' she murmured.

'All right to play the field before,' he said, 'but after marriage it's time to settle down and concentrate on your goal.'

'Umm . . . mm. . . .'

'Would you like to have a baby with me, Amanda?'

No answer came; but greatly to his surprise two big tears welled out under her eyelids. No piece of clothing, no edge of sheet was handy, no corner of it to dry her eyes. So he wiped her tears away with a forefinger and kissed her lids.

'Why are you crying, darling girl, when I'm so happy?'

'I'm happy too.'

'You've got a funny way of showing it.'

She slipped off the bed to find a paper tissue in the *cabinet*, and blowing her nose loudly she said, 'Except for two absolute no-hopers in my twenties no man has asked me to marry him, you see. That's what you're doing, isn't it?' She climbed back on to the bed and sat up crosslegged in the position he loved; and because he couldn't see her when he was flat on his back he sat up to look at her. 'Plenty of men wanted me for fun on the mattress, but not for children. No commitment, you see.'

303

'D'you think I'll do?'

She glanced at him. 'I can't think of anyone better, Jamie. You're the nicest man I've ever met. So I don't see why not.'

He leaned forward and kissed her knee. Then he ran a finger down the groove of her groin and stroked the soft white velvet skin on the inside of her thigh. He put his head in her naked lap and kissed her lovely crisp pubic hair, and was immediately lost in a torrent of desire. She was not only a recipient of love, she was generous in giving it: she loved loving, and he knew now that she loved him.

They were rather silent over breakfast next morning. There were not many other tourists in the dining-room. After two cups of strong black coffee he leaned across the red and white checked tablecloth, and looking furtively from side to side, whispered, 'Do you suppose we could get married in Paris – the British Embassy – or Protestant church – *hôtel de ville*, or what?'

'Oh! I don't think so, Jamie,' she replied loudly. 'I don't see how that could be done. The consul, or registrar, or priest or mayor, or whatever – he'd never know' – she suddenly dropped her voice – 'that we weren't committing bigamy, would he?'

'No, I suppose not.'

'We'll have to get home for that, Jamie love. But first,' she added briskly, 'could we have a few days in Paris?'

It was just what he wanted. 'In another week,' he said, 'the chestnuts will be coming into leaf, and the braver cafés will be pushing out their tables on the sidewalks. What do you say?'

'Magical!' cried Amanda enthusiastically. 'You're no hornet, Jamie. You're a Welsh wizard! But today,' she assumed a serious expression, 'it's Amboise, where all those Prods were hanged from the Plotters' Balcony, and the rest were tied up in sacks and thrown into the Loire.'

'France is making you bloodthirsty, Amanda.' But she only smiled complacently. 'We'll have to wash away the taste of Amboise with a draught of Vouvray. That would be a good way to end our last day here. My Wine Society catalogue describes Vouvray as a full and honeyed wine with just a hint of sparkle.'

'Our last day beside the Loire, Jamie, but there'll be many more such days to come.'

'You think so?' Only a few months ago he would never have believed so much joy was still in store for him.

She jumped up and moved quickly to the door; but

there she paused, and turning, her face alert with happy expectation of the day's pleasure, she said: 'I know it.'

Postscript

No heatwave has hit Fossbury this summer, but there have been enough hot days for farmers to harvest their barley and begin cutting wheat from their arable fields. This is the time when they need extra hands. Mrs Pewsey is no worse, she says. Holding her own is Dr James's description of her current state of health, but she doesn't do any outdoor work on the farm now, and Pewsey has had to take on a couple of unemployed school-leavers at a low wage to help him out. There have been other changes. Mrs Sims has passed on and into Fossbury folklore, along with the hunting doctor of the twenties and the even older barbaric memories of bull-baiting by the market cross. The delicatessen and one of the boutiques have shut up shop; but none of the pubs has been closed down by the recession.

An air of festivity hangs over the west end of the town on this August Sunday. The driveway to the Barn as well as a good stretch of the road outside are lined with parked cars, because Julia and Peter, who have recently taken possession of the house, are giving a Sunday lunch-party. It is a housewarming and a belated wedding reception too. Old Dr Doynton and his Dorothy have driven all the way from Shropshire to be present on this happy occasion. Young Dr Barton and Belinda in a blue flowery dress have taken a carrycot upstairs to place its precious contents, a sleeping infant girl, on Julia's bed before tiptoeing down to drink healths. Dorothy and Belinda, when they get together on the terrace, agree over their champagne that Peter, with his lean frame and iron-grey hair, certainly doesn't look like an old-age pensioner. Gerry Foster is there, nodding kindly to one and all, and so is Maisie with her sharper but still kindly eye. She has discarded her frayed jeans this morning for an emerald and navy two-piece she picked up in the July sales in Swinester.

'Very fetching too!' Thomas Verdi Parry tells himself as he edges towards the terrace, balancing a drink in one hand and preparing in his mind a little old-fashioned flattery for Maisie.

There are a lot of Peter's friends for Julia to meet, and a crowd of hers who want to meet Peter. James and Amanda have arrived rather late, and are embraced and kissed. 'So glad,' Julia murmurs. 'So glad to see you both.' James, entranced, she notes silently, and Amanda looking like a classical Aphrodite, so cool and elegant in that sleeveless shirt-dress of coffee-coloured silk, with a long string of pearls round her neck. The muted colours enhance the wonderful glow of her skin and the brevity of the dress reveals the beauty of her smooth long limbs. Later, when the caterers and helpers have departed and Julia and Peter sit on the terrace sipping her good Viennese coffee, mulling over the day's events, Julia will comment on Jamie: 'Absolutely punch-drunk with sex!' and Peter will ask, 'Are you surprised?' which will make her glance at him sharply, provoking him to say, 'She's easy on the eye.'

She is, of course, more than that, as Julia has discovered, rather to her surprise. She had expected, when they decided to employ Amanda as accountant and business manager for the practice, that in spite of her recognised skills she would turn out to be a bit of a bimbo (the collective wisdom to which Julia has fallen victim always assuming that beauty cannot abide with brains). But soon she learned that behind that smooth forehead framed in Botticelli tendrils the skull housed a very efficient computer. Within a couple of months Amanda, working only twenty hours a week, had sorted out any number of tangles and turmoils, and made one or two intelligent suggestions for the future as well.

'I'm wondering if she could be pregnant?' Julia will muse, stirring sugar into her coffee, which she likes very strong and very sweet. 'Something tells my practised eye that she is. She looks so rounded and content, somehow. Of course it must be early days. She hasn't attended my antenatal clinic yet. I do hope James doesn't intend supervising her pregnancy himself. That would be foolish.'

Julia has hired a young couple from Malmsford to cater for the party, and Mrs Roxby and Sandra are helping them. Mrs Roxby has agreed to continue working at the Barn, and Sandra is doing for Amanda at No. 3 Main Street, Dr Doynton's old house, into which she and James have moved. James sold Owl House remarkably quickly, perhaps too cheaply for the sake of a speedy move into a home his bride preferred. Julia does not like her new neighbours; and her heart sinks at the sight of them at the front door. She had hoped that since they were in the middle of rebuilding, extending and renovating Owl House into a Residential Home for the Elderly they might be too busy to turn up. She should have known better. The Tillys are not people who could miss a party with free drinks provided *ad lib*. They are Cockneys with hearts of gold, or at any rate in a rush to find it, with a buoyancy unchecked by any weakness such as imagination. Mrs Tilly is a fat woman who finds herself attractive in a billowing see-through trouser-suit of pastel pink. Mr Tilly is an entrepreneur.

'Better late than never!' Julia greets them deceitfully, but manages to avoid the hearty kiss he proffers.

'I'm a businessman,' he has explained to Julia over the fence. 'I'm in it for the money, I needn't tell you. In four or five years when we've made our little pile we're off to the Costa del Sol. *Olé*!'

'Well, don't make your individual rooms like prison cells,' she begged him. 'Not too small. Old people like to sit alone sometimes in their own rooms, so there must be enough space for an armchair and a reading-lamp as well as their own TV set. They don't all want to sit forever together in a semicircle in the lounge waiting for *Neighbours* to appear on the box.'

'There 'as to be a lot of little rooms, Dr Orchard, or 'ow can we make our profit?' He grinned, judging her a fool. 'What's more, the old darlings likes company. Keeps 'em 'appy. The more the merrier.' He laughed. 'I'm not Mother Teresa, you know.'

'I can see that,' Julia agreed. 'I can't see Mother Teresa living it up on the Costa del Sol on her takings.' She is glad that Lizzie is not there to meet her new neighbours, but realises that she mustn't antagonise Mr Tilly as no doubt she'll have to beg beds from him in due course, for some of her patients – when the silver cord is loosed and the golden bowl is broken, but the tattered shreds and fragments still lie indecently around. Oh! Medicine what have we done? Oh! Welfare state what have we left undone as we move into the senility boom we can't cope with and have to leave the care of the aged and infirm in the hands of people like the Tillys?

James and Amanda don't stay too long at the party. They are rather glad to escape from all the noise and strange faces and sit quietly on their own little terrace, whose Cotswold stone glows honey-coloured in the afternoon sun. James is about to remark that parties at the Barn aren't what they were in the days of Lizzie and Larry, but checks himself in time. There are still some no-go areas between them. Another of these is the denture-pink bathroom suite in Owl House, which luckily for Amanda she has had no need to throw out. James agrees with her completely that Dr Doynton's old house must in some respects be modernised, and certainly redecorated, but leaves these matters entirely to her; and Mary seems to have no objections. He no longer hears her voice. He believes she is happy now to relinquish the reins. That nice girl Sandra Parsons is coming daily for a couple of hours to help, and will be invaluable when the baby comes. Sandra, he knows, loves babies; and since no overtime is now available at Vince's workplace, and possible redundancy lurks in the shadows, Sandra is glad to earn a bit extra. He watches Amanda pick up a pair of secateurs and walk towards the climber roses on the garden wall to snip off the dead heads of scented Zephyrine Drouin. He doesn't think of her as Diane the Huntress now, or as Aphrodite, but he does still see her as a goddess, the most ancient one in human prehistory, and the most sacred of all: the goddess of fertility.

A Selected List of Fiction Available from Mandarin

☐	7493 0780 3	**The Hanging Tree**	Allan Massie	£5.99
☐	7493 1224 6	**How I Met My Wife**	Nicholas Coleridge	£5.99
☐	7493 1064 2	**Of Love and Asthma**	Ferdinand Mount	£5.99
☐	7493 1368 4	**Persistent Rumours**	Lee Langley	£4.99
☐	7493 1068 5	**Goodness**	Tim Parks	£4.99
☐	7493 1492 3	**Making the Angels Weep**	Helen Flint	£5.99
☐	7493 1364 1	**High on the Hog**	Fraser Harrison	£4.99
☐	7493 1394 3	**What's Eating Gilbert Grape**	Peter Hedges	£5.99
☐	7493 1216 5	**The Fringe Orphan**	Rachel Morris	£4.99
☐	7493 1510 5	**Evenings at Mongini's**	Rusell Lucas	£5.99
☐	7493 1509 1	**Fair Sex**	Sarah Foot	£5.99

In the tradition of Mary Wesley and Joanna Trollope, *Sunday Lunch* is a gentle yet powerful story, full of heart and deft characterisation.

On a fine summer Sunday a lunch party is being held in an architect's house with big rooms and a terrace, and a garden leading down to a stream with fields beyond. It is a lovely party in an idyllic setting, and everybody is enjoying life.

Yet before the day is out a scandalous death will have occurred which will change the lives of all the guests at the Sunday lunch, leaving them to come to terms in their various ways with new selves and new destinies.

'An intimate and fascinating glimpse into the unexpected improprieties behind civilised behaviour in a perfect commuter village'
MOLLY KEANE

'Eminently readable . . . there is humour here, and the wry wisdom of age'
SOPHIE KERSHAW, *Time Out*

COVER ILLUSTRATION: RUTH RIVERS

ISBN 0-7493-1558-X

MANDARIN
FICTION
UK £5.99
Canada $11.99

9 780749 315580